The Kiss of a Stranger

OTHER BOOKS AND AUDIO BOOKS
BY SARAH M. EDEN:

Courting Miss Lancaster

The Kiss of a Stranger

a novel by

SARAH M. EDEN

Covenant Communications, Inc.

Cover photography by McKenzie Deakins.
For more information please visit www.photographybymckenzie.com

Published by Covenant Communications, Inc.
American Fork, Utah

Printed in the United States of America
First Printing: January 2011

17 16 15 14 13 12 11 10 9 8 7 6 5 4 3 2

ISBN:978-1-60861-175-1

To Raul and Ed, the man of many names

Chapter One

England, October 1814

"Blast it all!" Crispin Handle, Lord Cavratt, did not generally resort to muttering under his breath, but an exasperating female could push even the most levelheaded gentleman to extremes.

He had retreated to the country to avoid Miss Cynthia Bower only to find her stalking the garden path of what he thought was an unknown inn. Miss Bower, with the painfully obvious encouragement of her mother, had decided that she ought to be the next Lady Cavratt and had worked feverishly to convince him of the same thing. The only clear conclusion Crispin had come to was that Miss Bower's only redeeming quality was that she did eventually go away. If only there were a way to keep her from coming back.

"Now isn't this a charming coincidence, Lord Cavratt." Miss Bower reached him with alarming speed.

If only his gelding, Hinder, moved that quickly.

"I thought you were remaining in London for the Little Season."

Miss Bower ignored Crispin's pointed lack of a response, following him as he continued to walk. She rarely required a reply when fashioning a conversation. "How pleased Mother will be to know you're here. We are visiting old friends, the Larneses."

"Of course you are." Old friends, indeed. Conveniently located friends, more like.

Miss Bower emitted a tiny wisp of a laugh, precisely the kind a lady of the beau monde would have spent her life perfecting. Society valued the most inane things. "Sometimes you are in such sour spirits."

"And you seem to always be nearby when I am," he answered.

If anything, Miss Bower smiled more broadly. "Providence, my lord. Simply an opportunity for me to elevate your mood."

The woman couldn't be insulted. She didn't seem able to comprehend a set-down no matter how blunt. Perhaps she simply ignored his obvious lack of enthusiasm for her company—blind ambition, as it were, though *deaf* ambition seemed more fitting.

Miss Bower's expression turned triumphant. "And I have come with just such an opportunity."

"I can hardly wait." He made no attempt to disguise the dryness of his tone.

A couple passed going in the opposite direction. Crispin acknowledged them with a bow of his head.

"The Littletons' Ball is a mere three weeks away." Miss Bower's rampant enthusiasm would have pleased Mrs. Littleton immensely.

"It will, no doubt, be a suffocating crush, as usual." Crispin did not care for balls. He did enjoy people—the genuine ones at least. Society functions rarely catered to the sincere and upright. If such stalwart character traits were required for admittance, the ballrooms of London would echo in their emptiness.

"You are so cross." Miss Bower executed a calculatedly dainty wave of her hand. "I think I'll punish you and not tell you *whom* they've invited. I know you will be quite pleased when you hear his name."

"Very well." If she talked long enough, perhaps she would wear herself out to the point of dropping onto the ground in a swoon. After enjoying the blessed silence for a moment, he could then make good his escape. "I shall take my punishment like a gentleman."

"You are insufferable at times."

If he was so insufferable, why did she continue smiling like a ninny?

"The Earl of Lampton will be there." Miss Bower's eyes grew wide in anticipation of his ecstatic response.

To own the truth, Crispin felt every bit as pleased as she had predicted he would. He and Philip Jonquil, the earl to whom Miss Bower referred, had been friends since their days at Eton. Lud, that felt like a lifetime ago.

"Surely you mean to attend the ball. The earl will be most pleased to see you, as will so very many others." Again Miss Bower failed to hit the subtlety mark.

Rather than being shackled for the first waltz and a country dance, to boot, Crispin sidestepped the question. "I see Lord Lampton quite often as it is. The ball, therefore, need not serve as the stage for a reunion, and I may remain at home with a clear conscience."

"I should just leave you here to your gloom and forget my intention to lift your spirits." Her sickeningly sweet voice threatened to undermine Crispin's determination to be civil.

"If only," he muttered under his breath for the second time in a matter of minutes.

"What was that?"

"Just admiring the flowers, Miss Bower." Crispin kept his eyes fixed on the few remaining blooms. The chill of early October had claimed all but the hardiest. He admired their determination. Survival required a certain degree of stubbornness.

"I do wish you'd call me Cynthia. I've asked so many times."

"And I have refused just as many times, Miss Bower." Crispin could feel the muscles tensing around his jaw. She irritated him almost beyond bearing.

"Although you are decidedly an intelligent, honorable gentleman—"

Ah. She'd moved to the nauseating flattery. Next would come feigned coyness with just a hint of a saucy temper. The ladies of society read far too much like a very predictable novel.

"—you certainly can't expect to make a match unless you are willing to attend a few crushes, my lord."

"I have attended far more than a few, I assure you." Crispin shuddered at the memory—feather-headed debutantes and their maddening mothers trailing him around all the drawing rooms of London, seeing nothing more than a title and lands and ready blunt. Even the gentlemen lost their forthrightness when tossed amongst the hypocritical throngs of society.

"You and I have spent time together at many such functions." Miss Bower compacted her lack of subtlety with a hint of desperation.

Time had come to formulate a reason to abandon the garden and leave Miss Bower to leech onto some other gentleman, preferably one who had a certain fondness for parasites.

"And we have met at Hyde Park," Miss Bower pushed on.

She'd practically thrown herself in front of his horse on two different occasions and *somehow* lost control of her own mount on another. Blast it, he needed to rid himself of her before she did something truly drastic. Crispin nodded warily, searching his brain for an excuse to flee.

"We have sat beside one another at dinner parties."

Something he'd done his utmost to avoid. The scheming of her mother had made that impossible at times.

"Attended musicales, the theater . . ."

She managed to show up everywhere he went. He half expected her to be waiting at White's on the nights he hid from her there. Miss Bower would likely not bat an eye at the thought of infiltrating a gentlemen's club in the interest of pursuing a title.

"We do certainly seem to run into each other a lot." Depressing thought. He'd once had a nightmare that Miss Bower had tied up his valet and hidden in his dressing room. The fact that he couldn't be entirely sure she wouldn't resort to such a thing made the image all the more disturbing.

"People are beginning to talk." Miss Bower offered an innocent look that wasn't innocent in the least.

Crispin silently acknowledged a woman standing near a hyacinth plant. She blushed in reply. Hers was not a practiced shyness. So there *were* still women in the world who weren't merely actresses. This particular woman most likely had no need to be. She was quite obviously a servant.

"Are you listening to a word I'm saying?" Miss Bower demanded, facing him with hands shoved impatiently against her hips.

A serious miscalculation, Miss Bower. Her clinginess irritated him—demanding his attention pushed him beyond mere annoyance. "No, as a matter of fact, I am not listening to a word you are saying, nor am I likely to begin doing so."

"I don't know why I even bother myself with this." She pursed her lips together, eyeing him with frustration. "All I am saying is the ton is beginning to wonder if you know how to court a lady or not."

"And what, pray tell, have I done to inspire such catastrophic doubt from all of society?"

"You and I have been seen together all over London and people have begun to talk—"

"Something you have pointed out already."

She didn't stop long enough to register his reply. "—and you have never once declared yourself."

Declared himself? He would likely strangle her within the first twenty-four hours of an engagement. No, when he married—an eventuality to which he did not particularly look forward—he would choose a woman with at least one original thought in her brain box, someone genuine who didn't see him as the quickest route to a title and pin money.

"You've never even attempted to kiss me."

Crispin shuddered at the very thought. Did the feckless female think he was dicked in the nob? Talking with her was repulsive enough—he'd have to be stark raving mad to kiss her!

"Perhaps you simply lack the ability."

"To kiss a woman?" He most certainly possessed *that* ability. A veritable talent, he'd been told.

She cocked her head to the side. He'd seen that look before. She was issuing a challenge, attempting to anger him into kissing her. As if any gentleman raised amongst the machinations of heartless women would fall into such an obvious trap.

"You need not worry about my abilities, Miss Bower." His patience slipped more with each passing moment.

"I always thought a true gentleman was born to woo, and yet your wooing of me has fallen remarkably short."

"Did you ever consider the possibility that I never intended to woo you?" Crispin dropped the civility, his temper barely held back.

"You need not be embarrassed." Miss Bower looked at him sympathetically. "I don't require the kind of attentions some ladies do when being pursued."

Crispin silently counted to five, not trusting himself to reply immediately. Five proved inadequate. By twenty, he felt better able to speak calmly. "You are not being pursued. My—"

"No one is about, Crispin. There's no need to—"

"It is *Lord Cavratt,* Miss Bower, and I have no intention of—"

"I realize that, as a gentleman, you have probably been hesitant to allow yourself a more ardent display of your affection." Miss Bower laid her hand on his arm.

He pulled back, probably more roughly than necessary, but she remained undeterred. He would never, no matter how old and frail a bachelor he might become, settle for the likes of Miss Bower. He would choose his own wife, and he would choose far better than this shallow, calculating young lady.

"A kiss would make your intentions quite clear, my lord, and would, I assure you, be most welcome." More fluttering eyelashes. More coy smiles.

She wanted a kiss, did she? Wanted a clear indication of his intentions toward her? "Fine."

Miss Bower's smile grew just a touch smug. That smile wouldn't last long.

Crispin marched to the hyacinths and the young serving woman still standing there admiring the few remaining flowers.

He offered her a quick bow. "Pardon me."

She curtsied, her blush returning once more.

Looking daggers at Miss Bower, Crispin gathered the unsuspecting maid in his arms and kissed her with as much fervor as he could gather in his irritation. Let the infuriating, clinging leech make of that what she would.

He'd intended to put Miss Bower in her place, perhaps to shock her from the garden and his life entirely. Mere seconds after pressing his lips to this stranger's, however, all thoughts of Miss Bower fled. He could think of nothing beyond how perfectly this nameless woman fit in his arms, how wonderful she tasted, how nice she smelled.

He'd quite thoroughly kissed her before her attempts to push him away registered in his befuddled mind. Her struggle snapped him back to reality. Crispin released her, trying desperately to catch his breath, to calm his racing heart. She had mesmerizing sapphire eyes. Crispin had the sudden urge to reach out for her again. But the poor thing had such a look of confused fear on her face he couldn't stomach the idea of misusing her further.

Crispin had never before thought of himself as a cad—he'd never had reason to. Just then, looking into the frightened face of the young woman he'd all but attacked, he, the pattern card of a well-mannered gentleman, knew he'd behaved little better than a jackanapes.

"Forgive me," he offered, sorely feeling the thoughtlessness of his actions. "That was uncalled for."

"It most certainly was," a deep voice rumbled behind him.

Crispin spun to face a stout gentleman, fifty years old by his face, though with the build of a man much younger. He was dressed in the first stare of fashion, marking him as a man of means. The young maid was probably a member of this gentleman's staff. Crispin did not generally fall into such ridiculous scrapes as this.

"My apologies . . ."

"Mr. Thorndale," the man introduced himself, "of Yandell Hall."

Crispin bowed. The man bent perhaps an inch in reply.

With a look of disapproval and a flick of his hand toward the woman who stood watching Crispin with those unbelievably blue eyes, Mr. Thorndale said, "And you, apparently, know my niece."

Niece? The woman he'd thought a servant was a gentleman's niece? Lud, what a bumblebroth. Miss Bower, he noticed, had fled the scene. The coward.

"You will both come with me." Mr. Thorndale turned back toward the inn.

The little slip of a thing hurried after him. Crispin, though unaccustomed to being ordered around, followed also. He was in far too deep to object to a little deserved bullying.

What was Mr. Thorndale's situation? If he proved a man of wealth and influence, this could, perhaps be worked around. A man in need of funds would be less obliging. Even so, the incident had occurred with almost no witnesses. Miss Bower wasn't likely to muddy his reputation—no point doggedly pursuing a gentleman with a reputation for being a cad. Although, in all honesty, the rakes did seem to garner far more attention from the ladies than they ought.

Mr. Thorndale's niece would not wish to propagate a scandal. She would be implicated in it, after all.

He had to have some name to assign the lady. "Miss Thorndale" would have to do until he learned differently. Crispin watched her follow Mr. Thorndale through the bustling front hall of the inn and up the winding staircase. Her faded, shapeless gown suggested the Thorndales had fallen on hard times. However, Mr. Thorndale's coat, though not Weston, was remarkably well tailored. *He* appeared bang up to the mark. Miss Thorndale didn't appear to have ever heard of the mark. The hideous gown she wore defied description. Her honey-colored hair had been pulled back in a severe knot, convincing Crispin she did not have a lady's maid.

The Thorndale family proved a study in contradictions. Mr. Thorndale was solidly built and self-possessed. His niece was wispy, pale, and withdrawn. She, Crispin decided, must take after the other side of her family tree—the quiet, colorless side, poor thing.

The threesome stepped inside a stuffy and wear-worn sitting area on the inn's second story. Mr. Thorndale instructed the upper maid to shut the door as she left.

Crispin began formulating an apology, but the words stuck in his throat when he looked at Miss Thorndale. She stood silently trembling, her eyes lowered to the floor.

Mr. Thorndale stepped to within six inches of his niece. She raised her head almost mechanically, as though she'd expected the sudden proximity. Mr. Thorndale glared at her. Tension filled the room with the thickness of London fog. Mr. Thorndale's hand flew through the air, landing soundly across his niece's face. The force set her nearly off balance, her delicate, pale hands instantly cupping her mouth.

Instinct propelled Crispin toward the quaking lady even as his mind froze in shock. The man struck his niece without warning, without provocation.

"Where was your woman?" Mr. Thorndale demanded of his niece.

"I thought she was with me."

Crispin reached out to touch her arm, intending to both ascertain the extent of her injury and to offer his support.

"Miss Thorndale?"

The poor lady was trembling.

"Just what is your name, sir?" Mr. Thorndale's tone turned to a sneer on the last word.

"I am Lord Cavratt." Crispin kept his tone civil. He would not let this man get his hackles up. He turned back toward the lady standing stoically silent beside him. "Miss—"

"Lord Cavratt, I expect you to do what honor requires of any gentleman who has compromised a young lady's reputation."

"You believe her compromised by a simple kiss?" The man truly was mad.

Mr. Thorndale looked down his long, overly hooked nose. "That, my lord, was no simple kiss. A true gentleman would not kiss a lady *that way* without intending to make an offer. Unless of course your intentions were not honorable."

How utterly ridiculous. To force an engagement over one kiss, and one with virtually no witnesses. Society would never require such a thing. Yet Crispin couldn't honorably refuse, not when Miss Thorndale's own uncle considered her reputation tarnished.

Miss Thorndale appeared as shocked as Crispin felt. She would never insist he go through with her uncle's demands. A brief and entirely foundationless engagement ought to allow the man time to cool off and regain his head. Crispin could endure a day or so of absurdity. He and Philip could laugh about it after the fact.

Crispin bowed and bit back an exasperated sigh. With as much grace as he could muster, he said, "If she will have me."

Chapter Two

Have him? Catherine didn't even know him!

He was apparently titled and probably wealthy. She'd certainly noticed his copper-brown hair and broad shoulders and the second and third glances he'd received from every female in the garden. More likely than not, Lord Cavratt was a complete cad. Just thinking of his kiss made her face burn hot again.

"Of course the chit'll take you," Uncle sneered. "Even *she* is not that brainless."

Catherine let her hand drop to her chest, trying to regain control of her breathing. There had to be a way out of this. Lord Cavratt was looking at her, quite intensely, actually. Did he expect her to say something? Thank him for the offer, perhaps? Declare herself fortunate or pleased? Cry off, was more like it.

Uncle could not force the poor gentleman's hand in this way. It was unconscionable.

"Uncle, you mustn't—"

Another resounding blow interrupted her plea. He hit her with enough force to split her lip. The radiating pain wasn't new, but it never hurt any less. How many times in the last eight years had she prayed for a means of escape from this tyrant?

"Maybe your husband will teach you to mind your place," Uncle growled.

Catherine held her hand tight to her face, trying to keep the blood off her dress. If she remained very still and remembered not to speak to her uncle, he might not strike again. No one should ever have to learn those sort of life lessons.

"That will be quite enough, Mr. Thorndale." Lord Cavratt stepped between her and Uncle, offering her a clean linen handkerchief and a look of obvious concern. Catherine lowered her eyes, uncomfortable with the pity she saw in this stranger's face.

Uncle ignored Lord Cavratt's reprimand and walked toward the door. "I'll go seek out the vicar."

Vicar?

"Vicar?" Lord Cavratt sputtered, sounding as shocked as Catherine felt.

"We'll have this mess settled tonight." Uncle gave Lord Cavratt the once-over. "Then you can't run."

"I haven't a Special License." Lord Cavratt stepped toward Uncle. She didn't realize until he'd left her side how much calmer she'd felt with him there.

"*I* have one," Uncle said.

He had a Special License? In his possession?

"You anticipated this sort of entanglement?" One of Lord Cavratt's eyebrows rose. He gave Catherine a questioning look.

Did he think she frequently found herself in the arms of complete strangers? She tried to look as dignified as possible with his now-bloody handkerchief pressed to her mouth. She had her faults, certainly, but she was no light-skirt.

"I would never have allowed an opportunity to rid myself of that brat to slip through my fingers." Uncle yanked open the door. "I'll bring back the vicar."

"Perfect," Lord Cavratt muttered.

"Keep an eye on the dandy," Uncle growled at the maid and sent her scurrying back inside the sitting area. She hung near the door and kept her eyes obligingly on the dingy window.

"Dandy?" Lord Cavratt said to no one in particular. "I am as much a dandy as that man is a saint."

Catherine had a sudden fleeting urge to smile at Lord Cavratt's jab. But smiling was unladylike. Uncle had told her so countless times.

"I cannot begin to apologize enough for all of this," Lord Cavratt said.

"Try," Catherine said under her breath.

Lord Cavratt obviously heard her remark. His brow raised in surprise as he regarded her searchingly. Catherine's heart raced as it did every time she'd managed to ruffle Uncle's feathers, which was alarmingly often. *Please don't let him be angry,* she silently pleaded.

"I am afraid we will have to marry." Lord Cavratt began a slow pace around the room. "I hope you don't object to a dandified gentleman." The caustic tone with which he spoke added an unexpectedly humorous quality to his words. He, obviously, objected to Uncle's evaluation of him. "But, I will see my solicitor in London and this will be cleared up quickly enough."

"I don't understand." Catherine's voice seemed minuscule contrasted with his rich baritone.

"We will annul the marriage," Lord Cavratt said, as though any peahen should have thought of as much.

So he thought her morals *and* her intellect were questionable—not the most promising evaluation from one's future husband. *Husband?* Good heavens, how very ridiculous!

"That sounded far more condescending than I intended. Forgive me."

Catherine nodded, feeling slightly appeased.

"The license cannot possibly be legal," he said, "which should make the marriage easily annulled. I think."

Catherine could easily believe her uncle had undertaken something illegal. Catherine dabbed at her lip. The bleeding had slowed, but the throbbing had not. She knew very little about annulments.

"I will secure you a room for the night." Lord Cavratt looked more than a little harried. "We'll be in London tomorrow and have everything settled day after next."

He had walked a perfect oval around the sitting area, talking as much to himself as to Catherine. Strangely, his words were calming. Their absurd situation could be rectified.

"Thank you, my lord."

"That will never do." Lord Cavratt shook his head at her and even smiled a little. "If we're going to be married—even for only two days—I'd like you to call me Crispin."

"I don't think I can." Catherine had been lectured on the rules of propriety more times than she could count.

"It is not a difficult name." He shrugged. "Two syllables. Fairly straightforward. Except my sister couldn't say it. She called me 'Crispy' for years, although that is a rather undignified chapter of my past I would rather forget."

"Understandably so." She had the oddest recurring desire to smile in Lord Cavratt's company. *Crispin's,* she corrected herself.

"And do I have permission to use your given name?" He looked oddly amused. The hint of a smile on his lips changed his entire face, rendering him a little less intimidating, though only a very little.

Catherine could feel herself blush as she nodded her agreement. A temporary wife ought to allow such a small familiarity, she supposed.

"Then would you mind telling me what it is? Or shall I wait to see it written out on the marriage license? Better yet, I'll guess." He made a face clearly intended to indicate deep pondering.

"Catherine."

"That would have been my first guess."

"Really?" She didn't believe a word of it.

Crispin looked surprised but amused. She really needed to rein in her tongue before she pushed him too far. Uncle rarely put up with cheek—she doubted Crispin would, either.

The door flew open, and Uncle marched in with the dyspeptic-looking vicar at his side. Two other men, obviously of the local gentry, followed close on their heels. Catherine lowered her eyes back to the floor. She heard the sound of paper being slapped onto the desk.

"I'd prefer to dispense with the ceremony and just sign the bloody thing." Uncle really was going to force them to do this.

Catherine repeated Crispin's reassurances. The marriage would be annulled, whatever that entailed. Everything would be set to rights. She would be back under Uncle's thumb—not as reassuring a thought as she might have hoped for.

"'Twouldn't be legal without the ceremony." The whiny voice could only be the vicar's.

"Very well," Uncle spat.

Crispin didn't offer any verbal agreement nor argument. Catherine heard the scratching of a quill on parchment.

"Miss Thorndale, you sign here," the vicar said.

Catherine summoned what dignity she could and strode to the desk. The vicar's bony finger indicated the spot where her signature belonged. She took the quill in hand and steadied her breath. She felt an inexplicable need to look at Crispin, to see some kind of reassurance in his face. Any expression short of complete disgust or utter panic would be more than welcome.

She glanced as covertly as possible. Their eyes met and she knew somehow that he understood her hesitation. He nodded calmly.

"Sign," Uncle snapped.

Willing her hand to not shake, she wrote neatly across the line *Catherine Adelaide Thorndale*. She couldn't even make out Crispin's signature. That seemed the way with men—indiscernible on so many levels.

"Get on with it, Vicar," Uncle ordered.

The ceremony, though everything that was legally required, proved quick, cold, and unfeeling. If Catherine hadn't listened closely, she might have entirely missed the fact that she and Crispin had just been pronounced man and wife.

Temporarily, she told herself.

Uncle waved over the maid, still loyally stationed at the window. She arrived in a swish of drab, colorless skirts, not unlike the ones Catherine herself wore. "Have Lady Cavratt's trunk brought from her previous room."

The woman looked thoroughly bemused. "Whose?" she asked.

Uncle flicked his hand in Catherine's direction. "Lady Cavratt."

Realization struck. *She* was Lady Cavratt. Catherine stole a look at Crispin, who stood in private conversation with the vicar. When the sour-faced man took his leave and Crispin turned to face her and Uncle, his eyes snapped with barely controlled temper. Catherine instinctively shrunk back.

"Now, Cavratt." Uncle addressed him in his usual self-assured manner. "I'd like a few moments with my niece."

Crispin offered a half bow and turned to go. Catherine felt her legs begin to tremble beneath her. She always avoided being alone with her uncle, especially when his mood was antagonistic.

"I am certain I don't need to remind you that your niece is now my wife."

Uncle nodded, though he looked a bit confused.

"Whatever you wish to say to her, you can say in my presence. I will stand across the room if you wish for greater privacy, but I will not leave her alone with you."

"You wish to eavesdrop on a private conversation?"

"I wish to make perfectly sure she comes to no further harm at your hands."

Catherine stared in shock. Was he protecting her? Why? She'd been anticipating a thorough lashing for this mess.

"Of course." Uncle's voice dripped with annoyance.

Crispin crossed the room and leaned against the wall, his eyes watching Uncle.

Uncle turned a venomous glare on Catherine. "Well, you've captured a title, which was no doubt your intention," he growled in a voice little louder than a whisper.

Catherine knew better than to attempt an explanation. Logic and Uncle were not particularly well acquainted.

"Two minutes in your company and he'll leave you in a ditch." Uncle eyed her with his usual dissatisfaction. "But—"

Catherine could feel her breath catch. Uncle's voice had taken on that tone of foreboding which always seemed to precede one disaster or another.

"—know this. Should he manage to unshackle himself, you will never be welcomed back to Yandell Hall." Uncle grimaced in obvious disgust. "I'll not have a good-for-nothing wench sullying my lands. Am I understood?"

Catherine nodded. Uncle did not make idle threats, meaning she'd just lost the only home she'd ever known. Since her parents' death, that home had held little but pain and unhappiness. Yet those familiar rooms had once been a place of peace.

Without a good-bye or a parting look, Uncle tromped from the room. His footsteps echoed down the hall and faded away. She never appreciated Uncle as much as she did when he left a room.

Catherine pressed the bloodied handkerchief to her mouth once more, though the bleeding had stopped. Uncle had washed his hands of her. Not such a terrible thing in light of what life with him had been like. Considering Uncle's temper, she'd come out of the mess less painfully than she'd expected. Crispin had even been thoughtful enough to protect her from the last moments of Uncle's anger.

Crispin stepped away from the wall and closer to her. "He is not the most tenderhearted of fellows, is he?"

Catherine shook her head.

"Well, no need to worry about him now. I sent a maid to prepare your room—I imagine it is ready for you by now."

"Thank you," Catherine said.

Crispin eyed her a moment. "Are you certain you are well? Do you need an apothecary, perhaps a tonic?"

She hadn't been expecting kindness. In all honesty, he'd shown her a great deal of kindness. “I am well, thank you.”

He nodded and indicated she should make her way to the corridor. They walked in awkward silence down the narrow passage and up another flight of stairs. She could hear the voices of guests gathering in the public rooms below. They passed closed doors; no doubt the rooms beyond were occupied by yet more guests of the very busy inn.

Crispin paused at a thick wooden door. “Right in here.” He motioned her inside.

She opened the door to a simply furnished room that smelled quite appetizingly of beef and potatoes. Candelabras were lit around the room, barely relieving the dimness. Nightfall must have come without her noticing. Jane smiled at her from across the room.

Bless Jane, Catherine thought. She’d been the only source of consolation in Catherine’s life since her father had died. Had it really been eight years?

She glanced back at Crispin, uncertain of what she ought to say.

He spoke first. “Do not fret, Catherine. This will all be put to rights soon enough.” He smiled and bowed before slipping out of sight down the corridor.

“’Is Lordship ordered a tray for your supper,” Jane said, motioning to the table once Catherine closed the door. “Seems you went and got married.”

Catherine recognized the curiosity in Jane’s face. She wanted to offer some explanation, but her embarrassment tied her tongue. To own the truth, she wasn’t entirely sure of the details herself.

“Mr. Thorndale forced the both of ya, di’n’t he?” As usual, Jane knew more than she ought.

Catherine nodded as she changed into her several-years-old night rail. Jane obviously expected more information. “Uncle happened upon Lord Cavratt as he was . . . kissing me.”

Jane whistled, bringing the blush to Catherine’s face in an instant. “Why’d ’is Lordship go’n do that?”

“Honestly, Jane, I haven’t the slightest idea.”

Chapter Three

THE JOURNEY TO LONDON REQUIRED eight hours. Though they had covered only half the distance to the metropolis, Crispin felt as though three days had passed since they'd left the inn that morning. Self-castigation did not make time pass swiftly.

He discovered very little about his wife during the first half of their journey beyond the fact that she didn't have very much to say and blushed every time he spoke or looked at her or moved. Despite the obvious drawbacks to a reticent traveling companion, he found he liked her company far more than Miss Bower's.

Catherine had nodded off within thirty minutes of retaking the road after stopping for lunch. She was a wisp of a thing, really. No obvious fuss had been made over her appearance. His servants had ascertained from the Thorndale servants that Catherine's uncle inherited an estate and a sizable fortune upon the death of his older brother, Catherine's father. Yet her dress and unobtrusive mannerisms would lead anyone to mistake her for a servant.

An intelligent, thinking, logical gentleman could reasonably make that exact misinterpretation. He kept telling himself that. The mistake had been understandable and excruciatingly unfortunate and, when it came down to it, rather idiotic.

Crispin's eyes settled on her bruised cheek. Her lady's maid had certainly applied some plaster or another to the bruise and fat lip—it looked much better than it would have otherwise. He didn't think Thorndale had hit her again, not after the first two times.

To hit a woman. Twice. Crispin shook his head in disgust. The man's own niece, even. And, worse, she hadn't been at all surprised by her uncle's actions. What kind of life had Catherine known? Not that Crispin's role in her life had been particularly ideal thus far, accosting her with unasked for and unwelcome attentions.

"You are a cad," he told himself. "A cur. A bounder. A scoundrel. A . . . human thesaurus."

The countryside flew past as the carriage rolled on toward London. Catherine slept on despite the jarring of the carriage on the rutted and ill-maintained roads. The sleep of the innocent escaped Crispin, however. The guilty, apparently, don't sleep at all.

That kiss. An unexpected smile began to cross his face. He hadn't expected the kiss to affect him at all. It was, after all, merely a display of his "talents," as he'd called them. And yet he'd spent half the night trying to pull his thoughts away from his ill-timed talent show. He'd never before held a woman who felt so perfect in his arms. Nor shared a kiss that left him unable to think.

The hinted-at smile disappeared, however, the moment he looked across the carriage at Catherine sleeping. Her bruised and swollen face was the price of that kiss. And neither of their reputations would emerge intact after an annulment.

"You *are* a cad," he whispered to himself and forced his gaze out the window.

Several hours passed without a moment's rest. Crispin didn't need to look out the window to know when they arrived in London. The smell of horses and humanity hung heavy in the air, which tasted vaguely of smoke and cinders. He knew from experience his senses would cease to notice the onslaught after he'd been in residence a few days. Time always numbed him to the impact of hypocritical society as well.

Welcome back to London.

Crispin glanced across the carriage. Catherine had awoken nearly an hour earlier but had not yet spoken. She sat in the far corner of the carriage, sunken so far into the deep blue cushions she nearly disappeared. Her eyes were fixed apprehensively on the dimly lit city outside the carriage window. He wondered if she noticed the taste in the air as well.

"London can be a little overwhelming." Crispin hoped to be consoling. It seemed like a husbandly thing to do. Husbands were usually consoling, weren't they? He might only be her maybe-legal husband for a day or so, but he could at least do the thing properly.

"I know," Catherine said, her voice little louder than a whisper.

Against the noise of the city, Crispin could hardly hear her. "You've been here before?" He leaned a little closer to hear her response.

She nodded. "When I was presented."

"You've had a Season, then?" Strange. He didn't remember seeing her in society.

Catherine shook her head but offered no further explanation.

The carriage came to a halt and Crispin glanced out the window. Permount House. At last.

A footman appeared on cue and handed Catherine out, something that seemed to surprise her. The "my lady" he offered appeared to startle her even more.

Crispin stepped out and motioned her up the steps where the butler, Hancock, held the door open for them. They stepped into the front hall and Catherine's eyes widened. She was impressed, he surmised. He felt an unexpected surge of pride.

"You received my instructions?" Crispin asked Hancock.

"Yes, my lord."

"And you've carried them out?"

"Precisely as requested." Hancock eyed him with amusement. This uncharacteristic formality between them felt uncomfortable. The butler, well into his seventh decade, had known Crispin from the time he was in leading strings. Many gentlemen would have replaced a retainer old enough to have known their grandfathers and familiar enough with their youthful peccadilloes to treat them with too large a degree of amused familiarity. Crispin liked Hancock far too much to dismiss the man simply because he knew enough to embarrass him before all of London.

Crispin had decided that, for the few hours Catherine would reside in his home, he'd not give her any reason to disparage his household or himself after the annulment. At least something should come out of this intact. Their reputations wouldn't, not entirely. His would, of course, emerge better than hers, he being male and the holder of an old and prestigious title.

"Will you have Miss—" He barely caught himself. "—Lady Cavratt shown to her rooms, please?"

Hancock bowed and disappeared to fetch an upper maid.

Crispin could feel Catherine's gaze on him. How did she do that? The half a dozen times she'd actually looked at him since they'd left for London he'd been able to sense her gaze before he'd seen her face. It was a phenomenon he could not at all explain.

Catherine looked at him expectantly. Did she need something? Could it be she didn't know the hour?

"So you can change for dinner." He kept his voice low. Best not give the servants anything further on which to speculate.

"Change, my lord?"

"Of course." He eyed her warily. Certainly she'd been taught society manners. Changing for dinner ranked among the most basic.

"This is the only dress I have." Catherine hung her head, the same defeated posture her uncle's presence had inspired.

"Then you can wash up," he answered, trying to seem unconcerned about her appearance for her sake. "And wear . . . that."

It really was an ugly gown. He'd never met a lady who'd have willingly worn something like that. It was only slightly more flattering than a potato sack and nearly the same color.

"This way, my lady," one of the upper maids bid. Catherine followed after a moment of confusion.

Crispin let out a tense sigh and stepped into the sitting room to gather his thoughts and his wits. His entire life was about to be turned upside down, he could feel it. Weren't kisses suppose to create widespread upheaval only in overly dramatic novels and fairy tales?

"Port, my lord?" Hancock offered with a little too much cheek.

"Brandy," Crispin replied, not bothering to hide his sarcasm. "Port later. Maybe you should search out some Blue Ruin and a long pint of Huckle My Buff."

"For a gentleman who does not drink, you have acquired a very colorful alcoholic vocabulary." Hancock hadn't moved a single inch to fulfill Crispin's directive. He obviously recognized the bluff for what it was. "Is the new Lady Cavratt so unbearable?"

"I have no idea how unbearable she is or isn't."

With a weary look, Hancock closed the doors of the sitting room behind him and, after checking to see if they were alone, gave Crispin a look that told him to unload his mind. After an honest and thorough retelling of the previous day's events, Crispin slumped into an upholstered chair and dropped his head sideways into his open hand.

Hancock shook his head in disbelief.

"It shouldn't be difficult to annul," Crispin said. "Probably nearly as easy as getting engaged. Perhaps if I kissed Mr. Brown, he'd push the annulment through as quickly as Mr. Thorndale pushed through the wedding."

Hancock took Crispin's grumbling in stride, not looking at all surprised. It was precisely why Crispin liked the man so much. No hypocrisy nor insincerity in Hancock. Crispin's father had trusted the man implicitly.

"Her abigail arrived a full hour before you and her ladyship," Hancock said. "Her Jane seems to be a woman who can assess a situation and determine with whom to share confidences."

"I take it you've learned something of my . . . wife." The last word stuck a moment before allowing itself to be spoken. *My wife.* A man really ought to have some warning before being required to utter that phrase.

Hancock nodded.

"You're better than Bow Street. I'm married to the lady and all I know is she hardly speaks a word, is scared to death of everything, and has abhorrent taste in husbands."

Hancock nodded his agreement, something Crispin found neither insulting nor surprising. "In addition," Hancock said, "she is an orphan, her uncle's ward, and she was married last night."

"Yes, I attended the ceremony—it was lovely. And I have met her uncle. Wonderful man. Makes Napoleon seem like a pleasant sort of fellow."

"Which may explain why the uncle never married."

"If he's in the market, I know a remarkably efficient way of finding oneself married with very little effort," Crispin said. "One does not even have to know the lady."

Hancock pressed on without acknowledging a single sardonic syllable. "According to her ladyship's abigail, the uncle was not at all pleased with this marriage."

"He rather insisted on it."

"Under the assumption you'd annul it as soon as you reached London," Hancock added. "He told Lady Cavratt as much."

"*I* told her as much," Crispin said. "I wouldn't be shocked if John Coachman mentioned it in passing. It is an assumption most of London is going to make."

"And, though her ladyship does not know the particulars," Hancock said, "she told Jane that she suspects, rightly so, that her standing in society and her reputation will suffer as a result of the annulment."

Crisping nodded. There would be an unavoidable scandal. She would be cut by most of society afterward, something that bothered him more than he would have guessed, considering she was little more than a stranger.

"Mr. Thorndale has cut her off," Hancock said, a cautionary edge to his tone that caught Crispin's attention. "In no uncertain terms, he informed her that, should the marriage be ended, he would not welcome her back."

"His generous nature warms the soul, does it not?" No reasonable man would throw out his own flesh and blood for an infraction he knew she hadn't committed. "Did you find out anything else?" Crispin rubbed his face wearily. "Perhaps this Jane told you if her ladyship is one who might murder an unwanted husband in his sleep."

"I didn't think to ask, my lord."

Crispin recognized Hancock's return to formality. He, too, had heard footsteps outside the door.

"Will you be dressing for dinner, my lord?"

"At risk of losing my title as a dandy,"—he was sorely tempted to roll his eyes—"I believe we will dine informally this evening."

"Very good." Hancock straightened his own blue livery and opened the doors of the sitting room.

Crispin stepped out, regaining his formal air. Catherine stood outside the dining room doors, dwarfed by the enormity and splendor of the hall.

"That is an ugly dress." Crispin had the strangest urge to run out that very minute and buy her the frilliest, fanciest dress he could find. Where on earth had that sudden inclination come from? He'd never been particularly eager to buy a dress for his own sister, though he'd never begrudged her any addition to her wardrobe she'd wanted.

"Quite hideous," Hancock concurred before hastily adding, "my lord."

Crispin watched Hancock disappear before turning his eyes back on Catherine. Why, he wondered, was she so quiet? He'd known several people who were naturally shy, but she didn't strike him that way. Did he, in particular, frighten her? Or was it people in general?

"Dinner is served," Hancock announced, pulling the dining room doors open.

Crispin stepped to where Catherine stood quaking. They were going in to dinner, not an execution. He offered her his arm and she simply stared at it, confused. Now what did he do?

Crispin opted for teasing her—the approach had generally worked with his sister, Lizzie. "It is a nice arm, isn't it?" Crispin said. "Perhaps you'd be willing to take hold of it for me—safeguard it from would-be thieves. I only have two and would hate for some unscrupulous ruffian to make off with one of them."

He held his arm out further still, trying to get across to her that he meant for her to take it. Catherine looked between him and Hancock.

"You want me to go in *with* you?" she asked.

Why did that prospect seem to unnerve her so thoroughly? He was not such an ogre. "Yes."

"*With* you?" she pressed again.

"And when we get in there, I'll probably even expect you to eat, heartless dictator that I am."

Hancock cleared his throat in an obvious attempt to stifle a laugh.

Catherine didn't laugh as Crispin expected her to. In fact, he didn't believe he'd heard her laugh once in the twenty-four hours or so they'd been acquainted. Granted, there hadn't been many lighthearted moments.

She cautiously slid her arm through his. It was progress, anyway. He practically had to drag her with every step, though. She actually looked shocked when a footman slid her chair underneath her. A bowl of mock-turtle soup was set before the both of them. Despite its less-than-worthy reputation, the impostor soup had become a favorite of Crispin's.

Catherine sat perfectly still, her hands folded in her lap. Her eyes darted in his direction but returned almost immediately to her clasped hands. After several minutes, Crispin's stomach wouldn't allow him another moment of patience.

"If this were consommé, it would be jelled by now," he said, hoping the hint would be sufficient. The soup would be little more than lukewarm after the delay. "Perhaps we should eat before it solidifies further."

Catherine nodded without looking up. She didn't reach for her spoon.

"It is customary for a gentleman to wait until after a lady has begun to eat," Crispin said.

She looked at him as though he'd just suggested she eat with her toes. She mouthed a silent apology and hastily stabbed a spoonful of soup into her mouth.

Crispin stared for a moment. No wonder she'd never had a Season. She hardly functioned at a simple meal.

The rest of dinner passed in almost complete silence. With the arrival of each course, Catherine shoved a spoonful of food into her mouth the moment the plate reached the table, all the while eyeing him nervously. Crispin shook his head in bewilderment. She was trying, he would give her that.

As the trifle was finished and cleared, Crispin found himself feeling rather obliged to say something to his silent dinner partner. He passed on the port he'd jokingly requested earlier, as Hancock no doubt had known he would do, and joined Catherine in the sitting room. Standing near enough for her to hear him, but far enough from the prying ears of any passing servants, he opted for the only topic in which he knew they both had an interest.

"I will speak with my solicitor in the morning. The whole matter should be resolved before most of Town is even awake."

Catherine looked directly into his eyes, her own pleading with him. She had strikingly beautiful eyes. Catherine's face slid into a look of resignation, and she nodded before hanging her head and stepping a little further from him.

Crispin abruptly turned away. Her distraught resignation made him decidedly uncomfortable. A more neutral topic, he told himself. "You said you've been in London before," he said, walking to the fireplace. "Do you come often?"

"I have been to Town three times, my lord." He barely heard her answer. She hadn't returned her gaze to his face, still studying the floor.

"Please call me Crispin."

"Of course. I'm sorry."

Blast, why was she apologizing as though she'd committed some enormous infraction? If he wasn't careful, he'd inadvertently convince Catherine she was a criminal. "You were in Town for your presentation and . . ."

"Twice as a child," she said.

"You consider the country your home, then?"

"I do."

"And do you have family there?"

"Only my uncle," Catherine replied as quietly as always. "My parents have passed on, and I was their only child."

Crispin tapped his fingers on the mantelpiece. She had no family. "Were you educated at home?"

She nodded.

"Were there any families in the neighborhood with whom you were close?"

"No."

"Were there many other young ladies your age there?"

"No."

"Was there *anyone* in the neighborhood?"

"Of course," she replied.

"Forgive me," Crispin said. "That was—"

"Uncalled for?" she finished for him. An instant later her eyes widened in apparent surprise. She clamped her mouth closed.

"Touché, madam," Crispin acknowledged. Throwing back the exact insipid phrase he'd used after their disastrous kiss certainly put him in his place. Though why she seemed upset by her own wit, he couldn't say. He found the show of backbone refreshing. "You seem to have had a lonely upbringing."

"Sometimes not lonely enough. Uncle was not always very good company."

"Really? I found him quite pleasant." Crispin rolled his eyes. "A jolly good chap."

He turned a little away from her and tapped his fingers on the mantel. Catherine had no family. No friends. No home. He ought to be able to annul their marriage—the license could not possibly be legal, after all, his name having been added long after it was obtained. That, however, would leave Catherine out on the streets, her reputation sullied beyond repair. But, he told himself, he could hardly be blamed for that.

He stopped tapping his fingers. She was looking at him. He could feel it. Cautiously, he turned. Her eyes were, indeed, fixed on him. How did she do that? And how could he get her to stop? The phenomenon was positively unnerving.

"I must apologize for all of the difficulty our situation must be causing you." She spoke with a quiet determination Crispin wouldn't have expected from one so reticent. "My uncle is a stern man, and often unfair. He should not have pushed you into this."

"I should not have kissed you."

Missing her cue, Catherine didn't offer platitudes of forgiveness. He felt more like a cad by the moment; a moderately executed lie might have appeased his conscience a little. It seemed like a wifely thing to do.

"I assure you this will all be remedied tomorrow," Crispin promised her. He hoped.

The reassurance left Catherine looking even less reassured. He obviously needed to work on the consoling husband bit. She twisted her hands around each other as she stood in uneasy silence and didn't look at him, didn't step away. Crispin watched her, his discomfort rising.

"I didn't rest well last night, my lor—Crispin." She reddened at her near oversight. "If you don't mind, I would like to retire early."

Mind? It would be a tremendous relief. Crispin had no idea what to do with a wife. "Of course."

Catherine turned and practically ran from the room.

He watched her go, intrigued by the conflicting aspects of her personality. She dressed like a servant and often carried herself like one. But she spoke like an educated lady of the ton, occasionally displaying an intriguingly quick intellect. She never smiled, but what little conversation she indulged in was not focused negatively. He had yet to hear her laugh, but he'd bet a monkey she possessed a keen sense of humor.

Alone, he had ample opportunity to examine the choices before him. He had grounds to absolve their forced marriage, but doing so would send her unprotected into what he knew all too well was an uncaring and unforgiving world. He didn't deserve to be tied to a complete stranger and couldn't imagine she did either. Which left him with a problem: what was he going to do?

Chapter Four

Catherine sat rigidly in a high-backed chair, listening to the sound of footsteps in the corridor. Her small traveling trunk lay packed on the floor beside her. She looked again around the rooms that had been hers for less than twenty-four hours. The walls were papered in shades of deep green and blue. The window dressings were lusciously thick and of the softest velvet. An ornate fireplace sat empty, though it had provided warmth during the long night she'd passed anticipating her fate. Never in her most imaginative moments had she dreamt of being surrounded by such luxury and beauty. Yet she'd found no joy in it.

She'd wandered from her bedchamber long after the house had settled into silent slumber and paced the cold wooden floors of the sitting area. Her future spread out before her in an unending tapestry of uncertainty. She had nowhere to go and no one to turn to. A night's worth of pacing and pondering had offered no answers.

According to Jane, Crispin had left at eight o'clock that morning and had informed his butler he would return within the hour. So Catherine had placed the trunk she'd never bothered to unpack beside the chair nearest her chamber door and sat to await her dismissal.

Four hours had passed. She, apparently, had not married a terribly punctual gentleman.

The footfall grew closer. A shadow crossed the threshold. Catherine steadied her nerves. He had come to throw her out.

She allowed her eyes to shift upward. Crispin strode through the door, apparently deep in thought. The air of assurance he generally exuded seemed to have significantly dissipated. His gaze fell on her.

"Good morning," he said.

His smile went a long way to soothing her badly rattled nerves.

"How are you?" he asked.

How was she? She had no idea where she was going, where she would be living the next day, the next hour. "Fine," she managed to whisper.

"Agreeable weather we are having, are we not?"

Catherine nodded. Was the gentleman a bit thick in the head? What had inspired a discussion of the weather, of all things?

"The sun appears to have cut through the fog and the breeze is . . . I'm stalling. Can you tell?" Crispin raised his brow in self-derision.

She nodded again.

"Should I keep stalling?" he asked with feigned hopefulness. "I believe I could manage it with very little effort."

"I would rather you didn't." Far better to know where she stood than to delay the inevitable.

"I was afraid you would say that." Crispin closed his eyes and rubbed them with his thumb and forefinger. He let out a long breath before opening his eyes again. He pulled a chair from the writing desk over beside Catherine and sat facing her. He seemed to debate over his words for a moment. "I have a confession, Catherine. Now brace yourself . . . I am more of an idiot than I originally suspected."

She hadn't been expecting him to say that.

"I see you do not disagree. A telling blow, to be sure."

"Are you stalling again?" She had the oddest urge to smile.

"Guilty." He let out a strained breath. "Obtaining an annulment is more complicated than I thought, and my two-day timetable is proving a bit optimistic."

More time? Catherine's heart throbbed in her throat. This was precisely what she needed. Catherine watched the muscles in his face tighten around his jaw, and she felt a twinge of guilt. His revelation had been a relief to her. A little unanticipated time would allow her to search out her options. Crispin, obviously, disliked the delay.

She wrung her hands together, fighting her conflicting feelings. "What are we to do until the annulment is granted?"

"Cards?" He looked almost serious. "Perhaps a parlor game or two?" He shook his head. "Forgive me. I would not want you to think I do not recognize the seriousness of the situation."

What an odd sense of humor Crispin had. Not unpleasant. Just odd.

Crispin rose to his feet and began treading a tension-thick circle about the room. "I won't sugarcoat the fact that all of Town will be speculating about the state of our marriage. For a gentleman who is well known in society to suddenly marry someone entirely unknown and without a single member of his family or any of his friends present . . ." He rubbed his forehead again. "People will wonder. For the sake of both our reputations, we need to attempt to convince them, for the time being, that we are a happily married couple." The obvious doubt in his face was not reassuring. "An annulment causes an uproar regardless of the circumstances, but an amicable ending keeps the entire thing quieter."

"You're not sending me away?"

"I am thinking of sending *myself* away. By nightfall I could be in Bedlam where I belong." Crispin paused at the fireplace, fingering the molding along the mantel. "I am certain you believed me completely mad within seconds of meeting me."

Catherine pinked at his reference to their ill-fated encounter outside the otherwise insignificant inn a mere two days earlier. Her color only deepened as she realized how often she'd thought since then that, under different circumstances, she would very much like to be kissed that way again. Perhaps she was the one who had gone a bit mad.

Crispin stopped his pacing and faced her, looking quite serious. "For the immediate future, you will be Lady Cavratt, and that comes with certain obligations."

Catherine felt her eyes widen. Obligations? What did he mean by "obligations"?

"Socially," Crispin clarified, amusement sparkling in his eyes. "Did you think I planned to make you clean my linens or something?"

She just shook her head, unsure what she'd thought he meant.

"I only meant you will be expected to attend dinners and balls and other forms of socially condoned torture."

Catherine bit down on her bottom lip. He wished her to appear in public as a titled lady of consequence? She'd never play that role convincingly.

"Were you educated in social proprieties?" Crispin watched her, obviously doubtful.

"I was." Catherine tried to hold herself confidently.

Crispin didn't appear convinced. "Last night—" he began awkwardly, "You didn't seem—"

"I never accompanied my uncle in to dinner. He insisted on preceding me, and I was instructed to wait for *him* to eat." She had realized quickly during her meal with Crispin that her uncle's rules were not observed in Crispin's house—probably in *any* house.

The explanation seemed to satisfy him. "Do you know how to dance?"

"I had a dance instructor before my presentation." Her training felt very inadequate in that moment. "That was a couple years ago, however."

"Do you play an instrument?"

"Several."

Crispin stared at her as though those musical instruments were protruding from her face. He opened his mouth to speak but closed it again and resumed his pacing.

Perhaps society preferred a lady to resign herself to only one instrument. "Is that a bad thing?" she asked.

"Not at all. It makes me feel a touch fat-headed, is all. I probably could not *name* several instruments, let alone play them."

She knew he was teasing her, exaggerating his ignorance. "Perhaps if you copied the names out a few dozen times you could commit them to memory."

He leaned against the mantel, looking far more at ease than he had since his arrival. "Did your governess require you to do lines as well, then?"

"She was merciless." Catherine had actually rather adored her governess. Uncle had dismissed her the day of his arrival at Yandell Hall.

"But she managed to teach you to play 'several instruments.' The merciless tyrant was efficient, anyway."

Her governess had laid the foundation for Catherine's musical pursuits. Her tenacious determination to master those instruments came later. Uncle generally let her be while she practiced. So long as music could be heard echoing from the frigid music room of Yandell Hall, Uncle left her alone.

"Lady Hardford extended an invitation to a dinner party Friday evening," Crispin said from the far end of the room. "We will, of course, be expected to attend. If the viscountess is convinced our marriage is nothing out of the ordinary, half the ton will be convinced of the same within hours. Minutes, maybe. With her, gossip spreads faster than Prinny's waistline, which is saying something. And though she rather looks like a vulture, she is far more like a hen. Clucks incessantly, but doesn't bite."

"Do you really think I can convince her?" Catherine knew well her shortcomings.

Crispin took up his pacing once more. She watched him take turn after turn around the small room. A man of obvious means, his clothes were precisely tailored and of the latest fashion, his home richly furnished and more than adequately staffed. She had gleaned from the efficiency of his home that Crispin appreciated his comforts and routine. Her presence must have upset both. He certainly couldn't be lacking in admirers. He'd been walking with one—a particularly beautiful one—the day they'd met.

Perhaps he was in love with some refined lady of distinction. What an explanation he'd have to make should he encounter his *amór* with his inconvenient wife on his arm.

"You look troubled." Crispin's voice interrupted her thoughts.

Catherine shook her head, not wanting to burden Crispin with more of her difficulties.

"Planning my imminent demise?" Crispin raised his brow the way he did when being sardonic. She'd come to recognize that look in the short time she'd known him. In all honesty, she enjoyed it. The expression bordered on playful and went a long way toward relieving her sometimes overwhelming worries.

"I hope I don't completely embarrass you," Catherine said quietly. "I am not very experienced with social engagements. I've led a very different life, I assure you."

A look bordering on sympathy crossed Crispin's face. He studied her for a moment. "Did you say that was your only dress?"

Catherine glanced down at the lump of hideousness she'd donned the past year. Age and wear had only rendered it more awful. Feeling embarrassed to her very core, Catherine nodded.

"Do you own a coat?" he asked.

"Yes."

"Put it on," Crispin instructed.

"Now? Am I leaving?"

"*We* are visiting Madam LaCroix."

Catherine had never heard of the woman.

"A mantua maker," Crispin explained. "And a miracle worker."

"I have no money to have a gown made." She had no money *at all.*

Crispin smiled and his entire face softened and brightened. "You, Lady Cavratt, are among the wealthiest ladies of the ton. An entire wardrobe will barely dent your pin money."

"An entire—" Catherine choked on the words. "I cannot. The expense!"

"I had always planned to be a generous husband," Crispin interrupted, his tone teasing. "You might as well take advantage of that."

Catherine rose to continue her protest. "I would never take advantage of—"

"Our little charade will fall apart in an instant if you are seen socializing in a potato sack, Catherine."

She felt her face catch fire. His assessment left little doubt of her unattractive appearance. "I did not choose the dress."

"Don't be angry with me." Crispin crossed to her, speaking gently. "Soon you will have plenty of fine gowns, and I won't chide you about this one again."

"I don't want to embarrass you, but I can't possibly accept—"

"I am generous, Catherine. But also stubborn, and I am determined to take you to Madame LaCroix the moment you get your coat."

Crispin smiled at her and, to her utter astonishment, Catherine felt better. She almost managed a smile in return.

"Much better," he said. His eyes rested on her face and Catherine could feel her cheeks flush. Crispin's expression grew more intense. He brushed his fingers against her face and her heart began to pound. "Try not to be too miserable. This will all work out one way or another."

With his hand so gently touching her cheek, she could not begin to fashion a reply. Breathing became something of a struggle.

Abruptly, Crispin pulled his hand away and stepped toward the door. "We also have to do something about your hair," he said, distant again. "Put on your coat. I'll be waiting below."

Catherine stood statue-still, her shock too great for movement. She could still feel his fingers on her cheek. She'd spent nearly a decade cringing from the slightest touch, so accustomed had she become to the violence of her uncle.

Crispin's touch had been gentle and frightening at the same time. She could feel her entire world tipping on end. She'd come to expect anger from every man she encountered, disgust at her appearance and complete indifference from society at large. Instead, she was on her way to a dressmaker, being treated kindly by a Peer, of all things.

The entire ordeal terrified her.

Chapter Five

CATHERINE LOOKED TERRIFIED. OR PERHAPS simply overwhelmed.

Crispin silently congratulated himself on selecting Madame LaCroix. She was not only a talented modiste, but one whose silence on Catherine's current appearance could be trusted.

Madame LaCroix declared that designing a wardrobe for Catherine would be "a challenge," which was probably the official dressmaker's term for "exorbitantly expensive."

"This is your only . . . dress?" Madame LaCroix eyed Catherine's ensemble with a look of utter disgust. Her French accent was, of course, not authentic, but being French helped a modiste pay her bills.

Catherine silently nodded.

"It must be burned. The shoes may be tossed into the flames beside it." Madame LaCroix turned to Crispin. "I can, of course, recommend a shop to replace the boots."

Shoes were definitely a necessity.

"Do you have bonnets?" the dressmaker asked.

Catherine shook her head.

"Stockings? Wraps? Pelisses? A reticule? Slippers? A riding habit? Shawl?"

Does Catherine have anything? Crispin wondered. Her head hung lower with each question. So Thorndale was a bully *and* a skinflint. How could he have allowed Catherine's situation to grow so ridiculous?

"I can only imagine the state of your underthings," Madame LaCroix mumbled. Catherine turned a very becoming shade of crimson. Crispin bit back a smile—he liked the fact that she blushed so easily. "She cannot obtain all of these things here, Lord Cavratt."

"I suppose I will have to lend her my bonnet and shawl, then." Crispin pretended to be serious. "Unless, of course, you wish to provide me with a list of where we might go to obtain them."

"So she could parade around the city looking like this?" Madame LaCroix waved her hand over Catherine, her nose turned up in obvious disapproval. "*Non!* Inexcusable, Lord Cavratt. The wife of a man of your position dressed as she is."

"Which brings us back to the reason for our visit to your establishment. You do still sell dresses, do you not?" Crispin eyed Madame LaCroix with a look meant to remind her who was paying the bill. "A decent dress would be a drastic improvement."

"Decent?" Madame LaCroix scoffed. "I have never made a 'decent' dress in all my life, Lord Cavratt. My creations are *magnifique*."

"I would trust no one but you to make the attempt." Flattery, he instinctively knew, would go a long way with the faux-Frenchwoman.

"You do not believe I could make her magnificent?" Madame LaCroix's eyes narrowed.

Catherine was pretty. She possessed a fine pair of eyes. But Madame LaCroix seemed to think she could be an Incomparable—a distinction very few ladies were granted.

"You doubt, but you should not. I am a worker of miracles." Madame LaCroix began circling Catherine, eyeing her with immense interest.

Crispin watched Catherine shrink into herself the way she seemed to every time anyone paid her any attention. She turned her eyes on him—so blue and so uncertain.

He'd seen something in them in her sitting area at Permount House, some hint of spark behind the fear, and it had pulled him in. Before realizing what he was about, he'd nearly kissed her again, his own too-vivid memories of the one kiss they'd shared clouding his judgment. She'd probably received little if any attention from men before and he wasn't about to confuse her for all the heart-wrenching looks in the world.

"Go. Go. Go. I must work," Madame LaCroix said, still surveying Catherine as she circled. "You have many purchases to make."

"I have always had quite an eye for stockings and slippers," Crispin replied dryly.

"Psh!" Madame LaCroix mocked. "And have her look worse than she does now?"

Catherine's head seemed to drop even lower. Crispin began to wonder if Madame LaCroix truly had been the right choice. Her bluntness was as legendary as her gowns. Catherine's obviously fragile heart might not be able to bear it.

"Ask Lady Henley to assist you." Madame LaCroix waved him off. "Her taste is impeccable."

Lizzie! Why hadn't he thought of his sister? She and her husband would most certainly be in Town. He had no doubt she would not only take up the assignment, but thoroughly enjoy it. Lizzie spent more time shopping than the entire House of Lords spent in Parliament. She would never pass up the rare opportunity to spend Crispin's money while enjoying her favorite pastime.

He thanked Madame LaCroix and turned to go.

"You're leaving?" Catherine asked, a thread of worry in her voice.

Crispin smiled reassuringly. "I will return in two hours' time. Your maid is here should you require anything, and Madame LaCroix will keep you excruciatingly occupied, I assure you."

"But you will come back?"

For just a moment he was tempted to throw out a cheeky remark about being unable to resist the opportunity to conveniently skip out. He realized not a moment too soon that their uncertain situation would likely render such a comment decidedly unfunny. "Of course I will."

She smiled at him, actually smiled. The miniscule effort would have gone unnoticed on anyone else, but coming from Catherine, the slightest lightening of her expression made those eyes of hers all the more striking.

A bit thrown off by the impact of a single tiny smile, Crispin made his way to Lizzie and Edward's home entirely by memory. He paid very little attention to the path he took. His sister and brother-in-law lived only half a dozen doors down from Permount House. To Crispin's relief, though not his surprise, they were at home and received him with enthusiasm and obvious curiosity.

"The rumor mill has been turning again, Crispin." Lizzie eyed him over her steaming cup of tea.

"And what poor sap is being grinded in it this time?" Crispin was fairly certain *he* was the poor sap.

"It seems the highly sought after but quite uncatchable Lord Cavratt has been snared," Lizzie said with an amused raise of her eyebrow before laughing out loud. "How many times have we heard gossip of that nature, Edward?"

"At least three times every Season." Lizzie's husband, Edward, grinned.

"But the gossips are quite frustrated in their efforts this time," Lizzie continued. "Lady Littleton was here not an hour ago fishing for information. I couldn't even give her a name."

"That is the easiest part," Crispin said.

"Oh, I could have rattled off several dozen names that could reasonably be connected to you." Lizzie waved her hand dismissively. "You are being pursued by at least that many. I didn't think you would appreciate my picking at random."

"What name would you have her choose?" Edward asked, obviously amused by the entire thing.

"Catherine is a nice name." Crispin shrugged as if it were merely a passing thought.

"To be sure." Lizzie eyed him quizzically. "But why choose it?"

"Because that is her name."

"You, apparently, have heard more detailed rumors than I. How did these rumors get started, I wonder." Lizzie sipped her tea. "Did you dance with her once too often?"

"No."

"Her mother is a little too anxious?"

"No."

Lizzie's lips pursed the way they always did when she felt her brother's teasing had gone too far. "You are going to torture your own sister by refusing to relate some humorous *on-dit*? Come now. How did this bit of gossip get started?"

Crispin shrugged. "It's quite simple, actually. I married her."

"Good heavens!" Lizzie's teacup clanked against its saucer. "You're serious! What convinced you to do that?"

"Her rather large uncle."

Crispin recounted the entire ridiculous ordeal, though leaving out Mr. Thorndale's rough treatment of his niece. Somehow he couldn't bring himself to further embarrass Catherine. Lizzie expressed disbelief and disgust when the story warranted it. Edward simply listened, mouth hanging in surprise.

"I have considered an annulment," Crispin said. "But that is proving more complicated than I'd anticipated."

"You obviously have grounds," Edward said. "The license was obviously forged."

"Why is it that gentlemen only ever think in terms of cold logic?" Lizzie set her teacup on the side table with a clink of annoyance. "Of course he has grounds for an annulment, but that does not make obtaining one a good idea."

Lizzie, then, thought a marriage contracted under threat of bodily harm between two people entirely unacquainted with one another beyond one shattering kiss ought to be considered ideal? Lizzie's thought processes had always been baffling.

"You will survive the scandal given time, but a lady, unless she is a duke's daughter or possesses an even higher rank, would not emerge from the aftermath with anything resembling a good reputation." Lizzie's expression clearly told him that she found her brother sadly lacking in intelligence. "This Catherine of yours would not be welcomed anywhere afterward. She could, perhaps, find a position as a governess, if such a position were located far from the eyes of society and if the family were desperate enough to overlook the smirch on her good name."

"Oh, but it is worse than even that," Crispin said. "The best chance for being granted an annulment lies in denouncing Mr. Thorndale for his illegally obtained license in the most public and inflammatory way possible. The ecclesiastical courts would most likely grant the annulment, but in the process, Catherine would, at best, be painted as a mindless pawn and, at worse, as a—"

"Coconspirator," Edward finished.

"Precisely." Crispin wouldn't wish such a thing on Catherine.

"But," Lizzie said, "to be forced to remain married to someone she hardly knows . . ." She shook her head. "I couldn't imagine being at all happy in a marriage I hadn't chosen."

Not being at all happy. Was that what Crispin had to look forward to should he remain married?

"Have you explained all of this to her?" Lizzie looked the very picture of their old nurse when she'd scolded them for irresponsibility.

He shook his head. "Being the picture-perfect husband I am, I lied to her. I told her there were legal complications and then very quickly changed the subject."

"Good strategy," Edward said with a nod of approval.

Lizzie did not appear to agree. "She will bear the weight of whatever comes of this. Either she will be shunned by good society and left to earn her keep by spending the remainder of her life in drudgery and necessary exile, or she'll be married to you."

"Why is it, dearest sister, that I cannot tell which option you consider the more horrid?"

Lizzie studied him a moment, as if piecing something together.

"She hates you, does she?" Sympathetic sisters were, it seemed, hard to come by.

"Oddly enough, I don't think she does." Catherine had every reason in the world to be storming through his house, looking daggers at him and despising him. But she had done nothing of the sort. "I seem to have married a saint."

"And when do I get to meet this pattern card of feminine virtue?" Lizzie asked. "Before you pack her off to slave away over a brood of destructive brats, I hope."

"Tonight at dinner." They never stood on ceremony with invitations. "You, of course, will be bringing carriage loads of presents."

"Will I now?"

"Bonnets. Shawls. Slippers. Even unmentionables, I think." Crispin tapped his lip thoughtfully.

"And why will I be bringing these, um, gifts?"

"Because I will be paying the bills."

"Ah, that does make a difference, doesn't it? Is there anything else on your list?"

Plenty. A return to normalcy. A wife he knew something about beyond her tendency to blush and cower in terror. A foolproof guide to what he ought to do about the messy situation in which he'd landed. "I have no idea. What do you think she needs?"

"What does she have?"

"A potato sack that is currently serving as a dress."

"Anything else?"

"A coat. A pair of boots that are, miraculously, still holding together. I have no idea if she even owns a night rail."

"Her uncle's generosity at work, I assume," Edward said.

Crispin nodded. "An oversight I very much want to rectify."

Lizzie looked far too intrigued for Crispin's peace of mind. "I accept."

* * *

Crispin watched Catherine throughout dinner that night. Lizzie and Edward were hardly intimidating, but Catherine seemed overwhelmed. How, he wondered, could she possibly survive a formal dinner party?

Lizzie completely monopolized Catherine after dinner, spending nearly an hour in a one-sided conversation Crispin didn't attempt to overhear. He stayed near the fire, pondering every upcoming social obligation he had scheduled and trying to determine the best way to help Catherine survive. Perhaps they could shrug off, say she was ill. But no. That would give rise to even more unwanted rumors.

If only he knew how to go forward. Crispin had sent a note to Mr. Brown, his solicitor, that afternoon. Though he had not committed one way or the other to the annulment proceedings, he instructed Brown to prepare the paperwork for either scenario. Brown would investigate the criminal aspect of Thorndale's forged license, as well as Catherine's situation so a marriage settlement could be drafted should they not obtain an annulment.

The clock chimed nine and Catherine excused herself, nearly running from the room as she'd done the night before. She would eventually grow accustomed to Town hours and Town manners and Town greediness. London had a tendency to corrupt with mind-boggling speed. He hoped she proved an exception.

Crispin turned his eyes on his sister and brother-in-law. "Care to place any wagers on the likelihood of her surviving anything beyond a poorly attended musicale?"

"I'll give you five to one," Edward said.

"Will you two stop it?" Lizzie had her fist propped on one hip. That look always preceded pain and suffering, usually in the form of a drawn-out lecture directed at him.

"Lizzie"—Crispin jumped in before she could thrash him too thoroughly—"you know I would never *actually* wager on any lady's chances for social success, especially not my own wife's."

She seemed only minimally appeased. "Catherine is quiet, but when she does speak, she is well spoken. With proper clothing and attention to her hair, I do believe she will prove herself an unparalleled beauty, which, as you know, goes a long way toward obtaining the ton's approval."

"Do you not think you're doing it a bit brown? Catherine is quite pretty, I grant you that. But—"

"You don't believe me." Lizzie's other fist took its place on her other hip.

"Now you're in for it," Edward muttered.

"I always believe every word you say, beloved sister." Crispin bowed for good measure.

"Mark my words." Lizzie waved her finger in warning. "When I have finished with dear Catherine, she will be the toast of the ton and every gentleman in London will be desperate to know where you've been hiding her."

"'Dear Catherine,' is it?" Crispin shook his head in amused disbelief. "I hope that you are absolutely correct and that Catherine will mesmerize all of society. In fact, if you can accomplish precisely that, I will buy you that ridiculous excuse for a bonnet you've been attempting to convince your husband to buy you for weeks."

Edward chuckled.

Lizzie squealed. "Agreed!"

Crispin would buy Lizzie the entire millinery if she could help Catherine in any way.

"Do you really mean to take her out amongst the ton?" Edward asked.

"I don't imagine I can avoid it."

"You most certainly could, which makes me wonder just what conclusion you've come to. If you were firmly set on tossing her out, I suspect you would have sent her to rusticate someplace inconspicuous."

"Oh, Crispin!" Lizzie looked very nearly giddy. "Have you decided to keep her?"

"You make her sound like an abandoned puppy. And no. I haven't decided anything yet."

There were too many complications. Regaining his freedom seemed to require sacrificing Catherine's future. But Lizzie's declaration earlier that day—that she couldn't be happy in a marriage she was forced into—made him wonder if ending the marriage might not be best, after all. What good was saving Catherine's reputation if she spent the rest of her life miserable? Maybe she would be miserable either way.

No, he hadn't decided anything yet.

Chapter Six

The day of the Hardfords' dinner party dawned without a hint of Madame LaCroix's gowns. Crispin did not generally spend hours on end watching the streets for a delivery, yet he'd been practically glued to the front windows all day. His agitation, though, was nothing compared with what he saw in Catherine.

She tiptoed around the house, avoiding everyone, including the servants, and wrung her hands in almost constant agitation. Her lips were pulled tightly together, her eyes constantly darting to the clock. A man felt like a failure seeing his wife so ill at ease in their home.

He'd done everything he could think of to lessen her anxiety. Lizzie made daily appearances, spending hours on end discussing what Catherine should expect at the dinner, topics of conversation, who would be in attendance—everything Lizzie could think of. The effort didn't seem to help.

Catherine looked more nervous with each passing day. If she could just make it through the dinner without crumbling, Crispin would consider the night a success. But they didn't stand a chance if Catherine had nothing decent to wear. A lady ought not feel self-conscious about her appearance at her first society function.

"Several packages have just arrived, my lord," Hancock said from the doorway. "Where would you like them placed?"

An entire day staring out the windows and he'd missed the delivery? "Bring them in here, and please send for Lady Cavratt."

Crispin laid aside his book, a pointless distraction after all. Three of the footmen entered, heavily laden with long white boxes and smaller parcels of red and blue. Crispin rose, relief seeping through him as he recognized Madame LaCroix's seal on the larger boxes. The dressmaker had cut the delivery time awfully close.

He counted four gown-sized boxes. Madam LaCroix's staff had been busy. The smaller boxes were most likely wraps or accessories. Lizzie's acquisitions had arrived the day before and she'd obviously enjoyed spending her brother's blunt. Catherine's abigail had placed it all out of sight, certain her lady would "swoon for days on end" if faced with so much finery at once.

Until she came into his life, he hadn't known more than a handful of ladies who did not have an insatiable thirst for all things fashionable and expensive. He liked that about her but wondered how quickly society would change her.

A moment later, Catherine appeared in the doorway, still bedecked in her brown-gray gunnysack, looking at him the way a child would look at a parent about to dole out a harsh punishment.

"I promise you are quite safe," Crispin said. "I have already eaten."

She slowly inched inside the doorway, her gaze flitting between Crispin and the pile of parcels. Crispin waited for her reaction, for a look of avarice to enter those bewitching eyes. Catherine stood completely still and obviously confused. She kept her gaze firmly on the floor.

"Have I done something wrong?" she asked after what seemed like ages.

"Wrong?"

"Hancock said you wanted me to come down here." Her voice shook a little as she spoke.

"To show you this." Crispin motioned at the enormous pile she couldn't help but have noticed.

"Packages?" Catherine's eyes suddenly seemed to register understanding. "Madame LaCroix," she whispered. Her eyes jumped around at all the parcels, her face growing more panic-stricken each second. "All of these are for me?"

"A couple of the gowns may be for Hancock." Crispin shrugged. "The Cavratt livery just isn't very becoming with his coloring."

"Really?" Was that a hint of sarcasm he heard in her voice? The thought made Crispin smile.

"The rest are for you."

Catherine looked up and stared at him, shaking her head. She looked unhappy. How could she possibly be unhappy with an entire new wardrobe? Buying things for Lizzie had never failed to improve her mood.

"This is too much." Catherine looked very nearly miserable. "I can't possibly accept all of this."

Crispin chided himself for what must have been the hundredth time that week. He'd assumed she was scoffing at his generosity when she'd simply been overwhelmed. She never seemed to act the way he expected her to. A wife really ought to be easily understood, oughtn't she? Surely other husbands did not find themselves so frequently and thoroughly confused by the ladies they'd married.

"I refuse to send any of it back, so you'll simply have to accept it." Crispin tried for a lighter tone.

Catherine turned those pleading eyes on him. "I've been such a burden already."

"Nonsense." Her look tugged at his heart in an increasingly familiar way. Something about those eyes of hers haunted him. "Consider it a thank-you for not scratching out my eyes during the past week."

Catherine turned toward the stacked boxes. "May I open one?" she asked, her voice so quiet Crispin hardly registered the hesitant question.

"Open them all if you'd like."

Her eagerness, though subdued, was refreshing. Catherine lifted a long white box from the pile. She knelt beside it, slowly raised the lid, and set it cautiously on the floor. Her long, slender fingers carefully peeled back a layer of thin paper. Then another.

Crispin stepped closer, glancing over her shoulder at the box. Madame LaCroix had promised him a miracle, and he wanted to see if she'd kept her word. The box Catherine had selected contained a cream-colored morning dress, its three-quarter-length sleeves edged in delicate lace. A thick ribbon of deep maroon edged the bodice and neckline.

Catherine stood, pulling the dress out as she did, the skirt falling gracefully to full length. Looking closer, Crispin spied hair-thin stripes of shimmering maroon interwoven in the delicate fabric. A pretty dress, to own the truth, but hardly the eye-catching creation Crispin had been expecting.

"That is not one of Hancock's." Perhaps a bit of humor would head off the disappointment Catherine must have been feeling.

She turned to face him, her eyes threateningly red-edged, her lips pressed together in an obvious attempt to steady them. She really was disappointed, Crispin thought.

"I've never owned anything so beautiful," Catherine whispered with inarguable sincerity.

Beautiful? The dress was very plain by society's standards, certainly nothing he'd expect a lady to become emotional about. At least not *pleasantly* emotional.

"Oh, I'm obviously already making a cake of myself." Catherine clutched the gown closer to her, watching him with growing concern. "I will try not to embarrass you tonight, Crispin. I promise." She'd moved to where Crispin stood evaluating the confusing scene unfolding before him. "I'm only . . . so overwhelmed . . . by your generosity. Thank—"

"That is not necessary," Crispin interrupted, taken aback by her sudden talkativeness.

"You must allow me to thank you for this." Catherine's eyes grew misty. Her chin quivered almost indiscernibly. "Please."

Gads, she was going to cry. He had no idea what to do with a watery female.

"I suppose. Though you risk puffing me up like a peacock." He folded his arms across his chest in an attempt to look unaffected.

Catherine stepped closer to him. She smelled of roses, he noticed. She had that day in the garden, as well. Gown still clutched tightly in her hand, Catherine kissed his cheek. He felt the hairs on the back of his neck rise. Catherine offered a quiet thank-you and slipped back to the mountain of parcels, eyeing the collection with obvious awe.

Crispin stood in stunned confusion. It was certainly not the first kiss he'd received from a woman. His own sister had kissed him in precisely the same way. So why did Catherine's simple kiss make his breath catch and his mind momentarily empty?

He simply hadn't expected it, he told himself. That was all. Catherine's reaching out to anyone would be understandably shocking. She'd spent the days since their arrival slipping around the house, obviously trying to go unseen, hardly speaking to a soul.

So where had her sudden boldness come from? With any other society lady, the kiss would have been a calculated attempt to garner his sympathies.

Catherine knelt beside the open box once more and painstakingly refolded the simple gown, laying it carefully back inside.

A slight smile edged its way across his face as he watched her. She fingered the packages like a child at Christmastime.

"What a sight this is!" Lizzie quite suddenly entered the sitting room trailed by her abigail carrying a box identical to the three large gown boxes currently on the sitting room floor. "I hope Catherine's gown for tonight is among these."

"Gown?" Crispin looked around as if in confusion. "Is Catherine expected to wear a *gown* tonight?"

"Very funny. I have the most delicious plan, Crispin." Lizzie waved her servant upstairs. "My abigail, Mary, is a wonder with hair, and I want her to arrange Catherine's for tonight."

"And sacrifice your own? Lizzie, you are truly a martyr." He knew full well Lizzie didn't make a move in society without a proper coiffure.

"That is the reason I am here so early," Lizzie said as if it should have been obvious. "I've brought my gown and everything I need. Mary can attend to us both and be done in plenty of time."

Crispin raised an approving eyebrow. Enlisting his sister's aid had proven an ingenious move, provided she didn't overwhelm Catherine right into the swoon Jane had earlier predicted.

"Is not this the most spectacular plan, Catherine?" Lizzie crossed the room and clasped Catherine's hands in her own. "You'll be radiant, I'm certain of it!"

Catherine smiled, though Crispin could tell she didn't believe a word of Lizzie's declaration.

"Except we only have two hours!" Lizzie said.

"Would not two hours be sufficient?" Catherine asked.

"Hardly!" Lizzie dragged Catherine from the room. "We have ever so much to do!"

"But I need to clear these." Catherine glanced back at the room and the pile of parcels left behind. "They'll be in Crispin's way."

"Oh, hang Crispin! The footmen will have it cleared before he's earned any right to be bothered by it."

"Your thoughtfulness, sister, astounds me."

"Oh, pish!"

Crispin chuckled as the ladies disappeared down the corridor. Lizzie, it seemed, had developed an instant liking for Catherine. Not that Lizzie could have helped herself—Catherine was inherently likeable. If she had turned out to be a shrew or a scheming harridan, he would have begun the annulment proceedings with hardly a hesitation. Instead, he had two stacks of papers awaiting his signature at his solicitor's office—one to end their marriage, the other to make it ironclad. And he still had no idea which set he intended to sign.

* * *

A person could only endure so much poking, prodding, and pinning. Two hours far surpassed Catherine's limit. Lizzie's abigail arranged and rearranged Catherine's hair. Jane, her own abigail, dressed her.

Lizzie insisted on keeping Catherine as far from any obliging mirrors as possible. The surprise, she said, would be far too fun to see.

Catherine occupied her time scolding herself for acting like such a wigeon in the sitting room. She'd been so overcome, so unspeakably grateful, she'd actually kissed Crispin—a Peer of the realm, for heaven's sake! A gentleman, she reminded herself, who was actively working on ending their marriage. Catherine knew so little of annulments. She could not even begin to guess how long the undertaking would require. Every time he spoke, she half expected to hear he'd finished whatever proceedings were required, the marriage was over, and her things were waiting for her on the curb.

Every stitch of clothing Jane dressed her in was new, from the silk stockings and unfathomably soft chemise to the exquisite gown. The color she couldn't quite identify, a scrumptious blend of blue and green, of the softest satin embroidered with delicate flowers.

The two abigails stood back in admiration after the tiny pearl buttons had been closed and Catherine had stepped into a pair of slippers perfectly matched to the gown.

"Beautiful," Jane whispered.

"The gown *is* quite beautiful." Catherine glanced down, trying to convince herself she was truly dressed so exquisitely.

"She was not referring only to the gown, Catherine."

Lizzie spun her around to face the gilded mirror atop her dressing table. Catherine gasped. She hardly recognized herself. Mary had pulled her honey-colored hair into an intricate twist, graceful curls framing her face. The pearl pendant Lizzie had insisted Catherine wear perfectly complemented the sprigs of baby's breath Mary had placed in her hair.

Catherine studied her reflection. Much to her surprise, she had a figure. Somehow she still pictured herself with precisely the same proportions she'd had at twelve. She'd never been beautiful but had always wanted to be. Her uncle would have set her down quite drastically to hear her think something so vain.

"The gentlemen will take us to task for keeping them waiting so long," Lizzie said with a laugh. "I suppose we shouldn't torture them further."

Catherine nodded mindlessly.

"You are nervous." Lizzie smiled at her in the mirror.

"I am." Excessively so.

Lizzie squeezed her shoulders reassuringly. "Now. Take a deep breath."

Catherine obeyed.

"I do that whenever I feel nervous," Lizzie confided. "It always helps."

Catherine doubted the confident Lady Henley was ever very nervous. Three very deep breaths later, Catherine walked out of her rooms. She didn't want to embarrass Crispin. She didn't want him to regret her presence any more than he already did.

Chapter Seven

"AND HOW DO YOU THINK the new Lady Cavratt will fare this evening?" Edward asked Crispin as they waited in the sitting room.

"Honestly, Edward, if Catherine doesn't cast up her accounts on the Hardfords' dining room table, I will consider the evening more successful than I am anticipating it being."

"No need to go borrowing so much trouble," Edward assured him. "I have a feeling Catherine will surprise all of us tonight. Lizzie has complete confidence in her."

Edward's innate optimism and cheerful nature were the very reason Crispin had so readily approved of his pursuit of Lizzie the year they were courting. She spent most of their childhood attempting to force smiles out of her "gloomy" older brother. He'd felt a tremendous responsibility for her since their father's death. Crispin would never have allowed *her* to be forced into an unwanted marriage, and he couldn't have parted with her to anyone less perfect for her than Edward.

Lizzie also claimed that love had brought them together. Crispin called it divine intervention. Another Season of escorting his sister and worrying over the unworthies who clamored for her attention, and he would have put himself out of his misery.

"Don't be nervous." Lizzie's amused voice rang out from the other side of the door, obviously speaking to Catherine.

If she needed reassurance among the three of them, she was doomed. Where was divine intervention when he truly needed it?

Lizzie slipped inside the sitting room alone. "Catherine will be but a moment. Mary insisted on one more pin in her hair."

He paced to the window. Crispin had half a mind to give Lady Hardford their excuses—Catherine had been through enough already. He could certainly invent some drastic enough reason to cry off at the last minute: illness, an unexpected trip to the country, leprosy. "Is she going to survive?"

"Mary is seldom dangerous with hairpins."

"Very funny. Of course I meant will she survive the dinner party."

Lizzie merely laughed at him. "I'm not sure *you* will survive. You are in a tizzy already."

"I am not in a tizzy." Crispin turned from the window to face his sister.

Lizzie smiled triumphantly. "I declared Catherine would be absolutely stunning, and so she is. You will have to humbly beg my pardon all the way to the millinery where *my* new bonnet is waiting."

"I never doubted she would look nice," Crispin said. "She has always been pretty. I just . . ." He pushed out a breath. He couldn't remember the last time he'd been so nervous over a simple dinner party. "Catherine is anxious enough as it is. She shouldn't also have to worry over her appearance."

"Crispin." Lizzie's smile turned a touch syrupy. "You want her to feel pretty."

"I only want her to not be entirely miserable." And yes, he wanted her to feel *confident.*

The doorknob turned and Lizzie, smiling quite unapologetically, moved toward her husband. "You are about to see the most beautiful woman you've ever beheld, Crispin," she said.

And with that introduction, Hancock stepped across the threshold. Edward burst into laughter, as did Lizzie.

Crispin's face split into an all-consuming grin as he chuckled quite uncharacteristically. "Truly a vision, Lizzie. Although not necessarily an improvement."

"I think you need to have a talk with that mantua maker," Edward chortled. "That dress didn't turn out right at all."

Hancock eyed them all quizzically. Looking thoroughly unamused, he stepped back across the threshold and motioned to someone just out of sight behind the doors. Crispin got his laughter under control but couldn't stop his smile. It felt wonderful to truly laugh. He seldom did.

Catherine stepped inside in the next second and Crispin gave her a second look. While anything would have been an improvement over the frock her uncle had provided, Crispin could never have envisioned the transformation that had taken place.

The woman—for she obviously was one—had a figure! Who would have guessed? The color of her dress made her eyes even more astonishing, adding a hint of green to their deep blue. Gone was the severe hairdo. Instead, her hair curled softly around her face. Crispin couldn't seem to keep himself from staring.

"Lord Cavratt, I do believe you owe my wife a bonnet," Edward said, his voice low.

Lizzie could have any bonnet she wanted. The change he saw in Catherine was well worth the cost of a hat or two.

"Your carriage is waiting, my lord." Hancock appeared to fight a smile.

"Thank you." Crispin offered Catherine his arm, still astounded by the change in her. "You look beautiful."

"I feel beautiful." She spoke as quietly as ever, but something in her voice had changed. She seemed a little less uncertain.

He threaded her arm through his and began walking toward the front door. Catherine paused as they passed Hancock.

"Thank you," she said to him.

"My pleasure, my lady." Hancock bowed. "And might I say, your plan worked splendidly."

Catherine nearly smiled. That seemed her way—hints of smiles, but never more. Even the tiny effort added a sparkle to her eyes that he rather enjoyed. But, almost before he'd registered it, the smile faded.

"Will it be a very large gathering, do you think?" Catherine asked after the foursome had settled inside the carriage and had begun their journey.

"Relatively." Crispin's answer seemed to make her more anxious. She pressed her lips together and tightly clutched her hands. "No need to worry. You'll do fine. And we'll all be there with you."

She did not seem appeased. Crispin eyed her nervously as he stepped out of the carriage at the Hardfords' home. Catherine stared like a frightened kitten at the front of the enormous townhouse.

"First"—Crispin slipped her hand under his arm—"we will be greeted by Lord and Lady Hardford."

"The vulture," Catherine whispered back.

Crispin smiled. Why was he suddenly so blasted cheerful? They were about to face the scrutiny of society and he'd spent an unusually large portion of the evening laughing and grinning? "I'd rather that conversation not be aired in public," he replied.

"Of course not." She sounded almost flirtatious. An intriguing change.

"After speaking with our host and hostess, we will proceed to their ballroom."

"Dancing?" Catherine barely whispered, her face suddenly panic-stricken.

"No," he quickly assured her. "We will take a turn around the room making polite conversation until dinner is announced."

He could feel Catherine tremble, no doubt unnerved at the thought of speaking to so many people. Crispin quickly glanced at her, expecting to find her a moment from fainting, but she looked perfectly at ease.

Catherine's hand tightened on his arm, and he distinctly heard her breath shake. She *was* nervous, but no one would be able to tell simply by looking.

"Lord Cavratt."

Crispin offered a polite bow to their host. Lord Hardford always wore bold colors. He'd selected a vivid purple for his well-tailored waistcoat. Crispin had always preferred the more subdued black though occasionally opted for white. Lizzie had scoffed at his "dullness" many times during the past three years.

Lady Hardford sported a high-necked dress of deepest blue silk with feathers fanning out at her neck. She looked precisely like a vulture, just as he'd described her to Catherine. Crispin barely kept an even countenance.

"This must be Lady Cavratt." The viscountess had a reputation for taking over every conversation in which she took part. "So pleased you could join us this evening."

Catherine curtsied prettily and offered a subdued smile, just as any lifelong member of the ton. "Thank you for extending the invitation." She spoke no more forcefully than ever but managed to cover the uncertainty Crispin knew she felt.

Good show, Catherine.

"Where have you been hiding this diamond?" Lady Hardford smiled, tapping Crispin on the arm playfully with her fan. "I am quite certain I have not seen her in Town before. Were you hiding her in some hamlet? Keeping us all in the dark until the opportune moment?"

"Do you wish me to give away all my secrets in one night, Lady Hardford?"

She smiled as he expected her to.

A bit of flattery and they could move on. "Yours is, as I'm sure you must realize, the first assembly we have attended since coming to Town."

The viscountess pulled herself up rather like a rooster, her feathered neckline ruffling appropriately as the realization of the status this distinction would lend her appeared to sink in. Crispin offered another bow and lead Catherine toward the ballroom.

"Well done, Catherine," Crispin whispered, leaning toward her so his words would not be overheard.

"She looked precisely like—"

"I know." Crispin barely held back a laugh.

"How have I done so far?" Catherine asked in an urgent whisper. "Have I embarrassed you?"

"Not in the least," he replied and laid his hand on hers.

"Then I will have to try harder," she said.

"To embarrass me?"

"You practically asked me to."

Crispin quietly chuckled. "I am beginning to suspect that you are a handful."

Catherine pinked quite attractively and her lips twitched but didn't turn upward. What would it take to coax an actual smile out of her?

"Lord and Lady Cavratt," the Hardfords' servant announced to the ballroom.

The room fell instantly silent. Catherine's fingers tightened around his arm. She looked entirely composed, though he could still see a hint of fear in her eyes in the split second she looked at him before they stepped inside the suffocatingly attentive ballroom.

Crispin could feel dozens of eyes upon them. Word of their sudden marriage had certainly circulated as, he was sure, had speculation about its future. He scanned the crowd for someone friendly whom he could count on being amiable. If Catherine's first introduction could be pleasant, she might relax. Her fingers must have been white from strain beneath her gloves. If she gripped him that hard any longer, he would have to summon the sawbones for an emergency amputation.

Almost miraculously, his eyes fell on Charles Ritfield, whose property adjoined his own in Suffolk. Though he was ten years Crispin's senior, they got on well. Charles was one of the most agreeable men of Crispin's acquaintance and not at all likely to devour an unsuspecting newcomer.

"I see someone I'd like to introduce to you," he told Catherine in low tones and began moving in Mr. Ritfield's direction. Around them the murmur picked up again in the room and the latest arrivals were announced.

"Lord Cavratt!" Mr. Ritfield smiled as they reached him. "A pleasure!"

Crispin undertook the introductions, miraculously managing to quite smoothly utter the phrase "my wife."

Mr. Ritfield paused only long enough for a breath before launching into a one-sided conversation with Catherine. "Only the other day I said to my wife, 'Lord Cavratt really ought to find himself a wife.' And now I find out he has. Capital! Capital!"

Crispin had forgotten Ritfield's tendency to grin unceasingly. That would either prove relieving to Catherine or unnerving. Crispin watched her, ready to move on if the encounter didn't look promising.

"Lord Cavratt is quite a favorite in the neighborhood. We've all been hoping he would find a lovely lady to bring home to Kinnley."

"Kinnley?" Catherine whispered to Crispin.

"My estate in Suffolk," he answered quietly.

"Lord Cavratt is quite the catch, I understand." Ritfield's grin only grew. "Quite sought after by the ladies—er, that is he *was* quite the catch. But then, you surely knew that."

Catherine nodded, not appearing at all overwhelmed by Ritfield's ceaseless flow of words.

"He is genial and polite. A gentleman to the core, of course. Bang up to the mark, I've always said. His estate is the envy of all of Suffolk. And we must certainly add to his talents that of discovering hidden treasures."

"I think that is sufficient flattery for one evening, Ritfield," Crispin said. The man really was a very good neighbor but had a tendency to be too effusive in his praise. "I will be sure to enlist your services if ever my good name is in question."

"Capital!" Ritfield laughed and slapped him on the shoulder. "Capital!"

The next three-quarters of an hour passed rather tediously and for Catherine, no doubt, in a blur. Each of the dinner guests had seemed quite anxious for an introduction to the mysterious Lady Cavratt. She managed to keep her composure if not all of her coloring. Crispin appreciated her continued ability to remain conscious—he'd expected a swoon within the first half hour. Catherine, it seemed, was made of sterner stuff.

Mr. Finley, a jack-a-dandy of deservedly poor reputation, held her hand longer than necessary only moments before dinner was expected to be announced. Catherine summarily extracted her fingers from his grasp. Crispin had the sudden desire to extract the man's head from his neck.

"And might I be so bold as to request the honor of escorting her ladyship in to dinner?" Mr. Finley asked.

Catherine's face blanched—the first sign of distress he'd seen her allow since stepping into the ballroom.

"That would be entirely too bold," Crispin said. "She quite outranks you."

"Of course, Cavratt." Finley did not appear at all put in his place.

"And," Crispin added, snaring Finley with his most determined glare, "should the question arise, you will not find yourself escorting her to supper at any future functions, either, as I have every intention of reserving that honor for myself." The declaration surprised him. He hadn't, until that precise moment, planned to live in his accidental wife's pockets. Strange that he didn't regret the impulse.

With a smile too much like a smirk, Finley bowed. Crispin didn't like the way the man's eyes lingered on Catherine in the moments before he walked away. Why he should feel such a possessive inclination he didn't know, but couldn't deny that in that moment he did. Perhaps it was simply his dislike for Mr. Finley. The man was, after all, a rake.

"Is it common for a gentleman to escort in to supper a lady to whom he is not married?" Catherine asked in a distressed whisper.

"That depends very much on the gentleman." Crispin's eyes burned a hole in Finley's retreating back. "And on the lady." He could think of a few who would undoubtedly enjoy Finley's company regardless of their marital status.

"And on the husband?" Catherine asked, her words laced with a hint of teasing he'd recognized from earlier that night.

"*Your* husband would never agree to such a thing." Crispin tried to match her tone but found himself entirely too serious. He would never have allowed another man to escort his wife anywhere. Catherine, of course, only fell into that category technically.

"Were the roles reversed," Catherine said, "would you allow a lady, other than your wife, to hang on your arm?"

Catherine sounded very nearly jealous.

Crispin distinctly liked the possibility.

Chapter Eight

CATHERINE SENT COUNTLESS SILENT PRAYERS of gratitude heavenward during their meal. Crispin was seated beside her, which relieved her mind enormously. Lizzie had spent most of the previous day explaining the expectations of a dinner party among the ton and even ventured to practice with her over a private tea in Catherine's sitting area. Without their combined efforts, Catherine would have made fools of them all.

"How long have you known your lovely wife, Lord Cavratt?" Lord Hardford asked, though his eyes were on Catherine.

A shiver of panic slid down Catherine's spine. How would Crispin explain this? *Three, four days. I kissed her quite scandalously in a garden and was forced to bring her home with me.* Surely he could think of something less humiliating to say.

"It feels as though a lifetime has passed since I first saw her, Lord Hardford," Crispin answered rather convincingly. "And yet the time has passed so quickly it seems only days."

Catherine bit back a smile. He'd managed to produce the perfect explanation.

"A lovely sentiment, to be sure." An ebony-haired lady across the table gazed at Crispin through her lowered lashes. Catherine couldn't say why, but she instantly disliked the lady.

"Where did you two first meet?" the viscount asked.

"In a garden, beside a late-season bloom of hyacinths."

Catherine was surprised to hear Crispin had noted the flowers. They were, of course, the reason she'd stopped—they'd been so immensely fragrant. She hadn't expected Crispin to notice them.

"I certainly hope you plucked one for her," their host said. "Women are forever wishing for flowers."

"I confess I had not the foresight," Crispin replied.

"Too overwhelmed by the beauty of the lady to note the beauty of the flowers." This compliment had come from Mr. Finley, she believed his name to be. Catherine avoided his gaze—something about the gentleman made her uneasy.

Crispin grew sullenly quiet beside her.

Had she done something wrong? She'd kept her facial expression neutral while doing her utmost to appear contentedly disposed. She'd eaten with delicate manners and had offered her attention to those speaking around her. She knew she hadn't said anything to discredit herself or Crispin. In fact, she hadn't said a word since the meal began.

Perhaps that was where she'd erred. Lizzie hadn't thought her reticence would give offense, so long as she didn't refuse to speak when spoken to. Not a soul had spoken to her, though, and she hadn't felt obligated to join in the conversations around her.

"What part of the kingdom do you hail from, Lady Cavratt?" the ebony-haired woman asked.

"From Herefordshire." Catherine spoke with as much self-possession as she could feign.

"Indeed?" The lady raised an eyebrow. Apparently Catherine hailed from the wrong part of the kingdom.

The lady turned to Crispin with the same eyebrow arched in a strangely amused display. "And you met her in Herefordshire, my lord?"

"As a matter of fact, I did not, Miss Glafford."

"Have you been to Town often, Lady Cavratt?" A heavy dose of condescension accompanied the question.

"Not very often, Miss Glafford," Catherine answered, managing to sound unaffected. "Herefordshire is a considerable distance from London, as I'm sure you are aware."

"It borders Wales, I believe." Miss Glafford sounded quite repulsed.

She apparently disapproved of Wales—the feeling was, no doubt, mutual. "Bordering Wales is a rather demanding job, I suppose, but someone must undertake it," Catherine said with forced indifference. "Herefordshire manages it quite well, I daresay."

Somewhere along the table someone snickered. Catherine held back a pleased smile. She could see by the annoyed expression on Miss Glafford's face that the remark had not been appreciated in that quarter. She probably thought Catherine would crumble under her scrutiny.

"I understand you have taken a new French chef," Crispin abruptly said to the viscount, a hint of anxiety in his otherwise calm voice.

Catherine glanced at him. Had her pointed response to Miss Glafford been a misstep? Lizzie had told her to be gracious and civil. She hadn't gone beyond those bounds, had she?

"Is this not the finest crème brûlée you have ever tasted, Lady Cavratt?"

Catherine recognized Miss Glafford's voice and she willed herself to reply evenly. "It is delightful." She offered the compliment to Lord Hardford, the viscountess being at the far end of the table, hoping that was the appropriate course despite the inquiry having come from Miss Glafford.

"You are a connoisseur of fine food, then?" Miss Glafford's look of pretended innocence marked her comment as a backhanded insult.

"I do not profess to be."

"Does she do herself an injustice, Lord Cavratt?" Miss Glafford turned to Crispin. "Or is her palate more discerning than she will admit?"

Catherine hated that Miss Glafford had discovered exactly how to disconcert her. Crispin had no idea what Catherine's tastes were, her likes or dislikes. Such a revelation would ruin the façade Crispin had been so dependent on her to help keep up. Miss Glafford's intention, no doubt.

"You must realize, Miss Glafford, I would never contradict a lady," Crispin answered quite civilly. "Most especially my new bride."

"But in doing so, you must contradict me." Miss Glafford once again gazed almost longingly at Crispin through her lowered lashes. "Is that not also inexcusable?"

"There are times, I fear, when offense cannot be avoided. One simply must choose which offense one is willing to give, however much one wishes to avoid doing so."

Miss Glafford smiled with marked satisfaction. Catherine tried to steady her hands. Which of them would Crispin "choose to offend"? She was certainly accustomed to having her feelings battered indifferently, but she hadn't yet endured such ill treatment from him.

Mr. Finley offered his own observation. "I am quite certain, Cavratt, you would suffer far longer for offending your lovely wife than you would any other lady in the room."

Catherine's eyes widened despite herself. Had Mr. Finley just labeled her as unforgiving?

"I fear I have offered the offense this time." Mr. Finley smiled a touch too broadly. "That was not my intention, Lady Cavratt. I only meant to refer to the unavoidable fact that, as husband and wife, ample opportunity would exist between you and Lord Cavratt to relive an offense long after this dinner has ended."

Perhaps not so long afterward. If she were failing as miserably as Catherine suspected she was, Crispin would likely push through the annulment proceedings with tremendous speed. Could such things be sped up? She had no idea, and yet her entire future hung on the answer to that and so many other questions. Eventually she would have to summon the courage to ask Crispin for more information.

Catherine forced her thoughts back to the moment only to find Mr. Finley's gaze still on her. His devilish smile grew. He went so far as to wink at her again. She shuddered at the unwelcome attention.

"I believe my wife has planned a musical evening for us," their host announced as the entire assembly made their way from the very formal dining room a few moments later. "Miss Glafford, I understand, is quite accomplished on the pianoforte."

Miss Glafford, escorted by Mr. Finley, blushed in a way that seemed more practiced than genuine. Only steps behind them, Mr. and Mrs. Glafford added their voices to the compliments Lord Hardford had already begun to offer their daughter.

Edward pulled Crispin aside and Catherine found herself unavoidably left for a tête-à-tête with Miss Glafford.

"Do not worry yourself, Lady Cavratt," Miss Glafford offered. Catherine didn't believe her tone of compassionate concern. "While Lord Cavratt could certainly have had his pick of any young lady in the ton, I'm certain he won't regret his choice." She then offered a painfully obvious look of unsatisfied analysis and shook her head as though discounting her previous assertion. "At least I hope not, for his sake."

Catherine had no response and didn't attempt to offer one. She didn't want Crispin to regret his choice either. Yet an annulment seemed rather pointed proof of regret.

"Catherine." Crispin abruptly stepped to them. "Lady Henley is suffering from a sudden headache."

Lizzie was ill? "Is there anything I can do for her?"

"Do you happen to have an apothecary chest in that reticule of yours?" That dry humor again. Catherine had quickly discovered she enjoyed it. "No? Well, then, she believes she must return home. However, since they arrived here in our equipage, they will need to use it again to return."

"Of course," Catherine answered.

"You would not be disappointed to leave earlier than expected?" Crispin asked, eyeing her uncertainly.

"I could hardly enjoy myself knowing your sister was suffering."

"I will offer our excuses to the viscount and viscountess." Crispin quickly disappeared into the crowd without another word.

"I've never known Lady Henley to suffer megrims before," Miss Glafford said as though deeply contemplating the development. "Something distressing must have entered her life recently."

Miss Glafford looked pointedly at Catherine then flitted away. The truth of her words stung. She had certainly unsettled the lives of Crispin, his sister, and her husband. Why was it she managed to annoy every person she'd ever lived with? At least Crispin hadn't locked her in her room yet—Uncle had taken that road rather quickly.

Crispin returned and offered her his arm. She took it but couldn't bear to meet his eyes, afraid his disappointment would be evident. She'd known him less than a week, and already his opinion of her mattered.

The carriage ride began in absolute silence. Catherine's gaze fell on Lizzie leaning unapologetically against her husband's shoulder, her gloved fingers raised to her brow. Edward had an arm around his wife's shoulder, whispering something into her ear.

Catherine watched the touching scene with a longing she'd felt countless times before. She'd certainly dreamed of a caring and gentle husband—someone who loved her.

Edward noticed her gaze. "She will be fine," he whispered.

The reassurance brought her some relief. Lizzie had become a fast and unexpected friend. Catherine hadn't enjoyed a single friendship in the years since her uncle had assumed ownership of Yandell Hall. She did not like the thought of her friend suffering.

"Is there anything I can do?" Catherine whispered as well.

Edward shook his head and turned his attention back to his wife.

Her eyes settled momentarily on Crispin. He kept his gaze on the window, his posture stiff and unyielding.

Catherine lowered her gaze to her own trembling hands before closing her eyelids altogether. Miss Glafford's cutting comments rang anew in her weary mind. Crispin must have sorely regretted ever stepping foot in that garden. She felt even worse realizing she, to a degree, was grateful he had crossed her path. For a few blessed days she had lived free of her uncle's tyranny.

She nearly jumped from her seat when a warm, gentle hand took hold of hers. The streetlamps outside offered just enough light to illuminate Crispin's face, his eyes watching her closely.

"Were you disappointed to leave?" he asked.

Catherine shook her head. She'd seldom been so happy to leave a place before.

"Jealous of Hancock's gowns?" Crispin managed to look entirely serious.

"You did give him the prettiest ones." The humor helped lighten her load a little.

"He is so very demanding." Crispin leaned toward her, his next words not reaching across the coach. "Are you concerned for Lizzie?"

"I am."

"But that is not the only reason for your tears?"

Catherine turned away, embarrassed by her lack of self-control. She wiped with her free hand at a tear hovering on her lashes.

"What has upset you?"

She felt Crispin slide closer to her. His leg barely brushed against her own, and the warmth of him so near made her shiver. Yet she wanted him to stay as close as he was, to continue holding her hand.

"Catherine?"

All at once, the sleepless nights, the tension, the upheaval she'd endured over the past week came crashing down on her. She promised herself she wouldn't cry. She refused to, even as several tears escaped just to spite her.

"I am sorry," she whispered.

Crispin didn't reply but kept her hand in his throughout the remainder of their journey. Her worries didn't disappear. Her uncertainty over the future remained. But for those few moments, she felt secure.

Chapter Nine

Crispin would have greatly preferred being almost anywhere else in London the next morning, but his anxiety for Catherine kept him pinned inside the sitting room. He worried about her more than he had about anyone before, even his own sister. But, then, Lizzie had never been as excruciatingly vulnerable as Catherine.

Which brought his mind back to their visitors: Mrs. Glafford and her daughter, who had managed to spout more barely veiled insults during the previous night's dinner than there had been dishes. Catherine had handled the entire ordeal with unfathomable polish, something that astounded him still. She'd even managed a crackingly witty rejoinder. He had been hard pressed not to laugh out loud at the unexpected show of steel. But she'd been teary during the journey back to Permount House. Catherine had said she was fine, but the tears had been real.

His sudden marriage had caused quite a stir. According to the ever-reliable servants' network of gossip, the possibility of an annulment was quite the hot topic. All of Town, it seemed, looked forward to being thoroughly scandalized.

And so Crispin had taken on the role of knight errant to a damsel in distress—a laughable mental image, to be sure. He would probably be one of those knights who managed to be thrown from his mount at the most critical moment of a battle, left sprawled on the side of the road, stuck in his rusty armor. Chivalry had never been a particular talent of his.

"I understand you hail from Herefordshire, Lady Cavratt," Mrs. Glafford said, not quite masking her critical evaluation.

"Yes. Outside Peterchurch."

"I don't believe I've ever traveled to that rustic part of the kingdom."

If her pointed remark had wounded Catherine, she didn't let on. "We receive few visitors," she replied demurely.

"With the exception of Lord Cavratt, I dare say." Miss Glafford fluttered her lashes at him as though she were trying to rid her eye of a speck of dirt. She most likely meant it to be a tempting flirtation. What he wouldn't give to be a rusted knight stuck far, far away from *her*.

"I understand your family resides in Surrey." Catherine turned the conversation with finesse. She may have lacked some of the polish of the Glaffords, but Catherine was not feather-headed.

"Yes. At Farrlow Park." Mrs. Glafford puffed up with obvious self-importance, jutting her chin out imperiously. Mrs. Glafford offered a description of their family estate that left out no detail, little or great. Catherine appeared to be listening, which was more than Crispin could say for himself. "And of course my Charlotte is quite the most beautiful young lady in the entire county, just as she is a favorite of all the gentlemen in Town. Dark hair is all the rage, as I'm sure you know."

"How grateful you must be that Lord Cavratt was willing to overlook such an obvious shortcoming," Miss Glafford said, leaning closer and lowering her voice almost enough to keep the remark private.

"I dare say he has overlooked other things and other people." Catherine emphasized *overlooked* with a pointed glance at Miss Glafford.

Miss Glafford appeared rightly ruffled. Crispin managed to choke down a laugh. His Catherine had more spirit than he would have imagined.

The laugh disappeared instantly. *His* Catherine? Where had that come from?

"Would you care for tea, Mrs. Glafford?" Catherine asked calmly.

"I would be delighted."

After seeing the tiresome lady satisfactorily provided with the refreshment she needed—hopefully enough to keep her quiet for a few minutes—Catherine offered the same to Miss Glafford, who accepted silently but not without a look of contempt shot in Catherine's direction.

"No cream, if you please," Miss Glafford said as Catherine turned her back to pour.

Catherine stopped in the midst of her preparations. "You do not care for cream, Miss Glafford?"

"Cream does not care for *her,*" Mrs. Glafford corrected. "Has a most decidedly unpleasant effect."

"Mother," Miss Glafford scolded, beginning to pink.

Catherine's expression, though hidden from the others, was unreadable. She bit down on her lip a moment, brow furrowing. What was she thinking?

"No explanation is necessary," Catherine told Mrs. Glafford. "An acquaintance of mine also chooses to omit cream from tea. I quite understand."

Why did Crispin detect a sense of mischief in Catherine's voice? Catherine, the quiet, demure young lady who'd tiptoed through his house for a week—he doubted she was capable of mischief. Although she had uttered a remark or two that made Crispin wonder if there wasn't more to Catherine than met the eye.

He watched her with immense curiosity but outward casualness. She prepared Miss Glafford's tea slowly. Crispin found himself mesmerized by the ritual. Was it the grace he saw in her slender fingers? Perhaps the way those often trembling hands were suddenly so steady. Or perhaps the fact that the look on Catherine's face was frighteningly reminiscent of Lizzie's expression during their many childhood acts of impishness.

Catherine quite smoothly took the cream pitcher and allowed three small drops of cream to drip into the cup. What was she up to? She stirred the cup silently before turning and presenting it to Miss Glafford.

Crispin had no idea what dreadful effect cream had on Miss Glafford. He hoped it was something drastic. Poetic justice, really.

"Crispin," Catherine said.

He looked up and found her directly beside him, holding a cup of tea for him. "Thank you." Before she could move away he caught her in his gaze and whispered, "What have you secreted into *my* tea?"

Catherine's face paled. She bit her lips once more, a debate obvious in her eyes. She seemed ready to form some excuse or another but glanced momentarily at Miss Glafford before sitting beside him and lowering her head. "It was not enough to have much of an effect," she answered, her whisper almost too low to be heard. "I—"

"Then you should have put in more," he whispered conspiratorially.

Catherine slowly raised her face until it tipped up toward him, her brows knit in a look of assessment she'd only once before given him, one that made him want to stand straighter, to adjust his cravat, to stay on his mount despite his rusty armor.

Her lips twitched ever so slightly. Then the movement became more pronounced. In a wave of transformation, Catherine's lips turned upward. That smile he'd long awaited proved utterly delightful. Her eyes danced under its influence.

"What was your maiden name, Lady Cavratt?" Mrs. Glafford asked.

Catherine's smile disappeared. Blast Mrs. Glafford! Crispin had been enjoying the rare sight.

"Thorndale," Catherine answered. Crispin could hear the uncertainty in her voice once more.

Mrs. Glafford watched him and Catherine over her cup. She seemed anxious to interrupt, though she couldn't possibly have overheard the conversation. Mrs. Glafford appeared to be on the "Anticipating an Annulment" list, and furthermore on the "Will Still Accept Lord Cavratt as Good Ton Afterward" list. Two lists of which Crispin did not approve.

"Thorndale," Mrs. Glafford repeated. "Not a name of significance, I fear."

"No, it is not," Catherine said. Why couldn't everyone leave her be? She did not deserve to be harassed.

He opened his mouth to offer a sharp set-down, but Mrs. Glafford spoke before he managed a single word.

"The Littletons' ball is quickly becoming the talk of Town," she said. "Do you intend to grace the event, my lord?"

"Of course." Crispin hid his scowl behind his teacup. "We"—He emphasized the *we*—"are quite looking forward to it."

"I am so glad to hear as much," Mrs. Glafford said sweetly. "Charlotte will, of course, be there. You must save a dance for her, Lord Cavratt. She has been given permission to waltz, you know."

Crispin let his eyes wander to Catherine. The spirit seemed to have drained from her, though she sat with a quiet determination to endure the remainder of the visit.

"She is quite an elegant dancer, my lord, though I say it myself." Mrs. Glafford smiled at her daughter. "I have no doubt the two of you would prove a very handsome couple dancing."

"I fear the world will never know," Crispin said. Before Mrs. Glafford could utter the question he saw behind her forced smile, Crispin continued. "I have every intention of spending the entire evening with my wife."

Mrs. Glafford gave an unladylike snort. Crispin's jaw clenched instantly. He'd had quite enough of these women and their insults. Even before his rumor-inspiring marriage, he'd endured every imaginable hint and insinuation from debutantes and mothers alike regarding hoped-for alliances and unions. They were the very reason he'd sworn off the Marriage Mart his first year in London.

"Mother." Miss Glafford's voice sounded pleading.

Perhaps she could keep her mother quiet. Crispin doubted it.

"Always modest." Her mother eyed her with overwhelming maternal regard. "Lord Cavratt, I'm sure—"

"Mother." The pleading had grown almost desperate.

"Yes, of course." Mrs. Glafford seemed to come to her senses. "We really must be going, I am afraid."

How tragic.

Catherine showed the women out with nary a word.

"A few more calls to make," Crispin heard Mrs. Glafford remind her daughter as they reached the front walk.

"I'm not quite feeling the thing, Mother," Miss Glafford answered, sounding as though she meant it. "I think, perhaps, we should return home."

What exactly had Catherine's secreted cream done to their unwelcome visitor?

"Miss Glafford didn't seem quite herself as they left," Crispin said when Catherine returned to the sitting room. He moved a little closer to where Catherine stood. "It was the cream, was it not?"

Catherine nodded. She looked as though she felt a hint of guilt.

"You seemed to know a great deal about the effect it would have." He managed a straight face despite his growing amusement. "Have you tainted tea before, then?"

Catherine turned her eyes on him, pleading with him again. Did she not realize he'd been teasing her? He'd wanted to see her smile again, but his jest seemed to have missed its mark.

"Who was it?" Crispin asked, a sudden curiosity sweeping over him. He understood so little about Catherine and found himself inexplicably wishing to find out more.

Catherine took a trembling breath, her face shifting to match the emotion. "My uncle," she whispered.

"Your—" Crispin almost choked on the admission. He would never have expected Catherine to stand up to anyone, let alone Mr. Thorndale.

"Please don't tell him! I shouldn't have. I know I shouldn't have. But I . . . I had to . . ." Her hand clasped his arm, her eyes never leaving his. "There were days when I simply couldn't endure it, Crispin. But when he was ill he didn't . . ." Tears threatened in those bewitching eyes. "Please don't tell him. He'll honestly throttle me. Please!"

Crispin took her face in his hands, forcing her to look directly at him. He could feel her trembling. "I won't breathe a word of it," he promised. In that moment he would have gladly taken on the role of rescuing knight in order to protect her.

Lud, where did that *thought come from?*

"Thank you." She looked immensely relieved.

He could smell the hint of roses that seemed to follow her wherever she went. At what point had he come to like that scent? And why was he so reluctant to release her?

Shaking his head at his own ridiculous thoughts, Crispin stepped back and pulled his hands safely away from her.

She seemed struck by the abruptness of his departure, but what choice did he have really? He naturally felt compassion upon hearing of her uncle's ill treatment. He'd simply reacted as any feeling human being would have. They were not truly husband and wife, but two people in an impossible situation. Holding her or remaining glued to her side made no sense considering their circumstances.

"I won't put cream in Miss Glafford's tea again," Catherine said, not quite looking at him. "That was unkind of me."

Apparently she thought he disapproved. Disapproved? It was a stroke of genius! "If you won't, I will," Crispin said. "I'll pour in the entire pitcher."

"She'd be done in for days." A hint of amusement colored Catherine's words, but still her smile had not returned.

"We would have the gratitude of every person who would avoid her company during her illness," Crispin said.

"Is that not a little malicious?" One corner of her mouth twitched up.

Gads, he wanted to see an actual smile again. "It is not *my* malice that concerns me, Catherine," he answered. "I am afraid I shall be on my guard from now on."

"And why is that?" Catherine asked. Her tone had lightened considerably. The sparkle in her eyes lit her entire face. She really was quite pretty—she had been even before Lizzie's ministrations.

Crispin leaned closer, the scent of roses greeting him as he did. "Because," he used the mock-serious tone he'd all but perfected, "I will inevitably question every cup of tea I'm offered for as long as you are here."

He watched for the sparkle to grow, for her smile to return, for her face to brighten. But, instead, she turned a touch more pale and seemed to retreat inside herself once more. The spark he'd seen in those brilliantly blue eyes extinguished in an instant. Her brows knit and her posture slipped.

There was no playfulness, nor was there the pleading he'd detected in her looks only moments earlier.

What had he done wrong this time?

Chapter Ten

Catherine had been married an entire week. She sat at a writing desk of deepest cherrywood beneath a tall window splattered by rain. From her position she could look out over the gardens, too wet and muddy for exploring that afternoon. A disappointment, to be sure. She had found she liked Crispin's gardens: well appointed, well maintained, and surprisingly peaceful in a world she found more and more in turmoil.

Rain pelted the glass as her thoughts wandered. They hadn't been out in society at all since the night of the Hardfords' dinner. Several bouquets of flowers had arrived for her in the days that had followed that remarkably uneasy night, offering congratulations on their marriage and flattering assessments of her character and beauty. Lizzie had assured her such gestures were customary and expected. Perhaps, Catherine thought hopefully, she hadn't proven too monumental a failure.

She'd narrowly escaped a hornet's nest with Miss Glafford. Her prank had been childish, she admitted to herself in retrospect—not at all like the times she had done the same to her uncle. She'd barely put in enough cream to give Miss Glafford a nagging stomachache. She'd often given Uncle enough to leave him indisposed for hours. Heaven help her, she didn't regret a single time she'd resorted to such desperate measures.

So much of the last eight years had been little more than perseverance. In the seven days she'd been at Permount House, survival hadn't been her foremost thought. With Crispin she felt safe, which seemed illogical. Without a moment's warning he could walk in and announce that their marriage was over.

She hardly knew Crispin. He fluctuated between personable and grumpy, between kind and distant. How could she find security in the company of a man whom she did not really understand? One who saw her as a temporary inconvenience? For just a moment after the Glaffords' visit, she had forgotten how uncertain her situation truly was.

She repeated his words. "For as long as you are here."

Catherine pushed out an uneasy breath. She needed a place to go after the annulment was official. Hiring herself out as a companion or governess seemed her most likely option. She simply needed to find someone who needed her.

With a sigh, Catherine returned her attention to the small expense book on the desk in front of her. Crispin had provided her with pin money, though it seemed more like a small fortune to her limited experience. Only Lizzie's insistence that not accepting would reflect badly on Crispin had convinced Catherine to accept it.

She'd spent very little, having bought only the accounting book and a new rivet for her reading spectacles. Catherine unfolded the tiny glasses and pulled them on, grateful they were repaired but as frustrated at her dependence on them as she'd been since acquiring them seven years earlier. She dipped the elegant quill in a well of blackest ink and added the rivet expense, which had cost nearly nothing, into the ledger. She was determined not to be irresponsible with such a generous allowance.

Expense added and columns checked, Catherine closed the book and slid it to the back of the desk's uppermost drawer. She folded her glasses, intending to place them with her account book but finding herself watching the rain again. She absentmindedly placed them on the desktop and wandered to another window to watch the garden being bathed in the unending downpour.

"My lady," Hancock said, interrupting her solitude.

She turned toward him, not unhappy by his company. Hancock had proven himself an ally early in her sojourn at Permount House.

"Lord Cavratt has requested to join you for tea here in the library if that is agreeable to you."

Catherine nodded and bit down on her lip, suddenly nervous. Had he completed the annulment? She had not yet found a position. There hadn't been time. She crossed on shaking legs to a chair and sat, her mind swirling.

"Would you like me to take your place, my lady?" Hancock asked, still maintaining his proper butler's posture but with a hint of conspiracy in his tone. "My well-timed appearance several days ago inspired quite a rousing round of laughter. And seemed to put you at ease."

Catherine half smiled in spite of her worries. "Thank you," she said. "But I believe I am equal to the task."

Hancock offered a bow and a look of unfettered sympathy before slipping from the room.

Sitting alone in the library, Catherine did not feel at all "equal to the task." How did one prepare oneself to be thrown out on the street?

Tea arrived in the next moment. The staff did everything with an efficiency that Catherine found both impressive and daunting. Crispin, she'd decided, liked things to happen a certain way. He liked his life to be predictable. No wonder he was eager to end their ramshackle marriage.

"Good afternoon, Catherine."

She recognized Crispin's voice and steeled herself to be calm. "Good afternoon." Heavens, her voice was trembling.

Crispin looked every inch the Town gentleman, as always, in his perfectly tailored superfine and pristinely tied cravat. He made his way across the room toward her, and Catherine's heart began pounding.

"I see you haven't poured yet," Crispin said, standing beside her at the table. "Now might be the best time for me to accept a cup—I can be certain you've done nothing to it."

"Are we soon to be at odds with each other, then?" Catherine tried to keep her voice from shaking, even as she felt her limbs doing just that.

"Not at all," Crispin answered with an easy casualness.

At all? she repeated to herself. Was that possible? Uncle had always considered the two of them to be constantly at odds, even when he and Catherine hadn't set eyes upon each other for days at a time.

Crispin actually seemed jaunty, happy. Did he feel no loss at her pending departure?

Catherine poured their tea, but her hands still trembled. Not a drop stained the pristine white table cloth. Catherine offered a silent prayer of gratitude. Uncle did not abide stains. Crispin likely didn't either. Willing her nerves to settle, Catherine held her cup and saucer as still as she could manage and sipped unenthusiastically at her tea.

"That is a new gown, I believe." Crispin watched her over his teacup.

"Hancock didn't want it." Catherine shrugged, the jest escaping from some hidden place inside.

To her relief, Crispin smiled at her. He selecting a finger sandwich from the silver tea tray. "I have some news."

Catherine swallowed. "News?"

"Yes. We are invited to a musicale this evening."

She could not reply immediately. Was that his news? "Lizzie told me as much yesterday afternoon. She provided me with a rather detailed description, in fact."

"Including the colors of the Yockings' music room and the breed of dogs who will howl from the stables during many of the evening's vocal offerings, I imagine." Crispin chuckled. "Lizzie is nothing if not a source of vital information."

He had come only to speak of the musicale? Perhaps the annulment was not finalized, after all. She had more time.

"She may not have adequately warned you, though."

"*Warned* me?"

"The Glaffords will be in attendance," Crispin said with a knowing rise of his brow.

"Heaven help us all," Catherine muttered. "So I should bring my cream pitcher, then."

"Malicious, Catherine." Crispin laughed, shaking his head.

Catherine sipped at her tea, relief and amusement easing her tension. Crispin had a wonderful laugh. And—she relaxed further—he wasn't sending her away yet.

"If only cream were an unfailing weapon against more than just Miss Glafford." Crispin's expression turned rueful. "Should you be forced to do her in, there will, I am afraid, be others who will seize the opportunity to—"

"Itemize my woefully obvious but overlooked shortcomings?" Catherine answered dryly.

"Something like that." Crispin exposed a crooked smile. "Society can be remarkably vicious."

"Worse than the Glaffords?"

"Unfortunately." Crispin's eyes dropped to his teacup. The humor was gone. Catherine missed it sorely. "You will be expected to play tonight. Or sing."

"I do not even remotely sing." Hearing a tinge of panic in her voice, Catherine sought for something lighter to say. "Every dog in the neighborhood would undoubtedly die from the pain of it should I even make the attempt."

Crispin's smile returned instantly. "Those poor dogs."

Catherine smiled back at him. A strange silence settled between them. Crispin watched her closely, and she tried to not squirm under the scrutiny. Quite suddenly, he seemed to snap himself from whatever had held him.

"You told me you play an instrument."

"I play four." Catherine endeavored to sound confident. Her musical talents, she knew, were her only redeeming quality.

"Only four?" Crispin clucked his tongue. "A shortcoming, indeed."

"A shortcoming I am rather fond of."

"As well you should be." Crispin shifted from jesting to genuinely intrigued in a moment. "Which four instruments?"

No one had ever asked her that before. Uncle knew only because he had taken a very detailed inventory of the music room upon inheriting. "The pianoforte. The harp. The cello. And the flute."

Crispin set his empty teacup on the tray beside him. "The Yockings will certainly have a pianoforte."

"They really will insist I play?" The thought of playing in public petrified her. "But I have never played for anyone." The teacup rattled in her hands as the reality of what she faced settled on her. "Not a single soul. I can't—"

"Refusing would be unacceptable."

"I'll be terrified." Catherine rose shakily, her head and thoughts swimming. "All those ears listening for mistakes. Eyes glaring at me. I couldn't—" She tried to set her cup on the table to stop its rattling but misjudged the proximity. It fell to the ground and shattered.

Fear surged through her as her eyes settled on the heap of broken china at the table's feet and the tea slowly seeping into the rug beneath. She snatched a napkin from the table and dropped to her knees. Her heart pounded painfully hard in her neck. He would surely send her away now, annulment or not.

"Catherine." Crispin's voice echoed above her.

He must be furious with her. Catherine grabbed at the pieces, trying to dab at the still warm tea. "I am so sorry."

"Catherine."

"I will replace the cup." Her hands shook so violently she could hardly continue cleaning the mess. "And I will scrub the stain out as well."

Crispin was at her side, kneeling on the floor also. Uncle only stooped to that level when he was livid.

Catherine grabbed more frantically. A jagged edge pricked at the smallest finger on her right hand, and she quickly pulled back in pain. Blood bubbled up from the small cut. Catherine dismissed it. She had to clean the mess. She had to.

"I am sorry. I am so sorry," she whispered frantically, tears blinding her as she desperately cleaned.

"Catherine. *Catherine.*" She felt Crispin's hand on her arm. "Stop. Look at me. Stop."

She turned her head, her heart pounding. That same sick feeling she'd been accustomed to under Uncle's roof seized her. She could feel her muscles tensing, bracing for punishment.

Crispin was watching her, his brow creased and eyes narrowed. He kept one hand wrapped around her arm, as the other rose to just above his head. On instinct Catherine flinched, hoping to lessen that hand's impact by pulling closer to herself. She closed her eyes, the pain beginning moments before it should have—the memory of what a beating felt like always preceded the infliction itself.

But there was only silence. No sounds, no movement.

"Catherine." Crispin spoke so quietly, so gently she hardly recognized the word as her name.

She opened her eyes and looked cautiously at him, still guarding her face as much as possible with her own shoulder. Crispin's forehead creased in intense concentration, his eyes studying her face. There was no laughter nor jesting, only confusion mingled with concern.

"Did you think I was going to strike you?"

"You weren't?" Her voice cracked on the words.

"No." He actually sounded offended by her assumption. With his raised hand he pulled a napkin off the tea table and wrapped her cut finger in it.

Crispin gently pulled her to her feet, still holding her injured hand in his.

"But the cup."

"The servants will attend to that," Crispin insisted. His gaze rested on the hand he held. "Would your uncle have struck you over a broken teacup?"

Why did Crispin sound upset? And why did his apparent concern make her feel like sobbing? She hadn't truly cried in the presence of another person since the day her father had been buried.

Catherine nodded, unable to meet his eyes.

"Among other things, I assume." His tone grew tense.

"He was not the easiest person to please."

"*I* am not always the easiest person to please," Crispin said. Catherine stepped back almost involuntarily, but Crispin took hold of her other arm. How was it that his touch could be both strong and gentle? She'd never known such a contradiction. "Please, hear me out," he said.

Catherine's eyes moved to his face. Uncle had never once attached a "please" to any sentence he'd uttered in her direction.

"I can be particular and grumpy and stubborn," Crispin said, his eyes boring into hers. "But I have never—*never*—struck a woman. Not even as a child. My sister pestered me to no end, but I never raised a hand to her. I wouldn't." His gaze locked deeper with her own. "So long as you are in this house, you have no need to live in fear for your safety. I promise you that."

Catherine closed her eyes to concentrate on those words. Fear for her physical well-being had been a constant concern of hers for nearly a decade. She hadn't dared imagine herself free of that burden.

"I would never hurt you, Catherine."

No. But he would eventually send her away, and she would lose the one place where she felt safe.

Chapter Eleven

Miss Eunice Johnford's singing was enough to put any ill-bred tomcat to shame. Crispin tried to maintain as neutral an expression as possible. He glanced at Catherine seated beside him as she endured the painful performance. Catherine, he'd learned in the week since they'd met, was incapable of completely hiding her feelings.

He leaned toward her. "This is truly an unparalleled performance," he said quietly in Catherine's ear, unable to keep from commenting.

"I quite agree," she answered in a whisper, her lips twitching.

Why did she constantly fight the urge to smile? At least she no longer looked scared out of her mind. The fear that had seized her that afternoon in the library still haunted him. To feel the need to cower over something as inconsequential as a broken teacup was unfathomable. And the way she'd cringed when he'd knelt beside her as if expecting him to lash out at her. He hoped his reassurances had eased her worries.

The moderately sized gathering politely applauded as Miss Johnford curtsied.

"How is your finger?" he whispered.

"I believe it will fully recover." Catherine's eyes twinkled up at him. "But only just."

"A near-run thing, was it?" He was finding the subdued appearance required at a musicale difficult when faced with Catherine's little-seen sense of humor.

"Shockingly near-run."

Miss Olivia Clarent stepped up to the pianoforte. Crispin had heard her play before. "You will enjoy this next performance," he said.

"I have your word on that?" Catherine asked.

"May I be forced to ingest gallons of adulterated tea if I am wrong."

The briefest flicker of a smile touched Catherine's face. Crispin reached for her hand—a completely subconscious gesture—before catching himself. He had never in all his life had such an urge. What was Catherine doing to him?

He forced himself to concentrate on the performance rather than his very confusing reaction to his equally confusing wife. *Wife.* That still felt strange.

His gaze drifted back to Catherine. She looked up at him and their eyes met. Leaning closer, Crispin whispered, "Miss Clarent is a talented performer."

"She plays quite well." An unexpected hesitancy accompanied her words.

"Except that . . . ?" Crispin was beyond intrigued. What did she find to censure in Miss Clarent's performance? "Certainly the mongrels in the stables cannot be suffering."

"They would have to be terribly fastidious mongrels to object to such a . . . technically flawless execution," she said.

"What is it you find amiss?" Crispin watched her closely. He'd never heard a single soul evaluate Miss Clarent's playing as anything less than perfect.

"I do not believe she understands the music." Catherine kept her voice to a whisper, but an uncharacteristic look of authority crossed her face, conviction entering her eyes.

"Really?" How could anyone who played flawlessly not understand music?

"Never mind," she muttered. "Forget I even spoke of it." She looked away from him, giving the impression to any who happened to look in her direction that she found the performance pleasing rather than lacking.

"I have offended you," Crispin whispered. "That was not my intention."

She didn't answer but kept her gaze firmly fixed ahead. He'd ruffled her feathers. Odd that the notion bothered him. He'd irked enough women in his days to fill Carlton House twice over. The others had deserved their set-downs, however. Catherine had done nothing but honestly answer his question. It was that honesty that had caught him off guard. Sincerity was, in his experience, a virtue few people embraced.

"What is it she doesn't understand?"

Catherine just shook her head, quite obviously dismissing his request for an explanation.

"I would really like to know." In actuality, he was nearly desperate to know. Catherine continually surprised him, and he found himself evermore interested in solving the mystery she presented him.

With an almost imperceptible sigh, she leaned a little closer. *Roses.* He was growing quite fond of the scent of roses. "The piece Miss Clarent is playing is intended to be emotionally urgent. Mournful, even. It is meant to convey an enormous, almost insurmountable loss. She plays it as though she were plunking scales. I dare say she doesn't understand the music."

Then Catherine pulled away again, barely masking the frustration in her eyes. Frustration with the music? Or with *him*? Crispin couldn't be sure, though he had a feeling the honest answer wouldn't be pleasant.

Crispin looked back at the pianoforte. Miss Clarent looked almost bored with her own performance. She did usually seem indifferent now that Crispin thought back on it. He'd always assumed this was merely from an abundance of skill.

Miss Clarent ended her piece and the room applauded, more enthusiastically than they had for Miss Johnford's butchered performance. Their host, Mr. Yocking, looked to the other young ladies for the next performer, though Crispin knew the evening to be at its end. Miss Clarent's skills were so legendary that no lady he'd ever encountered had been willing to follow her. She'd been given the distinction, whether prearranged or not, of ending every musical evening as the final performer.

"I should so like to hear Lady Cavratt play," Miss Glafford said with a look of utter adoration on her face—one she'd no doubt spent hours in front of the looking glass learning to produce. What Crispin wouldn't have given for a cream pitcher! "I'm quite certain her skills are polished enough to follow Miss Clarent tolerably well."

The entire room turned to look at Catherine, and Crispin watched her turn pale. He hadn't anticipated this complication. He'd wondered why Catherine had not been invited to play, but he hadn't pressed the issue, thinking perhaps Catherine would appreciate being left off. It seemed she'd been the victim of a well-plotted conspiracy.

"Of course, if Lady Cavratt doesn't feel equal to the task, I'm sure we all understand." Miss Glafford looked a touch too smug. So much for her social mask.

"Perhaps Miss Clarent would indulge us with an encore," Mr. Yocking suggested.

"I would not wish to deprive Lady Cavratt of her opportunity," Miss Clarent answered. Crispin could tell she felt more curiosity than concern for Catherine's social standing, as her look wasn't poisonous like Miss Glafford's.

"Gracious of you, to be sure," Miss Glafford praised with no hint of their well-known rivalry. "I am sure she would not presume to possess the talent to adequately follow you. Though I am told she is quite a diamond."

Every eye turned to Catherine, including Miss Glafford's and Miss Clarent's. Crispin tensed. This was an all-out attack. If Catherine accepted and fell short, she'd be seen as a presumptuous failure. If she declined to perform, she'd be deemed inferior in the eyes of everyone in the room.

"You don't have to do this," Crispin said in her ear.

"The gauntlet has been thrown, my lord," she answered as she rose to her feet.

Her response more than surprised him. What an approach to take in such a situation. Catherine, apparently, recognized she'd been dragged into a battle and had no intention of backing down.

She walked quietly to the pianoforte. Miss Glafford had the audacity to look on the verge of laughter. Crispin barely refrained from glowering at her. So help him, if she so much as brought an embarrassed blush to Catherine's face—

He dismissed the thought before it could fully form. What had come over him lately? He was behaving like an overprotective nursemaid. No, *nursemaid* wasn't exactly right.

Catherine sat at the pianoforte; no music, no curtsy. Crispin hoped she wasn't also sitting there with no talent.

The room took in a collective breath. Her actions were unheard of in this circle. Miss Clarent was the pièce de résistance musically. Crispin kept his eyes on Catherine's face. She'd told him she'd never played for another living soul. How terrified she must have been sitting there before a crowd of at least thirty anxious spectators.

He had a terrible feeling that very soon his wife would be in need of rescuing. He could just see the scene play out in his mind. Amidst jeers and guffaws, she would succumb to a fit of the vapors and collapse in a heap at the pianoforte. He, her ill-qualified knight in lackluster armor, would scoop her limp frame from the cold, unfeeling floor and whisk her off to Permount House. Several quarts of smelling salts later she'd regain consciousness, eternally grateful for his heroism. Or, more likely still, demand to know why he hadn't ended their marriage yet.

A hushed melody floated from the pianoforte, snapping Crispin back to reality. The piece Catherine had chosen was vaguely familiar. He glanced nervously around the room. Several people were leaning forward, obviously concentrating on the music. Others had closed their eyes, as if needing to rid themselves of any distraction in order to better hear the quiet refrain.

Subtly, skillfully, the melody grew. Complicated trills and runs interwove throughout, crescendos giving way to notes little more than whispered. How different from Miss Clarent's scales! Not a single comment or conversation interrupted the performance. All ears were on Catherine, if not every eye. Many of the assembly kept their eyes closed as they seemed to lose themselves in the beauty of the music. So much for his desperate damsel in distress. Crispin found he much preferred the actual solution to their difficulties over the one he'd imagined.

Catherine seemed entirely unconcerned with everything except the music. She swayed when the piece grew melodic, struck the keys with passion when the composition required it. A thousand feelings and emotions could be read on her face as she performed, and Crispin was hypnotized by her.

She came alive at the pianoforte. The timidity and uncertainty that seemed to always accompany her vanished as she played. Could one attach a pianoforte to a delicate wisp of a female? She seemed so much happier with the instrument. The mental image such an idea conjured was absurd to say the very least.

Crispin's errant thoughts reigned themselves in as the music grew enormous in its complexity and volume and Catherine seemed to feel the intensity of it. Her face glowed; a fire flickered deep behind her eyes. Crispin watched awestruck, his heart pounding in his chest.

A single, reverberating chord filled the music room then faded into silence. Catherine pulled her hands from the keys and glanced up at the room. Amidst the complete silence of the audience, Crispin saw uncertainty in every inch of her face. The music's spell over her had broken.

In a boom of thunder, the room exploded in applause. Crispin let out a breath he didn't realize he'd been holding. The room was on its feet, accolades and praise directed toward the instrument and performer. Catherine turned decidedly red. She managed a curtsy before moving toward Crispin.

As she took her seat, cheeks flushed becomingly, Crispin took her hand in his and pressed his lips to it. "Marvelously done, Catherine."

She didn't reply but glanced nervously across the room to where Miss Glafford and Miss Clarent were looking daggers at her. Crispin expected Miss Glafford's response, but Miss Clarent hadn't struck him as ambitious enough to refuse to recognize a talented musician.

"Miss Clarent is upset," Catherine whispered, anxiety in her voice. "I probably should have chosen a different piece. But . . ."

"I think you couldn't have chosen better. How could Miss Clarent possibly object?"

"I . . ." A look of resolution crossed her features. "You didn't believe me, and I wanted you to. For a moment I forgot you were not the only person listening."

"I don't understand."

"I played the same piece." Catherine looked precisely like a penitent child admitting some heinous crime.

"The same—?"

"As Miss Clarent."

The same piece? It hadn't sounded a thing like Miss Clarent's. Catherine's selection had been moving, entrancing, emotional. Miss Clarent's had been . . . well . . . not unlike fifteen minutes' worth of scales. No wonder she looked ready to storm and rage. "If the two of you were male, I do not doubt she'd call you out."

"*They* issued the initial challenge."

"Ah, yes, the gauntlet. And you appear to have chosen weapons." Crispin nodded appreciatively. "What is left?"

"Perhaps you could serve as second," Catherine suggested, the slightest twinkle of amusement behind her eyes. "For them." She indicated the two fuming young ladies with a tilt of her head.

Crispin fought down a chuckle he knew would be de trop in a formal gathering. Catherine had backbone. He liked her all the better for it.

Mr. Yocking declared the evening a success and the entire room moved to obtain refreshments. Catherine and Crispin were accosted ceaselessly the rest of the evening. The guests praised her talent as well as his good judgment. In a single spectacular performance, Catherine had taken her potential critics by storm.

Mr. Finley cornered Catherine as the guests began to disperse. Crispin made his way across the room to where the two stood. He couldn't hear their conversation but didn't like the nervous look on Catherine's face. Finley could be overpowering and had little sense of propriety when on the prowl.

Feeling a decided inclination to do the man some drastic injury, Crispin pressed his way past the guests dividing him from Catherine and Finley. "I think it is time for us to be on our way home, Catherine," he said as he reached her side.

"I was only beginning to praise your lovely wife on her performance this evening, Cavratt." Finley smiled far too much as he looked at Catherine. "Certainly you wouldn't wish to deny her the accolades she has earned."

"I thank you," Catherine answered, "but I am anxious to be going."

"As am I." Crispin shot a look of utter dislike at the man.

"I would be in a hurry as well," Finley added after Catherine had moved toward the door, his voice lowered so only Crispin could hear, "if I were on my way home with Catherine."

"You do not have leave to use her Christian name, Finley. And I advise you to remember that she is my wife."

Finley laughed as though he doubted the importance of Crispin's last assertion. "A technicality most of the ton expects you to address shortly."

"The ton can hang," Crispin snapped. He would have said more if not for the increasingly familiar sensation that grasped him. Somewhere, Catherine was looking at him. Why was it he could always sense that?

Finley's gaze slid past him and his brow rose seductively. Crispin turned to see Catherine behind him, far enough not to overhear, but close enough to see the exchange.

"Tell Catherine I look forward to seeing her again," Finley said.

"Take care when speaking of my wife, Finley. In a less-civilized setting, the consequences would be swift and painful."

"A threat?" Finley smirked, but Crispin thought he saw a hint of uncertainty in the man's face.

"A promise." Crispin left without another word. He held his arm out to Catherine, doing his best to look unshaken. They offered their farewells and climbed inside the carriage for a long and silent ride home.

Finley! Crispin's blood boiled. How dare he insinuate what he had. And to profess his intention of meddling with Catherine. He'd have the bounder thrown from Town! No man had the right to speak about Catherine so vulgarly.

The rake was fortunate Crispin's temper did not match that of others in society. The Duke of Kielder probably would have run Finley through on the spot. Crispin found the idea extremely appealing.

He stomped up the steps to Permount House, flung his outer coat at Hancock, and stormed into the sitting room. Finley had always pushed the bounds of propriety, but this was the outside of beyond. Using her Christian name. Looking at her the way he had. Catherine was a married woman. A married woman. Married to *him*!

"Crispin?" Catherine stepped past the sitting room door, half hidden in shadow.

Finley's scheming look and pointed remarks came back again with force. Crispin continued his tense pacing.

"Are you angry with me?" Catherine asked from somewhere behind him.

"Of course not," he grumbled.

"You sound upset."

"I'm not upset." He took a calming breath. "Not with you."

"I probably did something wrong. Without Lizzie there to help tonight, I . . ."

"No, no." Crispin forced all thoughts of Finley from his mind. Catherine did not deserve to be snapped at. He turned back toward her and motioned her inside the room.

With just the moonlight spilling in from the windows, she looked like a fairy. Yet another uncharacteristically sentimental thought. He'd had a lot of those of late.

"You played quite well tonight," Crispin said once Catherine had crossed to where he stood. "I doubt anyone but Miss Clarent realized you had both played the same piece. They sounded nothing alike."

"We played all the same notes."

"But it was not the same. You . . ." Crispin searched for the right explanation. It came with a healthy dose of irony. "You understood the music."

Catherine smiled up at him. With the moonlight illuminating her face and stray strands of hair wisping in front of her bewitching eyes, she was a vision.

"I won the duel, then?" Catherine asked, a twinkle in her blue eyes.

"You dealt your opponents a disarming blow." Crispin stepped closer to her.

"A *disarming* blow?" The same mischievous tone she'd used earlier crept back into her voice. "But not fatal?"

"I'm afraid not." He moved closer still. "I am certain they will rally again."

"Then what is my best course of action?" She smiled, entrancing him. "Do I wait for them to regroup? Or do I retreat?"

"You must face their second." He stood so close he could smell roses once more. "That is the proper protocol."

"Didn't *you* agree to be their second?" Catherine asked, her eyes focused on him.

Crispin reached to finger a wisp of honey-colored hair, guiding it back behind her ear. She looked so like a sprite he half expected her to vanish under his touch. Crispin's heart pounded, his breath catching in his lungs. He leaned in.

Catherine stepped back. He stood frozen for a fraction of a moment, feeling the loss more acutely than he could have imagined.

Had he almost kissed her? He opened his mouth to apologize, to offer some kind of excuse, but the look of confusion in her eyes silenced him.

"I . . ." Catherine continued backing away from him, her confusion giving way to a look of concern. "Uh . . . good night." She offered the final words with tremendous speed before spinning on the spot and nearly running from the room. She hadn't run from him in days.

"Blast," Crispin grumbled. He'd let himself get carried away by moonlight and music. And he'd frightened her.

Chapter Twelve

Catherine had no desire to entertain a caller. She had a great deal to think about.

Crispin was acting strange. Her *heart* was acting strange, pounding every time she thought about the look on his face as he'd stroked her cheek after the musicale a few nights before. There had been something in his expression she couldn't define—gentle and kind and intense all at the same time—and she was absolutely certain that for a moment he'd intended to kiss her.

In a flash of panic, she'd realized what a horrible misstep she'd made. At some point between his kiss in the garden and that moment in the moonlight, Catherine had begun to fall in love with him. An unrequited attachment would only further complicate their situation.

She stepped inside the sitting room where Hancock had placed their unexpected visitor, a pretty young lady seated near the window whom she didn't recognize.

"Good morning," Catherine said.

"Good morning, Lady Cavratt." Her visitor laughed the last words out, though she did condescend to rise.

This stranger had come to laugh at her, apparently. Why could she not simply be left alone to sort out the confused state of her life? She needed to ascertain just why a gentleman who was actively pursuing an annulment would come so excruciatingly close to kissing his wife. Further, she'd like to find some reasonable explanation for why that wife would spend four nights in a row wondering what it would have been like if she'd allowed him to do just that.

"Hancock." She turned toward the door where Crispin's ever-faithful butler still stood. "Would you ask Cook to send some refreshment, please?"

"Of course, my lady."

Perhaps if she fed the visitor, she would go on her way and leave Catherine to her recollections. The lady seemed vaguely familiar, though she couldn't place the face. "Please be seated, Miss—"

"Bower. Miss Cynthia Bower."

"Won't you please be seated, Miss Bower?"

They sat in awkward silence for several minutes. Catherine had never been equal to small talk, and Miss Bower seemed unwilling to take the initiative. Something in Miss Bower's gaze proved disconcerting, as if she were taking a mental tally of all Catherine's flaws.

"So Crispin still hasn't untangled himself, then?"

Catherine was too taken aback to reply.

"I imagine he will do so at any moment—once the wrinkles are ironed out. The law, I understand, can be a bit complicated."

"I wouldn't know, as Crispin and I have never discussed anything of that nature." She managed the lie with more aplomb than she had in the past.

Miss Bower simply smiled in patent disbelief.

A kitchen maid entered, setting a tray of tempting pastries and a tea service on a table before curtsying her way out.

"Would you care for tea, Miss Bower?" Catherine asked. She heard her voice break but did her utmost to keep her expression composed. She had yet to discuss the annulment in detail with *Crispin.* She certainly wasn't going to do so with an overly critical busybody.

"Certainly." Miss Bower did not attempt to hide her amusement.

The china clanked embarrassingly. Catherine handed Miss Bower her teacup before turning back to pour a minuscule amount for herself. She had absolutely no appetite.

"I heard Cook sent up fairy cakes."

Catherine looked up at the sound of Crispin's voice and saw him step inside the room. The look of annoyance he gave Miss Bower significantly lessened Catherine's anxiety.

Crispin's eyes locked with hers, and his expression changed completely. A look of concern crossed his features and it pulled Catherine to her feet. She met him halfway inside the room, a very hastily filled teacup in her hands.

"Are you in need of a second?" he asked quietly, his lips turned up in amusement.

"Desperately," she whispered in reply, carefully setting the cup and saucer in his hand.

"Come, then," he whispered in her ear. "Off to battle with us."

The sensation of his breath tickling the stray strands of hair waving atop her ears was almost unnerving. Her heart pounded, her insides tying themselves in fierce knots. Crispin slipped her arm through his and they turned back toward Miss Bower. He set his teacup on an obliging table.

"Miss Bower." He offered the customary, if abbreviated, bow. "You have, I assume, met my wife, Lady Cavratt."

A smirky smile crossed her lips. "I have."

Catherine took a deep breath, remarkably emboldened by the strength of Crispin's touch. She felt braver with him beside her, even if his presence did tend to make breathing more difficult.

"How are your country friends, Miss Bower?" Crispin asked

"My country friends?" Miss Bower appeared quite baffled.

Crispin offered no further explanation but watched Miss Bower expectantly.

"I cannot claim any great acquaintance in the country just now."

"Is that so?"

"Quite." Miss Bower gave Catherine a rather smug look.

"How odd. I distinctly recall you were visiting friends in the country very recently." Crispin raised an eyebrow.

"My . . . er . . ." Miss Bower creased her eyebrows a moment before understanding crossed her features.

"The Dawning of Realization," Crispin muttered, guiding Catherine to sit on the sofa. Much to her shock, he sat directly beside her and quite calmly retook his tea.

"What, pray tell, was *your* reason for being away from Town, Crispin?" Miss Bower asked in turn, her own look just as challenging as Crispin's had been.

"That, *Miss Bower*"—He seemed to place a tremendous emphasis on his very formal use of her name—"ought to be obvious."

"It ought to be?" Miss Bower asked.

A mischievous smile crossed Crispin's face. Catherine had discovered he possessed a remarkably sharp wit.

"While Miss Bower attempts to unravel this rather simple riddle," Crispin said to Catherine, "would you retrieve a fairy cake for your famished husband?"

"Famished?"

"A fairy cake may mean the difference between a long, prosperous life and expiring right here in the sitting room."

"I would sorely hate to be a widow after only a couple weeks." Catherine shook her head and sighed a touch dramatically. "It is terribly inconvenient to have to change households so often."

"*Inconvenient*?" Crispin's feigned shock proved even more amusing than his exaggerated hunger. "You would mourn the inconvenience? I am wounded, Catherine. You have pierced my heart."

"Oh, I doubt that very much." The effort required to conceal her smile was almost too much. *A true lady does not smile like a ninny,* Uncle's voice rang in her mind.

Crispin's expression grew instantly more serious. "You needn't hide your amusement, Catherine. I only tease you because I dearly love to see you smile."

They sat nearly touching on the sofa. Crispin brushed the back of his fingers along Catherine's cheek. She felt her cheeks burn bright. He really needed to not do that if she were to have any hope of emerging from their time together with any semblance of a whole heart.

"A very convincing performance," a voice suddenly interrupted.

Catherine had completely forgotten about Miss Bower.

"Performance?" Crispin asked, casually retaking his tea.

"I understand your effort to avoid a scandal, Crispin," Miss Bower said. "But there is no need to playact for me. I was there, you will remember."

She was *where*?

"Yes, you do seem to possess an abhorrent sense of timing," Crispin answered dryly. "You took all the romance out of our reunion, and, I fear, cast quite a shadow over our wedding."

What were they talking about?

"An annulment will stir up a scandal regardless of your efforts," Miss Bower said.

Crispin rose, agitation obvious in his posture. Was he upset about the possibility of a scandal? At the enormity of that scandal? Catherine had been too little in society to know precisely what the aftermath of an annulment would truly be.

"I, of course, will be willing to stand by you when the gossip begins to fly," Miss Bower said, her assurances directed exclusively at Crispin. "And, I have on good authority, so will most of the Upper Ten-thousand."

"It is a shame you have to be going so soon, Miss Bower." Crispin motioned toward the doors.

Miss Bower rose and made her way toward the double doors. Catherine managed to get to her feet, though she remained safely beside Crispin. His hand slipped around hers as Miss Bower collected her bonnet and gloves. Catherine's breath caught in her lungs. Her heart was most certainly in danger if the mere touch of his hand could cause such an immediate blush.

"It was a pleasure to meet you, Lady Cavratt," Miss Bower said. Her gaze drifted to Catherine and Crispin's entwined hands—a sight that didn't seem to please her at all. "Crispin, always a pleasure."

"Thank you, *Miss Bower.*"

Their very unwelcome visitor made her way out of the house. Catherine held more tightly to Crispin's hand. She knew that leaning on him was not wise—learning to stand on her own two feet would be far more prudent. She would work on that, but in that moment she didn't want to let Crispin go.

Despite Miss Bower's acidic comments, Catherine had found some enjoyment in the visit. Crispin had shown that witty side of himself that Catherine found she liked very much. He hadn't laughed—she loved his laugh—but he'd smiled. And, quite surprisingly, he'd told her he liked to see her smile. He "dearly loved" it, he'd said. The warm strength of his hand wrapped around hers helped lighten the lingering weight of Miss Bower's remarks.

"She is always a ray of sunshine," Crispin said as they reached the windows, Miss Bower's carriage just then disappearing up the street. "Makes a man want to . . . jump in the Thames with an anvil tied to his ankle."

Crispin released her hand and much of the courage she'd found evaporated.

"She seemed . . . to . . ."

". . . know a great deal about us?" Crispin still gazed out the windows. "She does. Miss Bower was in the garden that day at the inn."

Everything suddenly fit. The familiarity. The smug sense of understanding. Miss Bower was the beautiful young lady Catherine had seen Crispin walking with that day.

"We have, hopefully, delayed her retelling of those events." Crispin wandered toward the tray of pastries, taking a fairy cake. "She wouldn't want to expose herself as a truthless gossip if our performance contradicts her assertions."

Our performance. Crispin had been pretending. Catherine shook her head in frustration with herself. Of course it had been an act—everything about their marriage was an act. He pretended to be happy with her and she pretended to be unconcerned about her future.

What was wrong with her lately? Even under her uncle's roof she'd managed to find ways to take control of her life. She had taken up instrument after instrument as a means of avoiding him, smuggled sweet biscuits to her room after tea to enjoy later, escaped through books she'd discovered amongst her mother's things in the attic. Uncle may have controlled much of her life, but Catherine had never been one to give up entirely. She should have been actively seeking out her options since arriving at Permount House rather than developing a tendresse for her temporary husband.

Crispin's voice interrupted her thoughts. "Are you all right, Catherine?"

Catherine nodded but refused to look in his eyes. A single kind look from him would undermine all her resolve—she would find a way to convince herself he hadn't been entirely pretending, that in some small way he wanted her to stay. Distance and neutrality were an absolute must.

She needed to get her emotions under control before she broke down. A few moments on her own ought to be sufficient to talk a little sense into herself before she allowed her heart to convince her head of the impossible.

Chapter Thirteen

"Wait, Catherine!" Crispin called after his wife's retreating form. "Please."

He knew she'd been near crying, though he had not been able to see her eyes. He'd spent many hours since his hasty wedding pondering why he could sense her feelings at times. It was both unnerving and empowering.

He couldn't remember the last time anyone had truly needed him. He saw to the needs of his tenants, temporal as those needs were. He patronized several well-deserving charities. But with Catherine it was different. He felt at times that she needed *him.* Him, personally. The slightest act of kindness brought her to life. A tender word or a gentle touch seemed to lighten her in a way he could never have imagined his attentions affecting anyone. Despite their situation and his guilt in creating it, she seemed to be learning to trust him. Crispin felt an inexplicable need to not break that trust.

"Catherine." He reached her just at the foot of the stairs.

She stopped but didn't turn to face him.

"Please tell me what has upset you. If I've said or done something . . ."

Catherine shook her head, her back still to him.

"Miss Bower, then?" She would try the patience of a saint.

But Catherine offered another silent denial.

"Won't you tell me?" Crispin laid his hands on each of her arms just below her shoulders, needing to comfort her in the only way he could think of. He felt her shudder as she breathed and heard a muffled sob escape.

Crispin stepped around her and, placing a finger below her chin, lifted her face toward his. Tear tracks stained her soft cheeks, puddles of unshed tears clinging to her lashes. "You're crying."

"I'm sorry," she whispered, voice shaking. "I usually can control . . . myself . . . more." Sniffles interrupted her words.

"You don't need to apologize, Catherine. I just want to know what upset you."

She dropped her gaze and shook her head.

"I need to know." He tried to coax her eyes upward by gently stroking her hair. The gesture didn't seem to impact her, though it had a most decided effect on himself. His heart raced, as it seemed to every time he touched her. Needing to lighten the moment at least a little in order to regain his own equilibrium, Crispin opted for a more teasing approach. "We can hardly be a successful dueling team if we don't talk to each other."

Crispin waited, unsure if she would reply, unsure if he really needed her to. She was no longer running from him, and he took comfort in that small improvement.

"You . . ." A jumpy breath cut off her words.

Crispin tensed. He *had* done something. If his unknown infraction had brought her to tears, he must have done something horrible. He'd find a way to make it up to her if he ever found out what he'd done.

"You ate the last fairy cake," Catherine whispered.

"I . . ." Her words were so unexpected Crispin could hardly digest them. "Fairy cake?"

"You didn't even save me one." Catherine gave him a look of complete disdain ruined by the twinkle of mischief in her still-wet eyes and the twitch he'd come to recognize as a smile fighting to be let free.

She was bamming him! How unexpected. He'd always thought her too shy to tease him.

Catherine must have had a genuine reason for her emotions, and a reason to not tell him. But, standing there, his fingers still brushing her hair, those deep blue eyes sparkling up at him, her rosy lips struggling to smile, Crispin was content with her evasion. For the moment she seemed to feel better. Eventually, he told himself, he'd convince her to trust him more.

Eventually? Where had that thought come from? He hadn't come to any concrete conclusions about *eventually.*

He shook off the thought. "I believe there are several more fairy cakes on the tea tray."

"I am quite certain you ate them all." She barely maintained her serious expression even as she wiped at a lingering tear. "And I'm not sure I can ever forgive you for it."

Her distressed pout absolutely undid him. How she'd managed to pull herself together when she'd so obviously been distraught, he didn't know. She had fortitude, he'd learned that about her in the nearly two weeks they'd been married. It was an admirable trait not enough people possessed.

"I do hope you'll forgive me," he said. "Lizzie will take a switch to me if you're upset when they are here tonight."

Catherine shrugged. "I suppose for your well-being I ought to concede."

"Very considerate of you."

Then, Catherine smiled, truly smiled. Crispin's heart pounded almost painfully in his neck, every breath growing more ragged. His hand, seemingly of its own volition, ceased stroking Catherine's silken hair and brushed her cheek instead, the other hand rising to mirror it.

Roses filled the suddenly warm air as Crispin took the last step toward her. Catherine didn't pull back or push him away. His eyes focused on her face, her eyes, her lips. She was beautiful. Mesmerizing. Breathtaking.

Footsteps echoed not far away.

Suddenly aware that he was moments, breaths from kissing Catherine, Crispin shook himself to his senses once more. How had she managed to get under his skin so entirely? Their entire future was up in the air and he'd nearly kissed her twice in four days.

"Shall I prove my innocence, then?" He forced lightness into his tone.

"Your innocence?" Catherine sounded and looked confused.

"I still maintain I did not, in fact, eat all the fairy cakes," Crispin reminded her. "And I plan to prove I have been falsely accused."

"Oh." Catherine's expression cleared a little. Then, with an exaggerated thoughtful expression, she added, "I suppose it is only fair you should have a chance to redeem your maligned character."

"Exactly." Enough distance had arisen between them to calm his racing heart. Feeling more in control of himself, Crispin offered her his arm, which she took, and led her back into the sitting room.

"Oh, dear." Catherine was obviously feigning her despair. "It appears I *have* falsely accused you."

Crispin smiled, his gaze settling, along with hers, on half a dozen fairy cakes untouched on the silver tray. "Perhaps I should call you out for such an insult."

Catherine's lips again appeared to battle against her determination to not smile. "But I get to choose the weapons, do I not?"

"That is one of the rules, yes." Crispin found it odd that she should know the intricacies of dueling. She seemed to know so little of society, yet understood this aspect of the realm of gentlemanly pursuits.

"I haven't the slightest idea how to fence." Catherine paced the room, her eyes twinkling delightfully. "I am afraid you would have the advantage at fisticuffs."

"Pistols, then?" Crispin couldn't remember the last time he'd had such a diverting conversation.

"No." Catherine's answer was quick, abrupt, and not at all playful. Every hint of color had suddenly drained from her face, the twinkle in her eyes had vanished. "I don't like pistols." Apparently realizing the marked difference in her tone, Catherine stammered, her eyes on the floor. "M-my uncle cleaned his every month and insisted I be present when he did."

Odd behavior, to be sure.

"He told me repeatedly that pistols were the ideal means of eliminating . . . enemies and . . . inconveniences. I . . . I do not like pistols."

A single glance at her pale countenance told Crispin that she was not at all equal to the task of further discussing her uncle's warped and threatening behavior. He wanted to see her smile again, to wipe away the lingering impact of her uncle's memory on her. "We've eliminated the usual arsenal. Something untraditional, then?"

Catherine bit her lips closed with her teeth, not taking the bait he offered.

"Frogs?" Crispin suggested.

"Frogs?" She looked up at him once more. Curiosity replaced some of the pain in her eyes.

Crispin couldn't help the mischievous smile he felt spreading across his face. "I once put frogs in Lizzie's bed out of revenge for a childhood spat."

"And so you won the duel?" Catherine asked, her voice still quiet, but not as heavy.

"I found snakes in my bed the next night." He shrugged. "So I threw her in the lake."

Catherine's lips twitched again. Why on earth didn't she allow herself to smile? He would get her to before the day was over. He had no idea how but swore he would manage it.

"It wasn't deep, then?" Catherine said.

"Lizzie is an excellent swimmer, though she flailed around enough to convince me otherwise. I decided to rescue her and she pulled me in after her." Crispin remembered that bit of trickery fondly. "I don't even remember what started that battle."

"You probably ate all of the pastries."

How unpredictable she was proving. The more time he spent with her, the more he liked her.

"And now I see I am going to be forced to adulterate your tea." Catherine produced a melodramatic sigh that would have put Lizzie's efforts to shame.

He was grateful she seemed to have recovered somewhat from her difficult recollections. He followed her lead and offered a lighthearted comment of his own. "We're having an argument, then?"

"It is a very convenient way for a wife to let her husband know when she's in a tizzy." Catherine looked far less burdened than she had a moment earlier.

"And, pray tell, what would be a convenient way for a husband to let his wife know that he's claimed the upper hand in one of their, um, tizzies?" His grin, a rare-enough indulgence normally, felt perfectly natural at that moment.

"He could always throw her in a lake," Catherine answered.

Her smile hovered very near the surface, Crispin could tell. He *would* make her smile. He would!

"Of course, *you* don't have a lake," Catherine added with a look of amused triumph on her face.

"No," Crispin said, slowly, mischievously. "But I do have a large fountain."

"I don't swim," Catherine said, emotions warring on her surprisingly expressive face. Doubt, curiosity, amusement, apprehension, joviality.

"It's a large, *shallow* fountain."

"But I am not actually in a tizzy."

"You've twice accused me of pilfering sweets." Crispin stepped toward her. "And since you refuse to choose the weapons for the duel my honor requires, I have no choice but to dump you in the fountain."

"You wouldn't." It was as much a statement as a question.

In Crispin's mischievous mood, the declaration stood as a challenge. "Wouldn't I?"

He took another deliberate step closer to her. She inched backward. He stepped again but kept a close eye on her face. He didn't wish to frighten or upset her. She needed to smile, to laugh, to have a moment's enjoyment in life.

"Surely I haven't disparaged your honor so drastically as all this." Catherine stepped back yet again. Any moment now that elusive smile would break the surface. He saw not a hint of the apprehension that too often marred her remarkably lovely face.

"Fairy cake theft is a serious crime," Crispin said.

"A hanging offense, is it?"

Lovely? Was that the insipid word he'd assigned her features only moments earlier? She was enchanting. He could think of at least a dozen simpering debutantes who would have spent hours in front of their looking glasses trying to perfect the look Catherine was giving him: her brow raised in challenge, unknowingly pulling him closer to her.

"You would mock my maligned reputation?"

"Perhaps I don't take your threat seriously." Her eyes crinkled in a smile, though her mouth still fought against her emerging smile.

A deep chuckle escaped Crispin's chest. "I *am* going to have to inspect my tea," he said, moving more quickly toward Catherine even as she skirted around the sofa. "After your thorough dunking, I have a feeling you will be in a monumental tizzy."

Then, it happened. Catherine's face split in a spectacular grin. That single reward was worth all the effort.

"I suppose I should be grateful I am married to a much older man," Catherine quipped, pulling Crispin out of his momentary reverie.

"*Much older man?*"

"I am counting on your advanced rheumatism," Catherine explained. "You can't throw me in the fountain if you're too stiff in the joints to even catch me."

"To the fountain with you, woman!" Crispin lunged after her.

Crispin momentarily froze as Catherine's laughter rang across the room. He had never heard her laugh.

"Poor old man." Catherine smiled without hesitation. "I suppose I should take pity on your aging limbs and slow down a bit."

Crispin came swiftly around the sofa, but Catherine proved too quick. He spun to follow her only to be outmaneuvered. He faked to the right and she sped toward the door. Expecting this, Crispin cut her off, grabbed her at the waist, and pulled her directly to him.

Catherine's eyes danced with amusement. Any moment her laughter would erupt once more. What an enchanting picture she made. Her cheeks had colored with the exertion and her eyes had brightened with happiness.

"You, my dear, are more evasive than I would have imagined. I would almost think you had practice avoiding deserved punishments."

With that, every hint of laughter in her countenance disappeared. The guarded, fearful Catherine returned instantly.

"I am sorry, Catherine," Crispin quickly said, recognizing his blunder immediately. Punishments had been far more than a teasing threat with her uncle, he was certain. "That was a thoughtless comment. I forgot about your uncle."

"So had I," Catherine said. "I can't remember the last time he wasn't somewhere in the back of my mind. It has been wonderful, you know." Catherine tilted her head back, her eyes boring uncharacteristically into his. She usually avoided eye contact.

"What has been?" Crispin's voice sounded a bit husky as he became ever more aware of how close they stood.

"Not worrying," she said, still gazing into his eyes. "Not being afraid. Of you."

"I wouldn't want you to be afraid of me."

"Then it is a very good thing I am not."

"Catherine . . ." Crispin began, no idea what he intended to say to her. That smile of hers. He was done for. He bent his head, wrapping his arm more snuggly around her to close the distance.

This time he didn't hesitate, he didn't stop himself. And Catherine didn't pull away.

His lips brushed lightly over hers. The scent of roses filled his nose. He could feel her breathing, feel the warmth of her so close to him. Their lips met again, still gently, but with more fervor. That same sensation he remembered all too vividly from their first kiss swept over him in waves—the inarguable reality that Catherine's presence in his arms felt absolutely right, that his brain was barely functioning, registering nothing but her.

"Good heavens!" a woman shrieked.

Chapter Fourteen

He wanted to continue kissing his bride, blast it. Who was making all that racket? Maybe if he ignored the noise, it would go away.

"Crispin," Catherine whispered against his lips.

He kissed her again, but she pulled back.

"Crispin, someone is here."

With a groan of frustration, he glanced over Catherine's head at the inconvenient visitors. Lud. "Mrs. Glafford. Miss Glafford."

"Oh heavens."

He nearly laughed at Catherine's tone of annoyance.

"This is quite a spectacle," Mrs. Glafford said.

"That is the risk you take calling on a newly wedded couple." Crispin shrugged, releasing his hold on Catherine but immediately taking her hand. For the sake of the appearance, he told himself, and not because his mind was still completely wrapped around that unexpected kiss.

"But, I—" Miss Glafford began.

"Hush, child," her mother whispered tersely. "Apparently, this is a bad time."

"On the contrary." Crispin kissed Catherine's fingers, bringing a blush to her cheeks. He looked away before he lost his head again. "Cook has sent down fairy cakes. They're delicious."

He distinctly heard the tiniest of laughs escape Catherine's lips. Crispin grinned unrepentantly.

"Well!" Mrs. Glafford shot her chin into the air, spun on her heels, and stormed out the door, her bewildered daughter in tow.

"I tried to tell them you were not home to visitors," Hancock said as he shut the door. "They bullied their way inside."

"I believe you." Crispin took a deep, much-needed breath. He hadn't fully refilled his lungs after that kiss. If Mrs. Glafford's wailing hadn't broken the spell . . .

He felt Catherine's hand shift inside his. How strange that merely holding her hand made his heart thump nearly as much as kissing her had. He needed a few minutes' respite from his unexpectedly charming wife to bring him back to his senses.

"So am I still to be resigned to the fountain?" Catherine's teasing tone seemed a bit forced.

Her words didn't immediately register. Why was it, he continued to wonder, that he seemed to make a cake of himself every time he touched Catherine? He was no lovesick young beau. What would the Glaffords make of the encounter? More important yet, what version of the afternoon's events would they bandy about Town?

Suddenly remembering that Catherine had asked him a question, Crispin stumbled for a reply. She had asked him something about the fountain. "I'm not going to—no." He shook his head absentmindedly.

He tried to think of every possible angle from which the Glaffords might depict what they'd seen. If he could anticipate any possible damage, he might be able to prevent it. The mess they were already in over this marriage and its future hardly needed further complications.

A knock echoed from the front door.

"We're not at home, Hancock," Crispin warned.

Hancock opened the door. "Lord and Lady Cavratt are not at home," Hancock declared, though Crispin heard a hint of sarcasm in his voice.

Crispin glanced to the heavens, wishing for patience. And why, he demanded of himself, was he in such a sour mood? The Glaffords weren't likely to make too much of the scene they'd stumbled on, not if it lessened their chances at a prize catch: he himself being the fish they supposed on their pole.

"I tried to stop her," Hancock said as Lizzie flitted into the room.

"Blast it, Hancock!" Crispin muttered. "Could I not have one moment of peace in this house?"

"Oh, fiddle." Lizzie waved a hand dismissively. "Hancock wouldn't have let me in if I weren't family. Ooh, fairy cakes!"

A smile tugged at Crispin's mouth. He'd never think of fairy cakes the same way again. He stole a glance at Catherine. She had retreated to the fringes of the room, studying her clasped hands. What had happened to the teasing, smiling Catherine?

"I have come on urgent business, Crispin," Lizzie announced, gingerly wiping a few crumbs from the corners of her mouth.

"Please spare me the dramatics." Surely Catherine hadn't found that unexpected kiss so very unwelcome. Maybe she found it revolting—sobering thought for one who'd always believed he possessed a talent in that area.

"You are awfully grumpy this morning," Lizzie said.

"I am not grumpy." He hadn't been, at least. The Glaffords could make the most amiable individual remarkably ill-tempered.

Lizzie obviously didn't believe a word of it. "Irritable, then."

His wife, apparently, hated kissing him. He had every reason to be irritable. "It has been an unpleasant morning." Crispin rubbed his face—an outward show of tension he rarely indulged in. "Out with your news, Lizzie." Crispin knew he was being too short, but couldn't seem to shake his bedevilment.

"What is the matter with you?" Lizzie tensely whispered, walking quickly to where he stood. "All this grumbling and snapping." She glanced quickly behind her before looking back at him. "Have you and Catherine quarreled?"

That at least would have made sense. "Of course not."

"She seems unhappy," Lizzie said rather pointedly.

Crispin looked across at Catherine. She had sunk into a wingback chair that seemed to engulf her suddenly tiny frame. Blast it! She *did* look unhappy.

Forcing his unwanted attentions on her had gotten him into this mess in the first place. Repeating the offense had probably made things worse.

Did all husbands do this much apologizing? How many of them regularly apologized for mistakes they didn't even know they'd made? A man certainly didn't expect to apologize for kissing his wife, especially when *he* had rather enjoyed it.

Catherine rose from her chair. "I have some things . . . I need to . . ." She slipped out of the room before Crispin could even begin formulating an apology.

"What did you do to upset her so much?"

I kissed her. What now? Should he ignore their kiss, act impersonal? Or was the opposite tactic the better idea? Marriage really ought to come with an instruction manual.

"What is your desperate business?" he asked Lizzie.

"*Urgent* business," Lizzie corrected. "I have thought of someone *perfect*!"

"Perfect for what?" He'd thought many times that no matter how much he loved his sister, he would have been forced to do himself some dire harm if he were ever to find himself married to a woman as theatrical as she. He far preferred a lady grounded in reality and calm and . . . not opposed to being chased around the sitting room. He smiled at the memory.

"I am going to find a husband for Catherine!" Lizzie declared.

"You—" Shock tied his tongue for a split second. "Catherine *has* a husband."

Lizzie waved off that rather important fact. "Neither of you wanted to marry the other. I can't imagine her opinion has changed, and I know yours hasn't."

His hesitation surprised him. He hadn't made any final decisions regarding the annulment. The solicitor had unearthed an inheritance of some kind that Catherine was entitled to through her mother's side, though he had no details beyond his belief that it should be sufficient for her to live on. The discovery relieved Crispin's mind on one point—Catherine would not be left destitute—but still he couldn't bring himself to make a final decision. Which would make Catherine more miserable: an unwanted marriage or a socially devastating annulment? And at what point had he stopped putting his opinion on the subject foremost?

"It is perfect, Crispin." *Ah, yes.* Lizzie was still there. "Catherine has already made a splash in society. Chances are excellent that someone will develop a tendresse for her. If that lucky someone happens to be a gentleman of consequence and rank, his standing would save hers after you destroy her reputation and hopes for the future by coldheartedly annulling the marriage."

"You want me to play matchmaker for my own wife?" What utter rot.

"Of course not. *I* am going to play matchmaker for her." Obviously Lizzie thought her logic infallible.

"Perhaps I should take out an advertisement. 'Found: one wife. Inquire at Permount House if interested.'"

"Do not be such a dunderhead." Lizzie set her hands on her hips, head cocked to the side. "It's not as if you want to be her husband, and she quite obviously doesn't wish to be your wife."

"'Quite obviously'? Did she tell you she didn't want to be married to me?"

If Lizzie gave him one more dismissive wave, he would throttle her. "You forced her into this. What reason could she possibly have to like the idea of staying?"

What reason, indeed? Crispin didn't think he was such a bad catch, though Catherine, apparently, objected to kissing him. "But she *would* like the idea of staying with this paragon of masculinity you've unearthed?"

Lizzie nodded enthusiastically.

"And who is he?" He spoke through his clenched teeth.

Lizzie regarded him with equal parts surprise and amusement. "Not jealous, are you?" She sounded moments from giggling.

Of course he wasn't jealous, and he told her as much. When she simply smiled at him speculatively, Crispin felt his patience slip further. "Well?" he pressed after slowly counting to five.

"Philip," Lizzie announced triumphantly.

"Philip?" Crispin practically shouted. "You want to marry her off to my best friend? Are you insane?"

"He is ideal," Lizzie said. "He's lighthearted and genial—precisely what Catherine needs. Her spirits are too often depressed, and, quite frankly, you are far too cynical for her."

Crispin paced tensely around the room. Philip? Lizzie had lost her mind. And *cynical*? Would a cynical gentleman chase his wife around a room or laugh over fairy cakes? No! He was lighthearted . . . sometimes.

"Catherine would be immensely happy with Philip. As the Earl of Lampton, he outranks you. Taking his name would save her reputation."

"They wouldn't suit."

"We'll let them see that for themselves." The picture of indignation, Lizzie flew from the room.

Crispin dropped into a chair. Lizzie had gone mad, completely and utterly mad. Just because he and Catherine had not had an ideal marriage did not mean Lizzie could go about arranging an even less ideal marriage. Catherine deserved better treatment than being tossed from one husband to another.

He slumped down in the chair, worn to the bone. Catherine also deserved better than the public humiliation and ruin of an annulment. She ought to have a say in her future.

Lud. Life should not be so confusing.

* * *

Catherine looked unseeingly at a day-old issue of the *Times* laid out on her lap. She took a deep breath. What a morning she'd had. Miss Bower's poisonous visit. Crispin's unexpected words of comfort. He'd actually seemed genuinely concerned about her. He hadn't scolded her for her tears nor scowled at her emotions. And she had laughed for the first time in years. Those few moments of lighthearted enjoyment had proven remarkably liberating, as if a tremendous weight had temporarily lifted from her.

He'd held her in his arms. Sitting alone in the leather wingback chair, she could still feel his arms around her. And that kiss! She'd absolutely melted. How easily he made her forget their real circumstances. For a moment, she'd even entertained the notion that he'd grown fond of her, that he'd kissed her out of affection, perhaps more.

She focused once more on the *Times,* adjusting her askew reading spectacles. If she were to find a position before their marriage ended, she needed to begin searching for one.

"How long have you used reading spectacles?"

Catherine jumped at the sound of Crispin's voice. She hadn't even heard him come in.

She quickly removed her glasses. "They are awful, I know," she whispered.

"No, not at all." Crispin leaned against the library fireplace mantel. "It is just unusual for someone as young as you to require them. Have you had them long?"

Catherine took a long breath. She knew she could not easily avoid offering an explanation. "Seven years."

"You would have been only a child."

"I was nearly fourteen."

"Did your parents have poor vision as well?"

Catherine shifted uncomfortably, doing all she could to avoid looking at him. "No. I . . . My vision was . . . damaged."

"What happened?" he asked.

She really did not want to talk about this. Crispin continued to watch her, his curiosity not abating in the slightest. Perhaps a quick retelling would satisfy him and she could once again push the memory to the quiet recesses of her mind.

"My uncle was not accustomed to children." She'd used that as an explanation throughout the original ordeal. The words had offered little comfort then and even less in the years that followed.

"I had a feeling your uncle might have had something to do with this."

"He did not want me underfoot when he first inherited after my father's death. I had to stay in my bedchamber, but the windows were darkened and there were no candles."

Crispin crossed from the fireplace and sat on the ottoman directly in front of her. "I suspect there is more." He sat watching her, his expression so kind and compassionate she couldn't bring herself to refuse an answer, even if she could no longer bring herself to look at him.

"I was locked in." She'd never told anyone about the time she still thought of as her imprisonment. How worthless must a person be to be locked in her room for so long? Crispin certainly deserved to know, she told herself. After all his kindness, she didn't want him to look back and feel he'd been misled. "I tried to leave once. As punishment he refused me food for several days."

A strange silence followed. Catherine warily glanced up. She expected to see disgust, the realization that he'd married someone who couldn't even secure the affections of her own blood relations. Instead, he looked angry.

"Surely the servants could have helped you leave or, at the very least, brought you a candle."

"Uncle replaced the entire staff after Father's death." Including her governess, the one advocate she might have had. "Jane told me years later that Uncle convinced the staff I was a bit mad and that he had locked me in my bedchamber for my own protection. Only Jane was permitted to see me when she brought me my food. She eventually realized I wasn't really a Bedlamite."

"How long were you locked in?" Crispin's jaw tensed, his hands balled up in fists.

"Thirteen months."

"Over a year!" Crispin abruptly stood. "The bloody—" Crispin stopped himself midsentence. "And the imprisonment is what damaged your eyesight?"

"The doctor was unsure if the culprit was the prolonged lack of light or . . ." She truly hated talking about those experiences. ". . . or an injury I sustained very soon after I was permitted to leave my chamber."

"An 'injury'?" Crispin gave her a look far too searching for comfort. "Did your uncle have anything to do with this injury?"

Catherine did not answer—she could see she didn't need to.

"I am surprised he had the decency to allow you to be seen by a doctor."

"The servants paid for the doctor." Catherine shifted, feeling herself redden—she never had been able to repay them for that kindness. "For a year they put aside what they could and when a doctor happened through the town, they arranged for him to see me in the kitchen. The local doctor would have told Uncle, and he would have been furious."

"Bloody—" Crispin grumbled the same half statement. "Doing that to anyone, let alone a child who had just lost her father! His own niece, even!"

"I tried not to be a bother when he first came." She wished Crispin would drop the subject.

"You were a child," Crispin interjected. "What could he possibly have been punishing you for?"

"He never told me." She'd spent a great deal of those thirteen months pondering what her grievous crime had been.

Crispin again sat on the ottoman. He took one of her hands in his. How different the grueling eight years she'd spent with her uncle would have been if Crispin had been with her. She'd needed the comfort his gentle touch offered.

"I didn't mean to imply that you could have done *anything* to deserve being treated that way," he said.

She understood that on an intellectual level, but deep inside the scars remained. A fleeting and uncharacteristically pleasant memory of those long months brought a hint of a smile to her face. "I used to imagine creeping around the house at night making otherworldly noises and frightening Uncle out of his wits, perhaps even enough to make him flee the house for good. I became very adept at moving around in the dark and could have easily managed it if the door had been unlocked. I drew a great deal of satisfaction from imagining his terror-filled face."

Crispin squeezed her fingers. "Either you are the most forgiving person on the planet, or your imagination was sorely lacking in your younger years. I am afraid I would have thought of more dire forms of retaliation than merely frightening the cad."

"I *did* devise the tea adulteration scheme," Catherine reminded him. "Uncle certainly found that ordeal dire."

"And I called that scheme of yours malicious." Crispin shook his head. "Under the circumstances, you could have put arsenic in his tea, and it would not have been in the least uncalled for."

She sighed, weary from the weight of unwelcome memories. "Life has not been easy with him."

"Obviously, you don't particularly want to talk about any of this. I shouldn't have forced the topic on you."

"Actually, it is something of a relief to finally talk about it," Catherine admitted. "I've never felt there was anyone I could trust enough to . . ."

"I am honored to . . . be a friend," Crispin finished awkwardly.

A friend. She valued his friendship likely more than he realized, but somehow the word felt bittersweet. She wanted more than that from this man who was anxious to be rid of her.

Crispin's smile looked rather forced. He patted her hand before releasing it and taking a chair some distance from her own and spoke not another word the entire evening. Catherine spent the night jotting down names of individuals who might be interested in a companion or governess and trying to devise a means of covertly inquiring about employment. Which would be best, she wondered: a position near enough to afford the occasional glimpse of Crispin or one far enough removed to keep him but a distant memory?

Chapter Fifteen

Lizzie dragged her poor husband to Crispin's sitting room the next morning in an attempt to further her plot regarding Catherine's future with Crispin's best friend. In response to his sister's continued attachment to such an ill-conceived idea, Crispin quickly and conveniently related a very detailed accounting of every reason in existence that the two would not suit. Truth be known, he'd spent most of the previous night accumulating the list. He'd thought back on every childhood misdeed he and Philip had undertaken during their Eton years, conveniently leaving out his own involvement. He knew enough of his friend's past to convince Philip's mother to denounce him. Perhaps not quite that much, but certainly a sufficient amount to dissuade Lizzie.

"And Philip is a dandy of the worst sort."

"I think you're doing it a bit brown," Edward said.

"I am not. He would make her a terrible husband."

"He can't possibly be worse than the husband she has now." If Lizzie hadn't been grinning just like an obnoxious younger sister would when ribbing her brother, Crispin might have given her a piece of his mind.

"Your plan is ridiculous," Crispin said. "Her husband, who the gossips are convinced couldn't possibly care less about her, is bandying her about to his friends as a possible wife. She would be married, unmarried, and remarried all in the course of a short few months. No amount of rank could save her reputation after that."

"You do not know that for sure. And even if she lost some standing, at least Catherine would have someplace to turn in her time of need."

Turn to Philip? And why couldn't she turn to me*?*

"Philip is a good sort of fellow," Edward said. "He would be good for her."

"Et tu, Edward?"

The man had the audacity to grin, an expression that clearly covered a desire to laugh at him. "Is there some reason you object to Philip's courting our sweet Catherine?"

The only reason he would admit to he voiced. "Catherine has already been forced into one marriage. I can't feel good about wrangling her into another."

"I am not suggesting you literally shackle her to him." Lizzie rolled her eyes heavenward. "Merely introduce them and let nature run its course."

"Perhaps if we introduced them in a garden," Edward suggested.

"Perfect." Lizzie clapped her hands together in obvious glee. "Philip could kiss her quite soundly and they'd be married in no time."

"Are you two done?" Crispin had seldom been less amused.

"Everything will work out splendidly," Lizzie said. "You'll see."

The library door opened and Catherine stepped inside. Her gaze settled on his face. Lud, she was crying. Crispin's stomach twisted at the sight. What had happened? And why was he suddenly convinced he was at fault?

Seemingly oblivious to the others' presence, Catherine rushed to where he stood near the fireplace and held out an opened letter. He didn't recognize the handwriting. Indeed, he could hardly make it out. After much effort he deciphered the chicken scratch.

> Niece,
>
> Will arrive in London shortly. You will come to Hill Street upon receiving my card.

Thomas Thorndale

"He is coming to London?" Crispin repeated aloud.

Catherine nodded. Tears trickled down her face at an alarming rate. Crispin had never seen her cry this way, not making any attempt to hide her distress. His heart lurched at the sight.

"I don't really have to go to Hill Street, do I?"

"Of course not." Crispin reached out and gently touched her cheek, brushing away tears only to have them immediately replaced by newly shed drops.

Catherine closed her eyes. "He sounds angry. He is horrible when he's angry."

He thought immediately of a helpless thirteen-year-old girl locked in her room for over a year because that bounder had been angry. Crispin pulled her to him and wrapped his arms around her. "I won't let him hurt you. I would never let him hurt you."

Catherine laid her head on his shoulder, and he felt her hands clasp his lapels. There in his arms, she shuddered through sobs and what he imagined were years' worth of anxious tears. She didn't deserve the hand fate had dealt her—being held prisoner in her own home, enduring the violent temper of an insufferable man.

Crispin wished he could make it all disappear somehow. He'd whisk her away on his daring steed and hide her from society and her uncle. Just beyond Catherine, Lizzie and Edward silently slipped from the room.

There you have it, Lizzie. I am perfectly capable of taking care of her. Philip can find his own wife.

Crispin kept Catherine enfolded in the relative safety of his arms and let her cry until her breathing steadied. She seemed calmer but didn't pull away.

"Uncle always told me I wasn't to allow myself to be emotional," Catherine said softly.

"Nonsense." Crispin stroked her hair. "You cry whenever you need to."

"But I've completely rumpled your cravat."

"The sole purpose of a cravat is for crying into." Crispin felt a tremendous amount of satisfaction serving as a shoulder to cry on.

"Your valet will be furious with me." Catherine fiddled with the drooping cravat, her head still resting on Crispin's obliging shoulder.

"My valet likes you better than he likes me," Crispin said, sighing as though he were pained by the admission.

"Your entire staff likes me better than you."

He chuckled and held her tighter. Crispin resisted the unexpected urge to kiss the top of her head. Catherine had the strangest effect on him, bringing out a side of him he didn't even know existed. He smiled more and actually laughed. He had felt protective of Lizzie but not to the degree he did with Catherine. It was simply chivalry, he decided. After all, Catherine needed someone to stand up for her in the face of her uncle's return.

"Maybe we should invite your uncle to join us here on an evening when Lizzie and Edward will be present. That would certainly dispense any obligation you might have to see him."

"But I do have to see him?"

"I doubt you could completely avoid him."

"But I wouldn't be alone?" Catherine stepped back a bit and looked up into his face.

Crispin found the added distance a blessing, though he could not bring himself to completely release her. He was merely being compassionate, of course.

"Perhaps he doesn't mean to stay in Town long," Catherine said.

"I am certain he won't be in London long." He was certain of no such thing but would have said almost anything to put her at ease. His baseless reassurances seemed to work—she looked immediately relieved.

"And I won't have to see him alone?"

Crispin shook his head.

"Thank you, Crispin." She rose on her tiptoes and kissed his cheek. A flattering tinge of pink touched her cheeks as she turned and slipped from the room.

Crispin let out a long, deep breath, shaking off the tingling he felt clear to his feet. She had managed to get under his skin. He worried about her. He wondered about her. And he had no idea what to do about her.

Chapter Sixteen

WITH COMPLETE AND UTTER HORROR, Catherine watched the familiar figure of her uncle take the steps of Permount House five days after his letter had arrived. He took his time ascending. From the sitting room window Catherine watched him assess the Grosvenor Square residence she'd come to think of as her sanctuary. Her heart pounded desperately in her ribs. She felt instantly sick to her stomach.

Crispin had gone with Edward to Tattersall's, and she would, in fact, be forced to face her uncle alone.

She held her breath as she listened: a knock, the opening of the front door, a muffled conversation, and the approach of footsteps. Catherine's legs shook beneath her. The sitting room doors slowly opened and Hancock stepped inside. A fleeting look of concern crossed the well-trained butler's face before he resumed the more appropriate look of impassivity.

"Mr. Thomas Thorndale," Hancock announced then stepped aside to let the visitor in.

Uncle stomped into the room every bit the perpetually angered man Catherine remembered. Nothing about him had changed in the short weeks they'd been apart, though Catherine felt completely different. She'd found people she could trust, had experienced moments of pleasure and enjoyment. She'd stood up for herself and had received genuine compliments. But the moment her uncle's eyes settled on her, Catherine felt every ounce of courage disappear.

"Put on airs, have you?" Uncle scowled at her.

Catherine kept silent. Her uncle far preferred her that way.

"If that husband of yours expects me to foot the bill for those fancy clothes you've dressed yourself in once he's rid himself of you, he is sorely mistaken."

Catherine turned to the doorway where Hancock was, uncharacteristically, still standing. "T-Tea, p-p-please," she requested.

"Of course, my lady," Hancock answered with a deep bow and stepped out to fulfill the request.

"You knew I was coming to London," Uncle growled.

Catherine didn't respond, verbally or otherwise. That, apparently, was enough confirmation for him.

"Yet you did not come to Hill Street as I told you to, ungrateful wench!" he spat. "How dare you ignore your betters!"

"I am sorry," Catherine whispered.

"When I want you to speak, I will tell you so."

Catherine nodded. Uncle circled the room, stopping to thoroughly evaluate the more exquisite furnishings and decorations. Catherine stood stock-still, not daring to move without express permission.

Uncle's eyes settled on her once more, his dissatisfaction quite obvious. "Keeping you around for a bit, is he?" He raked her with his eyes. "Obviously you've married a man with very low standards."

Catherine waited for him to continue his diatribe. Weeks away from her uncle had done nothing to erase her vivid memory of how their encounters always played out.

A young maid set a well-appointed tea tray on a table before bowing herself out of the room. Catherine took up the task of pouring in order to steady herself. She knew precisely what Uncle's preferences for tea were: sugar, no cream. She noticed as she poured that Cook had provided her famous fairy cakes, and suddenly Catherine missed Crispin terribly.

They would have exchanged knowing looks over the pastry. Crispin would have pretended to inspect his teacup. He would have smiled and perhaps even laughed. She would likely miss him every minute of every day for the rest of her life after they parted ways.

She allowed her thoughts to wander to Crispin and the distraction had disastrous results. Catherine over-poured, scalding liquid spilling over the teacup. Suddenly realizing her mistake, Catherine panicked and allowed her hand to slip beneath the scalding liquid. The pain caused her to momentarily lose her grip on the teakettle. She caught it before a monumental disaster ensued but not in time to save the teacup from shattering beneath it.

"You are useless." Uncle walked toward the window as if inconvenienced by her pain.

Catherine attempted to clean up the mess she had created, wincing as her burned fingers throbbed.

Hancock appeared at her side. "Allow me, my lady," he said, quickly cleaning the mess. A moment later a maid came as well and carried the ruined tea from the room.

"Your fingers appear burned," Hancock said in a low voice, his eyes darting between Catherine and her uncle.

"I will see to it later." If she left, Uncle would only grow angrier than he already appeared to be.

"It seems painful."

Catherine tried to convey with a look the necessity of her remaining. Hancock bowed, looked one more time at Catherine's uncle, then left the room.

"I won't be paying for that cup, either." Uncle still watched the street through the window.

Her fingers grew steadily more painful. She tried to cool them off.

"Stop that ridiculous blowing."

"My fingers hurt."

"No more than you deserve." Uncle turned back toward her, his look one of pure disgust. "Come here, brat."

Catherine took two faltering steps, knowing she would be punished if she disobeyed. Uncle glared down at her. She could not force herself to close the remaining distance. He stepped forward, his massive hands taking hold of her upper arms and yanking her closer.

"You listen to me," Uncle snarled. "No matter the title you've gotten attached to your name, no matter the money and airs you think you've claim to, I know you're no better than the feather-headed wench you always were. You see to it you remember your place."

His painful grip dug into her arms.

"I won't hesitate to knock you back where you belong. Am I understood?"

Catherine nodded anxiously, praying he would release her. Her hand throbbed, her arms ached, and she had to desperately fight the feeling she was about to cry. Uncle would beat her black and blue over a single tear—he certainly had before.

"Mr. Thorndale," an angry voice said from the doorway.

Uncle gave Catherine one more intense look before releasing her arms and condescending to glance across the room at the most recent entrant. Catherine didn't need to look. She'd have known Crispin's voice anywhere.

Every fiber of her wanted to run to him, wanted to feel the increasingly familiar security she'd found in him, but she didn't dare risk incurring Uncle's wrath.

"Lord Cavratt." Uncle didn't even attempt to appear deferent.

"I see you've arrived in Town," Crispin said. "I trust your journey was uneventful."

"Quite."

Crispin reached her side. Relief poured over her. He took hold of her hand, and she pulled back at the surge of pain. He immediately let go.

"What happened to your hand?" he whispered.

Catherine just shook her head.

"Did he—"

"No."

"What brings you to Town, Mr. Thorndale?" Crispin asked, slipping his arm around her waist, holding her against his side.

"For one thing, I decided to learn what had become of my niece, since she doesn't feel the need to write to the only family she has."

Catherine leaned against Crispin. He wouldn't allow her uncle to hurt her. The skin of her hand turned ever redder, pain pulsating through it. Still, she felt better.

"I hope you have found her well," Crispin said.

"She is much changed."

"And are you in Town for long?"

Catherine found the courage to look up at her uncle again. She hoped his time in London would be quite short.

"My plans are still unsettled," Uncle answered.

"Perhaps you would like to join us for dinner while you are in London."

Catherine held her breath. Uncle at Permount House again? She could endure it, she told herself.

"Fine. I'll be here tonight."

A heavy silence followed. Uncle's high-handedness must have shocked Crispin. A person didn't invite himself to dinner, it simply wasn't done.

"Eight o'clock," Crispin finally said. "My sister and her husband, Lord and Lady Henley, will be here as well."

Uncle sniffed, obviously unimpressed. Without a proper take-leave, he stomped from the room and left.

Even before the sound of the front door closing echoed in the room, Crispin turned toward her. "What happened to your hand?" He tilted her chin up and looked in her eyes. Catherine flinched; there was something bordering on anger in his eyes. "Did he hurt you?"

She shook her head. "I dropped the teakettle and burned myself. He makes me nervous."

"I should have been here."

Catherine's breath shuddered out of her. She always trembled after an encounter with her uncle, a delayed reaction to the tension his presence created. She wrapped her arms around herself in an attempt to ward off the chill that seeped into her.

Crispin gently brushed an escaped hair from her face. His look was infinitely gentle, and she simply melted against him.

"I am sorry, Catherine," he said, holding her as he had the day Uncle's letter arrived. "You should not have had to face him alone."

She knew she must learn to survive on her own, but in that moment she needed the strength he lent her.

* * *

Mr. Thorndale arrived at precisely eight o'clock that night. With some effort Crispin kept his fists unclenched. Although Catherine hadn't said anything, Crispin knew Thorndale had done something to her.

Crispin glanced across the room at her. She stood in the shadows, her head lowered. He hadn't heard a word from her since that afternoon. He could *feel* the vibrant lady he'd come to know slipping away. Crispin could throttle Thorndale for the fear he brought into Catherine's eyes.

"Lord Cavratt." Thorndale offered a short bow.

"Mr. Thorndale." Crispin tried to hide his anger. "Allow me to introduce Lord and Lady Henley. Edward, Elizabeth, this is Mr. Thomas Thorndale of Herefordshire."

The expected bows and curtsies were exchanged.

"Dinner is served," Hancock announced.

Crispin repressed a smile. He'd specifically instructed Hancock to announce the evening meal before Thorndale had any opportunity to create havoc. Hancock had obviously taken his instructions to heart.

"Catherine, dear." Crispin turned toward her and held out his hand.

She looked up at him, the first time in hours she had looked directly into his eyes. He smiled encouragingly. Catherine's gaze shifted to her uncle. She seemed to debate for a moment before walking to where Crispin still stood waiting for her. She didn't slip her hand in his as he'd hoped, but her gaze had returned to his face, anxiety written in every inch of it.

"Uncle always precedes me into meals."

Crispin matched her whisper, but with firmness. "Not in this house."

He slipped her arm around his own and began the procession into the dining room. Crispin noticed with satisfaction that since Edward accompanied his wife, Thorndale walked alone in to dinner. It was socially unacceptable. Crispin could not have cared less. Thorndale, with any luck, would turn tail and run before the end of the night. Then—Crispin smiled at the thought—he'd have his Catherine back.

There it was again: *his* Catherine. This possessiveness wasn't at all like him.

Propriety required that Catherine be seated at the foot of the table and Crispin at the head. He would have greatly preferred to keep Catherine at his side. However, the more formal seating arrangement clearly indicated Catherine's position and importance in his home, something Thorndale needed to understand.

"How long were you guardian to our dear Catherine?" Crispin heard Lizzie ask Thorndale several minutes into the meal.

Crispin smiled at the endearment. Lizzie wasn't backing down from this undeclared war.

"My brother died eight years ago."

"Your brother was her father, then?" Lizzie somehow managed to look and sound pleasantly curious when Crispin knew she fully intended to draw blood. "And her mother had passed on then also, I assume."

Thorndale grunted an affirmative as he swallowed a generous mouthful of fish. "Died seven or so years before her husband. Left the worthless girl on my hands."

It was the outside of enough. To insult a lady in her own house! Crispin opened his mouth to firmly set Thorndale in his place, but a fleeting look from Lizzie told him not to.

"How fortunate for Catherine that you took her in." An almost undetectable look of scrutiny entered Lizzie's eyes.

"Didn't have a choice," Thorndale grumbled. "The will stipulated it."

"That does happen sometimes," Edward observed dryly.

"George was an imbecile." Thorndale continued stabbing at his meal, oblivious to the censure that had settled around the room. "Most ridiculous will I'd ever seen. Challenged it, of course, but it couldn't be broken. Wasted an entire year with worthless solicitors."

The year Catherine spent locked in her room, no doubt.

Dinner conversation moved to remarkably neutral topics and remained so through the rest of the meal. Crispin continually glanced at Catherine. She didn't participate in the conversation around her. Her gaze remained firmly locked on her plate, though she did little more than push her food around.

"What brings you to London, Thorndale?" Edward asked after the ladies had left for the music room, leaving the gentlemen to their port.

Thorndale took a generous swallow. "Business with my solicitor."

"Bothersome profession," Edward grumbled. Crispin watched him look away from Thorndale. Crispin knew Edward had no such dissatisfaction with solicitors. He too, it seemed, was fishing for information.

"I generally ignore the infuriating man," Thorndale said.

"Must have seemed worth the effort this time." Edward gave Crispin a conspiratorial glance.

"Seems the man only just learned of some complication with my late brother's estate." Thorndale looked thoroughly annoyed. "Had to come to Town to ensure he got it right. He'd have given away a blasted fortune if I hadn't stepped in."

"I hope you completed your business to your satisfaction," Edward said.

"Not yet. Soon."

Crispin digested this bit of information as well as the momentary look of triumph Edward shot in his direction. That, then, had been the purpose of Edward's strangely friendly conversation with the man they'd all agreed they disliked. Thorndale didn't intend to stay in London long. Of course, the length of his residency depended on the nature of the problem with his brother's estate. Did the complication involve Catherine? Surely Brown would have come across any significant problems. Still, it might warrant looking into.

Thorndale didn't seem to expect to remain in Town much longer. Crispin would tell Catherine the good news. She would be relieved, and he could relax—just as soon as he knew the man was back in Herefordshire.

When they reached the music room, Catherine was nowhere to be seen. Crispin headed directly for Lizzie. "Where is Catherine?"

"She needed a moment to compose herself," Lizzie said. "She seemed particularly concerned about showing emotion in front of her uncle."

"He punished her for becoming emotional."

"I can tell she is afraid of him. Horrible man."

Crispin nodded. "With good reason. I'd hoped inviting him here tonight would fulfill, in the safest way possible, any obligation she has to see him."

Quite suddenly, Lizzie's eyes grew wide in alarm. She motioned with her head over Crispin's shoulder toward the door. Crispin turned. Catherine, barely past the threshold, nodded in response to something her uncle said to her. He was likely berating her—she stood with her head hung and shoulders slumped—and Crispin was not going to stand for it.

He crossed the room, visions of pummeling the man to a pulp filling his mind. Thorndale deserved to be taken down a few pegs, and that seemed a very justified means of doing so.

Catherine looked up when Crispin reached her side. The sparkle had gone out of her eyes. Thorndale had a great deal to answer for once Crispin had Catherine safely away.

"Catherine, dear." Crispin stepped between Catherine and her uncle.

"I am having a word with my niece."

"Yes, but I am requesting the presence of my wife." Crispin slipped Catherine's arm through his. "I believe my claim outweighs yours."

Without allowing Thorndale a response, Crispin guided her away. "Shall I ask Lizzie to add a few drops of cream to your uncle's tea?" he asked in a low whisper.

"Yes, please." A hint of a smile hovered on Catherine's face.

Resisting the urge to kiss her nearly smiling mouth, Crispin pulled her hand to his lips and kissed her fingers. She blushed quite flatteringly. "What was he saying to you?"

He regretted the question almost immediately. Catherine's whole countenance fell once more.

"He felt the need to remind me of my place." She lowered her eyes. "He thinks I am acting *better* than I am."

"Better than—? He said that to you?"

"Crispin, please don't make a scene."

"He can't treat you that way. Not in this house. Not in front of me."

"You'll only make him angry."

"He has certainly made me angry." He turned back to where Thorndale was making himself comfortable on the sofa. The man was going to get the set-down of his life. Crispin could almost hear the trumpets announcing the start of a jousting match.

"Please, Crispin. Please don't. If we leave it be, he'll leave. Please. That's all I want."

Catherine's pleas hardly registered. Crispin made his way to the sofa, his anger steaming hot, his eyes burning a hole right through Thorndale's overstuffed waistcoat.

"Thorndale," he said through clenched teeth.

"Crispin, please."

"Shut your mouth, wench," Thorndale snapped at Catherine.

A muffled sob was all Crispin heard before Catherine fled past him in a flurry of skirts and ran from the room.

"She never did have any sense of propriety," Thorndale sneered.

"You will speak respectfully of and to my wife." Crispin barely repressed the urge to grasp the man's thick neck in his hands.

"I will speak however I—"

"Catherine is obviously not feeling well," Lizzie interrupted them both. "We should leave early so she won't be overset."

"I'll have the grooms bring your carriage around as well, Thorndale." Edward's tone allowed no argument.

At what point had Crispin lost control of the situation? Catherine had run out of the room like a frightened child. Edward was ordering the carriages, with Lizzie orchestrating Thorndale's removal from the house. Meanwhile, Crispin stood seething in the middle of the room, anxious to bloody the nose of a man who'd been permitted to leave without so much as a scratch.

He was supposed to be looking out for his wife. *He* ought to have been her rescuer, not the bystander. Thorndale's departure would have been far more satisfying had he been the one to toss the cad from the house.

"We had his carriage parked out front all night," Hancock admitted after Lizzie and Edward had departed as well. "Thought it would facilitate a quick removal should one be necessary."

"Which it was," Crispin grumbled.

"Lady Cavratt's woman tells me her ladyship was quite overset," Hancock continued. Most of the ton would be shocked at Crispin's easy relationship with his butler. But in moments like this, Hancock was invaluable. "Jane's given her a small amount of laudanum to help her sleep."

Laudanum? Catherine required sedatives? His presence during

Thorndale's visit should have been supportive, preventative of disaster. True to form, Crispin seemed to have disappointed her. Again.

Chapter Seventeen

"I AM NOT RECEIVING VISITORS," Catherine told Hancock almost desperately the next afternoon when he announced a visitor awaited her in the music room.

"I attempted to say as much. He didn't consider himself a visitor."

"Who is it?" Catherine had her suspicions.

"Mr. Thorndale."

Catherine's stomach made a full turn inside as it inched its way toward her throat. Crispin had left earlier to meet with his solicitor. She'd barely managed to hide her dismay when Crispin had announced his destination. What else could they be discussing but the annulment? Now she had to face Uncle alone again.

"Shall I attempt to send Mr. Thorndale off?" Hancock asked.

That would certainly be the easier course of action. Catherine had no desire to see her uncle. But she couldn't avoid him forever, especially if she was a few signatures away from being left to her own defenses. Steeling herself for the encounter ahead of her, Catherine straightened her shoulders.

"No," she told Hancock. "I will see him. Briefly."

"Of course, my lady." Hancock sounded as though he were attempting to convince her of her own statement. "If his lordship should return during Mr. Thorndale's visit, shall I send him in?"

Catherine's heart sank. She had very quickly come to depend on Crispin. She needed to learn to survive without him. "If he wishes to join us, he would certainly be welcome, though I do not anticipate Mr. Thorndale remaining long." That sounded far more confident than she felt.

She opened the doors to the music room, her heart pounding in her ears. Uncle sat near the pianoforte as if he were master of Permount House.

"Have you begun your daily practice?"

Catherine shook her head.

"Sit."

She very nearly complied. Obedience had always been her instinctual response to her uncle. Catherine remained standing and took a breath to steady her nerves. "Did you have a particular reason for your visit, Uncle?"

The look of shock on his face bolstered Catherine's courage. She stood straight, shoulders back, and didn't cower. But his surprise slid into annoyance, and Catherine involuntarily took a step back.

"You dare question me?" Anger laced his words.

She swallowed and reminded herself of her determination to stand on her own two feet. "This is my home," she said. "I have every right to know why you are here."

"How much longer do you think Cavratt'll keep you around? Can't take much longer to get the annulment."

"Perhaps he does not intend to obtain one." Crispin absolutely intended to obtain an annulment, was seeing to it at that very moment, in fact. But Catherine had no intention of telling her uncle as much.

"My brother would not have wished you to be turned out on the street." Uncle offered this, what could have been a kind sentiment, with as much tenderness as a rabid dog. "I will be returning soon to Yandell Hall and you will return with me."

Catherine could feel her jaw drop. Return with him? Panic gripped her insides. She could not live with her uncle again. She had been free of the pain and the beatings and the humiliation for weeks. Going back was not an option.

"In fact"—Uncle rose and strode determinedly toward the door—"I will instruct your things be packed at once for your removal to Hill Street."

She forced her voice to remain calm even as she felt herself begin to shake. "No."

Uncle spun around, his face registering complete shock. He began to sputter.

Catherine's heart pounded. She could not go back to Yandell Hall. "I am a married woman and will stay with my husband." Her voice remained level, though her knees quaked beneath her.

"Wretched wench!" Uncle apparently found his voice again. He stormed to where she stood only a few feet from the closed door. "How dare you talk back to me!"

"My place is here." Defying her uncle had never seemed an option over the past eight years, yet there she stood, refusing to be bullied.

"I'll show you your place!"

Living at Permount House had so unaccustomed her to Uncle's trademark violence that the sting of his hand across her face came unexpectedly. She stumbled backward, barely keeping her balance.

"Grown mighty high in the instep, have you?" Uncle grumbled. His massive hand wrapped hard around her arm as he pulled Catherine closer to him. "You'll pay for your impertinence."

"I am not leaving this house." Catherine struggled against him with all the strength in her body, but his grip held fast. "You have no right—"

"We will depart without your personal effects," Uncle decreed. "That dandy can keep the fripperies he bought you."

She refused to be dragged from the house in disgrace to live another eight years in misery. Catherine dealt a swift kick to Uncle's shin and his grip slackened. She pulled away and grabbed the door handle, throwing the doors open.

Hancock stood in the doorway. "My lady?" he asked. Catherine heard the concern in his voice.

"Mr. Thorndale will be leaving now." Catherine stood as tall and confident as she could manage with blood trickling down her chin.

Hancock motioned to two footmen just out of sight in the hall. They took hold of Uncle's arms and accompanied him from the room. As he passed the threshold, Uncle shot Catherine a glance that told her with chilling certainty that they would cross paths again.

She hadn't precisely defeated her foe, but she had stood up to him.

* * *

Crispin stepped into the back sitting room of Permount House, his mind heavily occupied. Mr. Brown had unearthed more information regarding the inheritance Catherine had received through a somewhat distant maternal relative. The amount was significant—at least £25,000—but the matter had proven complicated. The solicitor had spent the better part of thirty minutes expounding on laws of inheritance and something involving order of death and the will of Catherine's father. Crispin had heard very little and understood even less.

Should she receive this bequest, Catherine's future would be secured and one more obstacle to the annulment would be eliminated. Crispin ought to have found relief in the knowledge. Instead, he'd grown increasingly more sullen.

"My lord." Hancock's anxious tone caught Crispin's wandering attention.

"Hancock? Is anything amiss?"

"*He* was here."

He? He *who*? Had Lizzie tracked Philip down and brought him here to court Catherine right in Crispin's own house? Behind his back? He'd ring a peal over Lizzie's head she'd not soon forget!

"I tried denying him entry, but he'd have none of it." Hancock walked with Crispin toward the front of the house.

Crispin eyed Hancock warily. How much did his ever-faithful butler know of Lizzie's schemes? And why did Hancock feel the need to prevent Philip's entrance? Did he know Crispin would disapprove? Good man!

"I believed the situation safe enough with both of them in the music room," Hancock said. "Her ladyship enjoys playing."

"The music room?" Catherine had played for Crispin's would-be replacement? His jaw clenched.

"But I never heard any music," Hancock said.

Crispin turned to face Hancock, silently demanding the story be completed.

"He began shouting. Then her ladyship threw open the door and—" Hancock stopped abruptly, shoulders squared in determination. "I had Thorndale thrown bodily from the house!"

"Thorndale!" Crispin felt his heart drop to the pit of his stomach. *Thorndale!*

"No lady should be treated that way in her own home." A muscle twitched in Hancock's jaw. He was angry. Livid, even. What had Thorndale done?

A sense of panic began settling in. "Where is Lady Cavratt?"

"In her room, my lord."

Crispin ran up the stairs. So help him, if Thorndale had hit her again, he would leave the man a bloody mess! He flew through the door to Catherine's sitting area without stopping to knock. Catherine sat wrapped in a blanket on the sofa facing the fireplace. Her eyes flicked to his for a fraction of a second before she snapped her head back around, facing directly away from Crispin.

"Catherine?"

She didn't look at him. Was she hurt? Angry?

Crispin crossed to where she sat, but the moment he reached her side, Catherine stood and stepped away from him, her back to him. She kept her blanket clutched around her shoulders.

He stood behind her and laid his hands on her arms just below where the blanket slipped over her sagging shoulders. He half expected her to pull away from him, but she didn't. Neither did she turn to face him. Crispin stood there, his hands lightly pressed to her arms, at a loss for something to say or do.

Catherine broke the silence. "I made him angry," she said quietly.

"Tell me what happened."

"I decided I needed to stand up to him. I'm not sure it was such a good idea, after all."

He felt her shudder. She should not have had to face her uncle alone. Crispin stepped around to face her. He immediately tensed, his eyes taking in her purpled cheek and split lip.

"Did he do this to you?" But he already knew the answer.

"I argued with him," Catherine's voice quivered, her eyes cast downward. "He was so angry."

"The bl—" Crispin turned toward the door. Thorndale would be nursing a broken nose within the hour.

A quiet sob stopped him before he'd taken a single step. Catherine needed his attention first.

Crispin gently laid his hands on her shoulders, trying to take hold of his own anger long enough to calm her fears. "I am going to tell Hancock not to let Thorndale in the house again."

"I would appreciate that," Catherine answered quietly, obviously fighting to maintain her composure.

"I can't believe that—" Crispin bit back a word that was entirely inappropriate to utter in front of a lady. "That he would do this."

Catherine didn't answer. Her fragile-looking hand, still red from yesterday's scalding, darted out from under the blanket to rub tensely at her temple.

What did a husband say to his wife in such a situation? She still wouldn't look at him. Maybe she was angry, but he'd never seen Catherine angry. More likely she was disappointed in him.

Crispin had an almost overwhelming urge to pull her close to him and wrap his arms around her. He, who'd never spoken nonsense in his life, was ready to spout hundreds of meaningless words of comfort if it meant seeing her at ease once more. Before he could utter a single nonsensical phrase, Catherine stepped further from him, turning to face the empty fireplace.

"How was the meeting with your solicitor?"

An abrupt change of topic, to be sure. "Fine," he blurted. "But, that's hardly—"

"You seemed anxious when you left."

"The message he sent sounded urgent."

"Did you complete the . . . the annulment?" Catherine's voice sounded smaller than usual.

"No. We, er . . . Not exactly."

Catherine turned to face him again, an odd look in her eyes that Crispin at first interpreted as relief, though he quickly dismissed the idea. *She* had asked about the annulment. Lizzie had insisted that Catherine would be miserable in a forced marriage. If anything, he ought to be seeing frustration in her eyes, especially considering his repeated failures to protect her from her uncle.

"But you went there to discuss the annulment?"

Why was she so insistent on discussing this? And why did that word grate on his nerves suddenly?

"The legalities make this very complicated." The legalities were hardly the most complicating factor. If Crispin could just make a decision, the entire thing could move forward. Still, he continued to vacillate.

"Complications?"

For a fraction of a second he was tempted to tell her about his indecision, that he felt an odd, inexplicable pull to her that he couldn't explain and couldn't ignore. He could have begun the annulment proceedings that first day, but weeks later he continued to postpone the decision. In the end, he wasn't willing to admit that she had somehow gained that hold over him. A man had to have some dignity. "There are a great many things to be done," he fudged. "Arrangements . . . for the future, that sort of thing."

"I have been thinking about that as well," Catherine said. "Where I'll go and what I'll do afterward."

Crispin couldn't tell if she'd been contemplating her future without him as a positive change or not. Attempting to sound unconcerned, he asked, "And what conclusions have you come to?"

"I have decided I will need to find some sort of employment, a means of supporting myself."

The image Lizzie had painted of Catherine slaving away on some remote estate for a family of questionable character reentered Crispin's mind with tremendous force. There was no guarantee these fictional employees would treat her any better than her own uncle.

"I don't think that would be necessary, Catherine."

"But I have nothing to live on." She still hadn't looked at him. Crispin didn't know what to make of her refusal to even glance in his direction.

"That is, actually, what I spoke to my solicitor about." That seemed to capture her attention and she glanced back at him. Her bruised face distracted him from the topic. He fluctuated between storming from the room to hunt down Thorndale and an almost crushing desire to pull Catherine into his arms and protect her from abusive uncles and heartless employers and the vicious gossips of society.

She is counting on an annulment, he reminded himself. Catherine had brought up the subject and had made her preferences on the outcome of their marriage obvious. Her only concern was where to go afterward, not whether or not the annulment should be pursued.

"You discussed with your solicitor what to do about me?" It sounded rather cruel and impersonal when she phrased it that way.

"No," Crispin said. "He discovered that you are entitled to an inheritance through a maternal relation, though he is still ascertaining the details. It should be sufficient for you to live on after the . . . annulment." The word stuck a bit in his throat.

She turned away from him again. Crispin resisted the urge to reach after her, to ascertain why she seemed unable to even look at him. Did she dislike him so much? Find him lacking in some way?

"You seem to have everything figured out." Her detached tone widened the chasm he felt growing between them.

"I am trying to help," he said. Why did her simple statement make him feel so blasted guilty? He'd gone above and beyond his duty in looking after her future. He'd delayed and debated against the most convenient course of action for himself out of concern for her. "Did you think I would throw you out on the street?" Her unspoken accusation stung.

"My own uncle did."

Now she was comparing him with Thorndale? Crispin leaned against the mantel, clenching his teeth in frustration. Thorndale! Did she truly think him as horrible as that man? Weeks of debate and worry and she thought him no better than her skinflint, heartless uncle. "Yes, except I am throwing you out with a small fortune to live on, gentleman that I am." The sarcasm was beneath him, but he'd never been particularly good at enduring misjudgment.

Silence hung heavy between them. She offered no smashing rejoinder or set-down, as Lizzie or Edward or Philip would have done. They did not put up with his cynicism.

"If you would please let me know when you have more details about this inheritance, I would appreciate it," she said with surprising authority. "I will endeavor to set my affairs in order as quickly as possible."

She thought he was pushing her out the door? Crispin turned back toward Catherine. She'd allowed her blanket to remain on the sofa. Deep blue bruises shaped suspiciously like thick fingers marred her arms. The bruise on her face had darkened just in the few minutes since Crispin had discovered her injuries. And yet she wasn't falling apart. Catherine seemed suddenly collected and dignified. She held her chin up and looked directly at him.

"If you'll excuse me," she maintained her almost-confident demeanor, though a tear slid down her cheek, "I am not feeling well."

Catherine walked quickly to the door leading to her bedchamber and slipped inside, closing the door behind her. Crispin heard it lock.

He crossed the room. "Catherine," he said through the door. "I . . . uh . . ." What was he supposed to say? *I am not a complete cad*? Or, *I'm not actually throwing you out*? Perhaps *I'm sorry*. Though he wasn't entirely sure what he'd be apologizing for, except that she seemed upset and he'd been a little too cynical.

He ran his fingers through his usually tidy hair and let out a long breath. If Catherine really was in favor of an annulment, he ought to be grateful. Shouldn't he be? That solved his dilemma. But he still felt unsure. She didn't seem precisely overjoyed at her future. Was she uncertain as well?

Crispin stepped away from the silent door, his mind spinning. His indecision wasn't fair to either of them. Mr. Brown would have details on Catherine's inheritance soon, and Crispin vowed he would come to a decision immediately thereafter. No more debate, no more delays. One way or another, they would know what their future held.

Chapter Eighteen

FORTY-EIGHT HOURS HAD PASSED SINCE Thorndale's visit, and Crispin had yet to see a glimpse of Catherine. She hadn't come down for dinner the night of Thorndale's forced departure and had bowed out of the evening's entertainment—a trip to the opera—claiming she did not feel well enough to attend. Crispin hadn't been alarmed, not really. She'd been upset and understandably so. Thorndale's visit could not have been an easy one to endure nor forget.

When she didn't appear at any meals over the next two days and firmly, through her abigail, declared herself not at home to visitors, Crispin began to wonder if Catherine might really be unwell and not simply overwrought.

"She has been a touch feverish," Jane confirmed a couple hours before Lizzie, Edward, and Philip Jonquil, the Earl of Lampton, were due to join them for a dinner en famile. Crispin had sent for Jane, wanting to know what he couldn't seem to find out for himself. Catherine didn't reply when he spoke to her through the door, and he didn't feel at liberty to simply enter, despite her being his wife and Permount being *his* house.

"Should I send for a doctor?"

"It will pass," Jane said. "It always does."

"Is she sick often?" Crispin hadn't guessed Catherine had a weak constitution. She seemed fit enough.

"After a harsh"—Jane seemed to search for the right word—"punishment, she sometimes isn't well. Fevers 'n' such. The doctor from Bath what checked on her now and again said it was nerves. Bein' frightened and all."

"She really has been ill?" Crispin moved toward the door of the library, intending to go directly to Catherine to check her condition himself. "Why wasn't I told?"

"She said to not say nothin', my lord. Said you wouldn't appreciate the bother."

Crispin turned back toward Jane. *The bother?* Catherine's well-being had never been a bother. It was an absolute essential! "Will you please inform me in the future whenever Lady Cavratt is unwell? Whether or not she thinks I would care to know?"

"O' course, my lord." Jane curtsied. Crispin thought he saw the momentary flash of a pleased smile.

"Will she be joining us for dinner this evening?" Crispin asked before Jane could slip from the room.

"She hasn't decided yet, my lord."

Crispin nodded his acknowledgment and the abigail left. Catherine's refusal to confide in him bothered Crispin more than he cared to admit. Their marriage really was little more than an overblown misunderstanding, and yet it troubled him enormously that his own wife didn't trust him. Or perhaps she didn't think he cared.

In fact, he'd spent the past two days debating what precisely he ought to do about the situation with Thorndale and Catherine. He'd been sorely tempted to hunt Thorndale down and plant him a facer or two . . . or ten. He'd very nearly done just that, but something nagged at him. While he wouldn't let Thorndale inside Permount House again, he knew he couldn't be everywhere with Catherine, and the possibility existed that Thorndale would take any revenge he sought for Crispin's retaliation out on her. She'd been so adamant the night Thorndale had dined with them that Crispin not cause trouble. She'd insisted it would make Thorndale angry. The very next morning that anger had been directed at Catherine.

Rather than undertake a very cathartic rampage at Thorndale's residence, Crispin had spent his time wondering if Catherine was angry with him or disappointed or simply ready to be rid of him. They hadn't parted on the best of terms and it bothered him tremendously. Knowing she'd kept to her rooms because she wasn't well, he worried ever more. Crispin wasn't accustomed to worrying about people.

Blast it all, someone should have told him his wife was ill! He could have sent for a doctor or seen to her comfort. She at least would have realized he wasn't entirely heartless. She might only be in his house a short while longer, but he did not want her to be miserable.

An idea struck a moment later that brought a smile to Crispin's usually somber face.

* * *

The young maid curtsied and scurried from the room, leaving Catherine completely at a loss. The package that had apparently come for her didn't appear to have been posted. In fact, the only direction written on it was simply "Catherine" in decidedly masculine writing. Catherine pulled at the strings, allowing them to fall loosely to the tabletop.

Mere minutes remained before she needed to be downstairs for their family dinner. She had already dressed. Her coiffure was complete. The maid from below stairs had entered with the mysterious bundle only moments before Catherine had intended to leave her rooms. She'd checked the looking glass one more time, hoping Jane's now-perfected formula for minimizing and covering bruises had worked well enough to make her presentable.

Her face she deemed passable. Her arms were another story entirely. She simply hoped her long gloves would cover the bruises enough.

Curiosity overcoming her, Catherine peeled back the parcel paper. A folded piece of paper lay on top of something wrapped in silver tissue. What could it possibly be? Catherine pulled her reading glasses from the bedside table, took the folded paper in her hands, and read.

My dear Catherine,

Please accept this as penance for one of the many crimes of which I stand, sadly, guilty. This being the most heinous—a hanging offense, I am told—it is the one for which I wish to first begin making restitution.

I hope you will be a merciful magistrate and not sentence me to anything too severe. My valet would not begrudge me a tear-stained cravat, but he would most certainly resign should my neck wear accompany me on a long incarceration.

I sincerely hope you are feeling recovered enough to join us this evening, as I am convinced not one of our party is coming for my sake, criminal that I am.

Repentantly Yours, etc.

Crispin

Catherine reread the note twice. *Recompense for his criminal activities?*

She pulled back the silver tissue paper. The package smelled of sugar. All the more curious, Catherine quickly pulled back the last layer of tissue. A single, perfectly round fairy cake sat centered on a porcelain tea saucer. Catherine stared for a fraction of a moment before understanding dawned.

He was, for the first time, referencing the lighthearted, wonderful morning they'd spent laughing over tea cakes and acts of treason.

Catherine refolded the note and held it for a moment pressed to her heart. A smile spread across her face. She read Crispin's note one more time. "My dear Catherine," he had written. *Dear* Catherine.

He didn't seem upset with her. She'd worried about that. He'd certainly been short with her the day of Uncle's visit. She hadn't been particularly pleased with him, either. Her heart had sunk at his admission that he was getting closer to finalizing the annulment. Until that moment, she'd held some hope that he would change his mind. She liked him—more than liked him, though she wouldn't allow herself to confess to more than that. She had wanted him to comfort her after the encounter with her uncle, to commend her for the show of backbone, despite its less than pleasing consequences. Instead he'd callously declared his intention to throw her out. The rejection had proven too much for her.

Perhaps, she thought, her mind replaying the tone of Crispin's note, he regretted the argument as well. She looked back at the fairy cake, something which only they would have found humorous, a piece of lighthearted banter that was theirs alone. He couldn't be so entirely indifferent to her, could he?

She needed to see him, to try to decide what he thought of her, *if* he thought of her. But she could not bring herself to do so with witnesses. Should he so thoroughly reject her again . . .

Catherine hurried to the door in her dressing room that connected with his and knocked. Would he be in his rooms still? He might not appreciate the intrusion into his private space. But, she told herself, she wouldn't stay long.

She turned the handle, opened the door, and stepped across the threshold into uncharted territory. No one stood in the dressing room. She passed into the bedchamber beyond. Her rooms and these adjoined one another but had very little in common. Her own bedchamber was decorated in light, pale colors. Crispin's was paneled in deep cherrywood, the floors covered in rich carpets of deepest blue. The room even smelled different: like sandalwood, like Crispin.

He stood framed by the doorway to his own sitting room, watching her approach with obvious curiosity and a look of confusion that bordered on alarm. "Hello, Catherine."

"May I come in?" she asked, uncertain.

"Of course."

"I received your parcel," she said.

A hint of a smile touched his face. "And have you come to absolve me of my crimes?"

"You, sir, owe me an inordinate number of fairy cakes." Relief surged through her. He was in a teasing mood. She loved that side of him. "One will hardly acquit you."

A corner of Crispin's mouth quirked a touch higher than the other, his eyes sparkling the way they had the first time she'd accused him of pastry thievery.

"I suppose I shall have to send you another tomorrow, then." Crispin shrugged, looking every bit the unrepentant rake.

"Bribing a judge is criminal, you realize."

"Hopeless, aren't I? Of course, I will probably steal another cake at tea tomorrow, which should negate the bribe entirely."

"Perhaps *I* should throw *you* in the fountain."

"That is a harsh sentence, my dear." Crispin chuckled. *My dear.* Catherine thoroughly enjoyed the way that sounded. "Can you not be lenient?"

Catherine waved him off in a display of mock disfavor. "'Tis no worse than you deserve."

"My mother would have been disappointed to know she raised such a hardened criminal." Crispin sighed dramatically. "But then she introduced me to fairy cakes in the first place."

"Then perhaps she is to blame." Catherine tapped her lip with her finger as if deeply considering the possibility.

Crispin stepped closer. He took her hand in his, pulling it away from her mouth. "Best not do that, dear."

Tap her lips? Why ever not?

Both of Crispin's hands encircled her one. "A less scrupulous gentleman than me might be unable to resist the temptation."

"What temptation?"

He didn't answer, his gaze seemingly riveted to her mouth. Catherine's heart flipped inside her. Suddenly her lungs refused to take in a full breath.

"We . . ." Crispin looked away, but his eyes wandered back to her lips once more. He cleared his throat. He released her hand but didn't step back. "We should probably go down to dinner." His gaze locked with hers, some unidentifiable emotion in his eyes.

She couldn't fight the impulse that seized her in that moment. Catherine closed the distance between them, rose up on her toes and kissed his cheek. She paused only a moment to take in the scent of him before stepping back once more. She felt a blush creep up her cheeks but did not regret the gesture.

"Do you usually kiss gentlemen after threatening to toss them in a fountain?" Crispin seemed to be attempting a light tone, but the intensity in his gaze had increased.

"I've never kissed anyone but you." She hadn't intended to make such a personal confession. Catherine bit down on her lip, waiting for his reaction.

His eyes returned to her mouth, though he pulled his gaze away almost immediately. Crispin closed his eyes a moment.

Catherine's heart pounded hard in her chest. She still couldn't seem to pull in a full breath.

"Catherine." He didn't open his eyes.

"Crispin?"

He almost looked in pain. Crispin ran his hand across his face, a tense breath breaking the silence between them.

"Crispin?"

He finally looked at her again, something like worry creasing his brow. "What are you doing to me?" His words were muttered, barely discernible.

"I . . . don't understand."

Crispin laughed humorlessly and opened his eyes once more. "Neither do I." He shook his head and looked evermore frustrated. "Perhaps we should go down to dinner."

Had she upset him? Only a moment earlier he'd seemed pleased with her company. Why must he be so confusing?

Crispin slipped her arm through his and led her out of his rooms. His demeanor hadn't become cold, precisely, but distant. "I wish you had told me you were ill," Crispin said as they made their way down the corridor.

"I didn't want to bother you."And she'd been afraid he wouldn't care. She could not have endured more rejection.

"For future reference"—He seemed to pull her arm more snugly inside his own—"I do not consider your well-being a bother."

The comment surprised her enough to glance up at him. His expression was closed and unreadable, but she could have sworn he walked a little closer to her than he had a moment earlier.

How she wished she knew him well enough to understand how to interpret his contradictory actions. Even more, she wished he planned to keep her around long enough for her to figure him out.

Chapter Nineteen

He was losing his mind. The fairy cakes and accompanying note had been meant as a peace offering, nothing more. Then Catherine had stepped inside his rooms, and an alarming sense that she belonged there had swept over him. They were in the midst of an annulment. Only a few days earlier she had been noticeably determined to map out her future without him. Still he'd stood there like a greenhorn mooning over her.

He'd managed to get his confusing reaction to her presence under control. Then Catherine had touched her lips and he'd barely stopped himself before kissing her again. A man couldn't go around lavishing kisses on a lady who fully intended to walk out on him and, if Lizzie's ridiculous plan played out, directly into the arms of his best friend. He had every right to be on edge.

"Is Lord Lampton a good friend?" Catherine's question brought him back to the present.

"So far." His grumbled reply understandably confused her.

"Have you two had a falling out?"

"Not yet."

"Does he . . . know about . . ." Catherine bit down on her lip—Crispin had to look away. She was too tempting for her own good—for *his* own good.

"He knows the circumstances of our marriage." A straightforward, factual approach seemed best. "He and I are close enough I'd have mentioned a fiancée, or a lady to whom I intended to propose. It was better to simply tell him the truth."

Catherine mouthed "Oh," but her look had grown more concerned even as her eyes looked more withdrawn.

"Rally your courage, dear." When had he started using that endearment? It wasn't at all like him. "You've faced worse than this—the Glaffords come to mind."

Catherine seemed to lighten a little. "For that battle I was armed with a cream pitcher." Catherine spoke quietly, but a spark of mischief returned to her eyes.

Crispin far preferred seeing her look less burdened. "You plan to poison my oldest friend?"

"Do I need to?"

If Philip had any intention of going along with Lizzie's harebrained scheme, Crispin would poison the scoundrel himself.

"Crispin?" She sounded nervous again. She *looked* petrified.

"If you adulterate his tea, I would most likely find it necessary to toss you into the fountain."

A smile of relief lit her face. Crispin pulled her hand to his lips and, without taking his eyes off her bewitching smile, kissed her fingers, smiling with amazement at how she continually made his heart pound with only a look. Why was it she wanted so badly to be rid of him?

"I do believe I am decidedly de trop this evening." Someone chuckled from the doorway just behind Crispin. "No unattached hearts beyond this point, I'm discovering."

Philip. Despite several days' worth of very un-Christian thoughts directed toward a man he'd known nearly all his life, Crispin found himself smiling. Catherine's fingers tighten around his as he turned around. He gently squeezed her hand. "I see you managed to evade Hancock."

"An old trick, as you well know." Philip smiled that bright grin that had broken so many hearts in their younger days. He held his hand out, and Crispin shook it enthusiastically. "Slipping in unnoticed allows for more discovery." Philip gave him a look far too full of amusement, which Crispin chose to ignore.

"Philip, this is my wife, Lady Cavratt." Catherine's grip on Crispin's hand had grown remarkably tight. "Catherine, this is Philip Jonquil, the Earl of Lampton."

After offering the appropriate curtsy, Catherine clung to Crispin's hand once more. Some of the ton's tabbies would disapprove of Catherine's reticence and what they would see as her neglect as a hostess, but Crispin found her nearness and her touch endearing.

"Lady Cavratt." Philip smiled at Catherine. Her fingers tightened almost imperceptibly around Crispin's. "I feel I need to confess that I came here tonight solely for the purpose of speaking with you."

Crispin tensed.

"With me?" Catherine's tiny voice replied.

"Ever since I received Crispin's, uh, rather informative letter, I've felt an almost desperate need to thank you."

Crispin recognized the teasing glint in Philip's eye, and he relaxed a fraction. The Earl of Lampton had a reputation for absurdity. While Crispin knew he could be serious enough when circumstances warranted it, Philip appeared to most of the world as little more than a court jester.

"You wanted to thank me for your friend's rather unenviable situation?" Catherine asked, her eyes smiling a little. She seemed to have taken Philip's measure quickly.

"I've anxiously perused the *Times* daily anticipating an announcement of Crispin's untimely demise." Philip shook his head in mock sadness.

"Indeed?" Catherine's eyes twinkled, her grip slackening.

"I would not have blamed you in the least if you'd murdered him in his sleep." Philip managed to look entirely serious.

Crispin bent closer to Catherine, intending to explain Philip's odd sense of humor but realized in an instant he didn't need to. She was on the verge of a smile, something Crispin seldom saw. He didn't at all like seeing her smile at another man.

"I *have* been sorely tempted to poison his tea," Catherine said.

"Which brings us back to my profuse gratitude," Philip said, "for sparing the life of my unfeeling friend." Philip bowed to her and Crispin heard Catherine laugh lightly. She laughed! Catherine almost never laughed.

The smile that had lit Crispin's face when Philip arrived disappeared in an instant. Catherine was smiling at the man and laughing with him. He didn't like it. With a little creativity he could probably manage to throw Philip out without being obvious about it. It was a shame Philip couldn't be done in with a bit of cream in his tea.

Dinner passed uneventfully, filled with lighthearted conversation and less than charitable thoughts on Crispin's part. Catherine seemed more at ease during the course of the night than he ever remembered seeing her in company. Lizzie watched Philip and Catherine interact without bothering to disguise her look of triumph. As Catherine's mood lightened, Crispin's darkened.

Catherine didn't cling to him as she had early in the evening. While he was infinitely grateful to see her happy and unafraid, he missed her nearness. She'd come to him earlier, in his bedchamber, practically begging to be kissed, and had remained by his side throughout the evening. He had rather enjoyed that, and Philip was ruining everything.

Later in the evening, his jaw tightened at the sound of one of Catherine's rare laughs escaping from where she stood on the far side of the room beside Philip. Crispin cut across the music room and planted himself at Catherine's side.

Philip was laughing. "And she was convinced that Crispin had written the poem."

"Poor Crispin," Catherine replied, fully smiling. "To be so smitten with Lady Garner's eyebrows!"

"Smitten, indeed."

Crispin felt himself redden. Lady Garner. That had been a mess. *Philip* wrote that infamous poem as a jibe against poetry in general and love poetry specifically. It was Finley who had delivered it to

Lady Garner rather heavily hinting that Crispin had been its author and Lady Garner its inspiration. If not for Lord Garner's distrust of Finley and Philip and Crispin's insistence that they had been victimized in the entire ordeal, Crispin might very well have been called out. Lord Garner was a notoriously jealous husband.

"I see you're enjoying yourselves at my expense." Crispin attempted a light tone he didn't quite achieve.

"Lord Lampton is attempting to make me jealous." Catherine smiled brightly at Crispin.

Her look had the dual affect of calming his affronted sensibilities and further igniting his own jealousy. Must Philip be so blasted friendly with her?

"Don't tell me Crispin has never written an ode to your eyebrows." Philip managed to sound and look shocked.

"Not once," Catherine replied laughingly.

"I have never penned an epitaph to *anyone's* eyebrows," Crispin quickly pointed out. "And that entertaining interlude nearly left me forever eating grass outside London."

"As you can see, my lady, poetry is still not an easy topic for our friend here." Philip cast a knowing look in Catherine's direction.

"Then perhaps we should choose another topic of discussion." Catherine looked far too entertained to be truly repentant. "We should ask him how he feels about fountains."

Philip gave her a momentary look of confusion, but, after looking at Crispin, he began laughing once more. Catherine quickly joined in.

Crispin had suffered quite enough of the frivolity. He bent a curt bow and walked away, tensed from head to toe.

Some moments later Philip announced his intention to depart, being expected to make an appearance elsewhere that night as well. Crispin was not at all disappointed to see the back of him. Philip had certainly made headway with his courtship of Catherine, meaning Lizzie had a great deal to answer for.

* * *

Catherine exhaled loudly and slowly. What a time to receive a letter from Uncle. Only a few minutes remained before they were to leave for the Littletons' ball. To make matters worse, Crispin had been distant and strangely ill-tempered during the past few days.

She scanned the missive once more, two particular sentences standing out to her.

> You will return to Yandell Hall before your folly further disgraces our family name . . . I am not an indulgent man and will not wait for your acquiescence.

Catherine slipped her glasses off and laid them on the nearest table. She glanced out the windows of the sitting room. The vaguely threatening tone of Uncle's letter worried her.

She tucked the letter into her reticule. Her experiences with Uncle left no doubt of his willingness to use force to reach his goals. She still bore a faint bruise from her last encounter with him. Still, she had come away from that experience with greater determination to stand her ground. Uncle would not bully her into submission, though she knew he would try.

"Are you ready, then?" Crispin's rather brusque address startled Catherine.

For a fleeting moment she considered telling him about Uncle's note, asking his opinion. But his behavior of late had been so distant. He might very well resent the bother.

I do not consider your well-being a bother. He'd said that the evening of Lord Lampton's visit. At the time he seemed to mean what he said. Perhaps she should confide in him after all.

They had passed several silent minutes in the carriage before she rallied her courage enough to broach the subject, though indirectly.

"I received an unexpected note this afternoon."

"You have a correspondent in Town?" Crispin's eyes never strayed from the darkened windows.

Catherine pushed forward, despite his less than encouraging demeanor. "I had not expected him to write to me."

"*He* must have some reason for doing so." His tone leaned more toward annoyance than concern.

Why was Crispin being so surly? Had she done something to upset him?

"I suppose he does," she said, opting for the safety of silence. There was nothing comforting about a bothered husband.

They arrived at the Littletons' ball without either speaking another word. Catherine had never seen a greater crush. Gowns of every imaginable design and in every color under the rainbow swirled about the ballroom. Her own dress seemed subdued in comparison. A deep blue precisely the color of her eyes with braided silver trim and no ruffles or bows to speak of, it had seemed extravagant to her at first. With palpable discomfort, she realized her mistake. Catherine felt ever more out of place.

"Lady Cavratt."

She turned to see Mr. Finley smiling quite confidently back at her. He always made her skin crawl. She stepped closer to Crispin—despite his coldness of late, she knew he would not allow Mr. Finley to mistreat her.

"So pleased to see you this evening," Finley said with a bow. "I was hoping to stand up with you. The supper dance, perhaps."

"Mine is the supper dance." Crispin looked daggers at Finley.

"Then I'll settle for this one." Finley didn't miss a beat. A waltz had only just begun.

Surely Crispin would claim the waltz as well. He disliked Finley, probably even more than she did.

Finley cupped his hand under her elbow and led her to the floor. Catherine looked back at Crispin, waiting for him to object, to interfere, but he had already turned away and appeared deep in conversation with none other than Miss Cynthia Bower.

Crispin, she silently pleaded.

"You look exceptionally beautiful this evening, my lady," Finley said, his eyes not quite on her face. "I believe we will soon be the talk of the room, if not of the ton."

"That would be unfortunate."

"On the contrary," Mr. Finley answered. "We make a fine couple. Even your husband seems to have noticed."

Catherine's gaze sought out Crispin and found him glowering at them. His look of disapproval did not appear to be directed only at Mr. Finley. What in heaven's name had she done to earn Crispin's irritation of late?

"I believe every man in the room wishes you were in his arms right now," Finley whispered in her ear.

Catherine attempted to step back from him, but he held her tight. She felt his hand push earnestly against the small of her back as he attempted to pull her ever closer.

"That is quite near enough, sir," Catherine said as sternly as possible.

"Good show." Finley looked amused. "But Cavratt cannot hear you. There is no point feigning dislike at a distance where his pride won't benefit from the words."

"My words were intended to dampen your enthusiasm, not to boost my husband's pride." Catherine pushed against him with every ounce of her strength.

By the time the dance ended, Catherine's arms ached from the effort of keeping her nemesis at a distance. Finley returned her to Crispin's side, where he proceeded to pull her hand to his lips and kiss her fingers rather longer than necessary. Catherine tried to free her fingers, but his grip was exceptionally strong. Crispin's mood seemed to darken further.

"You waltz very well." Crispin sounded more disgruntled than complimentary.

She'd spent the entire set fighting off Finley's unwanted advances and had hoped to find some respite, some comfort in Crispin's company. He kept his eyes glued straight ahead at the dancers. He hadn't yet looked at her and she felt the wall between them thicken. She felt bereft, disappointed.

"Lord Cavratt, how pleasant to see you again," a syrup-sweet voice said into the icy silence.

"Mrs. Bower." Crispin sketched a civil bow.

Catherine glanced at the woman who stood next to Crispin. She was small and plump with eyes far too penetrating to bode well for anyone who dared cross her. The last name alone told Catherine this woman was the enemy.

Crispin undertook the proper introductions. "May I introduce you to my wife. Lady Cavratt, this is Mrs. Bower."

Catherine attempted to affect a dignified countenance despite her growing displeasure with the evening and the company. Mrs. Bower glanced down her overly long nose at Catherine and gave a barely audible sniff. She stepped across Crispin and stood directly in front of Catherine.

"Not a very pretty thing, are you?" she said under her breath. She tipped Catherine's chin with her index finger and looked her over with a scrutiny that would not have been out of place at Tattersall's. "A shame."

Catherine stepped back as far as the crowded nature of the ballroom would allow and kept her chin as high as she could manage, unwilling to show Mrs. Bower that her pride had been nettled by the unflattering assessment.

"You don't mind, do you, my lord, if I introduce your dear wife to a few friends?" Mrs. Bower asked, turning back toward Crispin with an air of complete delight. "There are so many anxious to meet the new Lady Cavratt."

"Of course not," Crispin replied dismissively.

In the blink of an eye Catherine was whisked none too gently to the far side of the room directly in front of a group of seated matrons. They looked her over unabashedly, one particularly fearsome woman even producing a quizzing glass as if she were the most dandified of gentlemen. A few cackled, several clicked their tongues in disapproval.

"*This* is the great specimen of womanhood who finally captured the illusive Lord Cavratt?" the woman with the quizzing glass sputtered. "The rumors must be true, then—Cavratt was bullied into it."

"On the contrary, Lady Genevieve," a second, less frightening woman countered. "I think she is perfectly lovely. Perhaps the rumor to be believed is that theirs is, indeed, a love match."

A few unladlylike snorts escaped the group and a low-voiced, heated debate ensued. Catherine could see no means of escape. Crispin was somewhere amidst the crush, though Catherine wasn't entirely convinced he would come to her rescue—he'd been so decidedly distant. Several of the matrons were actually circling her in order to glean more details for their criticism.

"Too short," one declared, retaking her seat.

"She has a pretty face, though," another chimed in.

"Painted, I daresay." With the help of her ever-ready quizzing glass, Lady Genevieve had discovered that Catherine's cheek was, in part, benefiting from the use of lightly applied cosmetics. Catherine felt herself blush. The paints had been necessary—the bruise from Uncle's fit of temper was still marginally visible on her face.

"Forgive me, ladies." The deep, rumbling bass sent unwelcome shivers up Catherine's spine. Her uncle had come to the ball. "I would have a word with this young lady."

A hand gripped Catherine's arm, and her blood turned to ice. Uncle never attended ton entertainments. What could he possibly be doing at the Littletons' ball? Catherine frantically searched the crowd for Crispin.

Fighting against Uncle's pull would only cause a scene, so Catherine allowed herself to be led through the open terrace doors and a short distance into the formal knot garden. Uncle's fingers wrapped around the precise part of her arm they had gripped only a few days earlier. The first bruises had not entirely healed, and the new injury stung more than Catherine would admit.

Far enough from the house for the noise of the ball to be little more than background din, Uncle spun Catherine around to face him. She steeled herself against the glint of anger in his eyes.

"Making a spectacle of yourself, I see," Uncle snapped. "You certainly gave those tabbies plenty to meow about back there. Parading your shortcomings to the world. I'll not have the Thorndale name dragged through the mud!"

Catherine stood as dignified and unshaken as she could manage, though inside she was terrified.

"You received my letter?" Thorndale demanded.

"I did." She took courage in the unexpected steadiness of her own voice.

"And didn't have the decency to send a reply?" A tint of purple framed Uncle's features.

"You did not indicate you were expecting a reply," Catherine said, willing her legs not to shake beneath her. She had stood up to her uncle once already. She could do so again. "You posed no question to which I could assume you awaited an answer."

"The time I should expect you at Hill Street, that is what I was expecting!" Uncle's patience had grown noticeably thin. "You are returning to Yandell House before you disgrace the both of us."

"No, I am not." She far preferred Crispin's sudden indifference to Uncle's violent temper.

"Serpent!" Uncle hissed back at her. "Ungrateful whelp!"

"My place is with my husband." *For as long as he is my husband.* Catherine did not allow her doubts to show.

Uncle's lips tightened until they nearly disappeared. Catherine knew that look. Anger. Absolute, unrestrained anger. She pulled back, her instinctive need to protect herself outweighing her determination to not be cowed.

"You will not embarrass me." Uncle leaned closer, his grip tightening painfully.

"Let go of me."

His eyes narrowed. "You little—"

"Catherine!" a woman's voice called out from not far behind.

Uncle's grip was unrelenting. Catherine couldn't turn in any direction.

"We wondered where you'd gone." Catherine now recognized the voice as Lizzie's.

"Is that you, Mr. Thorndale?" Edward was with her.

Catherine breathed a sigh of grateful relief. She pulled back once more and found Uncle's grip relaxed just enough to allow her to escape. She turned toward Lizzie and Edward.

"Dear Catherine, we were quite lonely without your company," Lizzie said.

Uncle harrumphed in an obvious display of disbelief.

"You will come back inside with us, won't you, Catherine?" Lizzie asked, seizing Catherine's hand in her own and turning her toward the house.

"Gladly," Catherine answered.

"I was not finished speaking with my niece." Uncle grabbed Catherine's arm once more. She winced at the strength of his grip. Lizzie and Uncle tugged her in opposite directions.

"Mr. Thorndale." Edward stepped closer.

Uncle leaned over and hissed into Catherine's ear. "You will come to Hill Street in the morning."

"I will not."

"You will come in the morning or you will arrive later in disgrace," Uncle snapped back. "I will not have you—"

"—embarrass you further," Catherine finished for him. "You've said so several times."

His grip tightened, his brows compressing deeper in a scowl. "Do not talk back to me, girl!"

"Lady Cavratt," yet another voice, deep and confident, entered the conversation. "I do believe this is the dance you promised me."

The Earl of Lampton stood mere inches from Uncle. Catherine

had hoped to see Crispin come to her rescue. But Lord Lampton's presence had the decidedly happy effect of loosening Uncle's grip and, apparently, his determination to intimidate her.

"Certainly you would not deny me the opportunity to flaunt my remarkable ability to execute the quadrille." Lampton spoke with an air of arrogance Catherine knew to be feigned. She had realized within moments of meeting him that the image he projected and the man he was underneath were decidedly different.

"Puffed-up dandy," Uncle grumbled under his breath, releasing Catherine's arm.

"Come, my lady." Lord Lampton offered his arm, which Catherine gladly took. "The ballroom awaits."

"Thank you," Catherine whispered the moment they'd stepped away from Uncle.

"Ladies do tend to be overcome with gratitude when asked to dance with me."

Catherine almost smiled, his exaggerated tone breaking through the panic Uncle had very nearly brought to the surface.

"That was the infamous Mr. Thorndale, then?" Lord Lampton asked, glancing over his shoulder, the affected airs having vanished instantaneously.

"I wasn't expecting him here tonight." Catherine let out a tense breath. "If Lizzie and Edward hadn't found me . . . or you, for that matter . . ." Tears prickled at the back of her eyes.

"Now, now," Lord Lampton said mock-scoldingly, "tears are not permitted at a ball."

"I am sorry. It has been a difficult night."

"Dry your eyes," he instructed kindly, handing her a handkerchief. "Your husband will have my neck if he thinks I've upset you."

"I haven't seen Crispin all night." Her emotions hovered precariously near the surface. "I think he must be upset with me. Or . . . ashamed . . ." Uncle's words came rushing back, pricking at her already tender emotions.

"I see a diversion is in order." Lord Lampton stopped their trek just short of the terrace doors and directed her, instead, to a quiet alcove away from the prying eyes of the guests. "Dab a few more times and take a few deep breaths. You'll put yourself to rights soon enough."

"I am sorry for this." Catherine took a shaky breath, sitting on an obliging bench. "First my uncle and then—"

"—your inattentive husband." Lord Lampton nodded sympathetically. "You have earned a few tears, I suppose. Though my skills at the quadrille have been known to leave sensible women weeping."

"Perhaps I should keep your handkerchief, then." Catherine managed a smile as she dabbed at what she hoped was a final tear. "You have said you intend to inflict your quadrille on me."

"Your feet may well be inflicted upon," Lord Lampton admitted with a shrug. "The splendor of my attire tends to distract those around me, making grace on the dance floor a difficult commodity to come by."

"Promise you don't have wandering hands, and you will be an infinite improvement over Mr. Finley." She grimaced at the memory.

Lord Lampton sat on the low wall of the terrace. "What did Crispin have to say about Mr. Finley's hands?"

"Crispin hasn't . . . I don't know that he noticed."

"Oh, I imagine he did. Crispin, I think, has been feeling a little confused lately."

"Confused?"

Lord Lampton spoke more quietly and quite a bit more seriously. "He is torn between the way he thinks he ought to feel about you and the way he actually does."

Catherine searched Lord Lampton's face, unsure what he meant. Did Crispin hate her but felt he shouldn't? Or—Catherine's heart fluttered inside her ribs at the sudden, unexpected thought—did he feel even an inkling of the affection she felt? That image did not precisely match the indifference she'd seen in him the last few days. Still, the idea planted a seed of hope in her bruised heart.

"This is cozy."

Crispin! Catherine's stomach leaped to her throat at the sound of his voice. He had come to find her after all. She turned to look at him, framed by the terrace doors.

"Afraid your wife will fall desperately under the spell of my not insignificant charms?" Lord Lampton said.

"Hardly. But Lizzie seemed to think Catherine was about to find herself in significant peril." Crispin seemed to scrutinize Catherine's and Lord Lampton's every move.

"Not at my hands, I assure you." Lord Lampton held up those hands in a gesture of innocence. "And, now that you have arrived on the scene, I relinquish her into your care."

"Thank you for your company," Catherine said quietly, returning his handkerchief. "And for your obliging linen."

"Happy to be of assistance, my lady." Lord Lampton bowed. "Now I shall go grace the assembly with the splendor of my new jacket." He smoothed his mulberry-colored sleeves. "If you need me, I will be at the center of the admiring throng."

Catherine allowed a shadow of a smile to cross her face as Lord Lampton disappeared into the ballroom beyond. His humor was a welcome diversion from her ever-growing problems.

"You and Philip seem to have become fast friends." Crispin didn't sound particularly pleased. "You are bound to be the talk of society by morning at the rate your friendship is blossoming."

"That is what Mr. Finley said," Catherine mumbled.

"So you've developed a friendship with him as well, have you?"

"No, I—"

"And whom were you in the gardens with for so long?"

Why did Catherine suddenly feel as though she were being scrutinized by a very suspicious governess? She had done nothing wrong, yet his tone was entirely accusatory.

"Several people noticed your prolonged absence." Crispin circled back to where she stood. "I was at a loss to explain why my wife, whom I have made every effort to convince society I wed for love, was so obviously not at my side. The gossip that this will create . . ."

A strange ache radiated around Catherine's heart. *Tears are not permitted at a ball,* she reminded herself. So why did she feel like weeping? Why did she so desperately wish Crispin had wrapped her in his arms instead of lecturing her? She needed the gentle, tender Crispin back.

"Would it have been so difficult for you to stand up with your husband?" Crispin grumbled.

"Would it have been so difficult for you to have *asked me* to stand up with you?" Catherine turned on her heels, not wanting to show the pain in her eyes. She was so tired of trying to trust this man who seemed so determined to push her away.

"Catherine." Crispin spoke more gently, but she hurt too much to trust that tone.

"I'm not feeling well, Crispin. Excuse me, please."

Catherine hurried back into the ballroom. She pushed past dozens of nameless faces, doing her utmost to maintain an even composure. Lizzie stood at the far end of the room. In less than a minute's time, Catherine had reached her side.

"Catherine, are you all right?" she asked, her hand immediately pressed to Catherine's.

A vocal reply eluded her. She shook her head, not willing to risk further disgracing herself with public tears.

"Your uncle?" Lizzie asked, her voice low.

Your brother. She took a shaky breath.

"Of course you are overset." Lizzie squeezed Catherine's hand. "We can call up the carriage if you'd like to return to Permount House."

Catherine nodded, swatting at a defiant tear.

"Come." Lizzie quickly guided Catherine from the room. "The tabbies will rip you to shreds if they see you crying."

"They will rip me to shreds regardless."

"Welcome to London, Catherine." Lizzie motioned to Edward, who joined them at the door to the Littletons' house. A few whispered instructions from Edward and the Henley equipage was summoned. Lizzie and Edward climbed into the carriage along with her.

"You need not leave on my account," Catherine said.

Lizzie waved off the objection. "I have no desire to spend the evening among the gossiping tabbies. Cats never were my favorite animal."

"Crispin will wonder where I've gone." If he even noticed she'd left.

Lizzie shrugged off Catherine's concern. "I sent word to Crispin that we'd taken you home."

An hour later, snuggled beneath the warm, heavy blankets on her bed, Catherine allowed her tears to fall. How could she still feel such deep, growing affection for a gentleman who confused and frustrated her? Exhausted, she fell into a dreamless sleep.

Chapter Twenty

Crispin read the note a second time.

> To quite the most beautiful woman at the ball,
>
> May these flowers bring you as much pleasure as your company brings me.
>
> Yours, etc.,
>
> R. Finley

It was, of course, customary—even expected—for a gentleman to send flowers the morning after a ball to a lady with whom he'd danced. But, generally, not a married lady.

The extravagant bouquet represented all the best the local hothouses had to offer. Although the action was decidedly beneath him, Crispin pocketed the note rather than replace it within the stems of roses for all the world to see. It was bad enough he'd made a cake of himself without everyone who passed knowing that Finley had not.

Crispin glanced down the entry hall to the staircase. Catherine still hadn't come downstairs. Hancock, though unwilling to offer any details—a change in loyalty that had Crispin wondering just what kind of spell Catherine had cast over his house—indicated that "her ladyship" was, indeed, awake but remained in her rooms. Tea time had already passed and she hadn't yet made an appearance.

He fully intended to apologize for upsetting her at the ball. He had been out of line snapping at her, when his frustration had been with Philip's ability to make her smile and laugh every time they were in company with one another. Crispin hadn't been able to even find Catherine the night before, while Philip had spent an obviously pleasant interlude with her on the terrace.

A knock at the door interrupted Crispin's musings and, within minutes, Hancock passed him with yet another bouquet. *Finley!*

"One minute, Hancock." Crispin stopped the butler as he walked the flowers to another half-round table.

Crispin pulled the card from within the flowers and opened it, his insides boiling all over again. Hancock gave him a very disapproving look, which Crispin completely ignored. He refused to stand idly by and allow Finley to send love missives to Catherine.

The handwriting on the card, however, didn't look like Finley's.

> To Lady Cavratt,
>
> With the hope that this day is better than yesterday and that Lord Cavratt's flowers are more impressive than these.
>
> Lampton

Philip? Was there a gentleman in all of England who wasn't sending Catherine flowers? And what on earth did Philip mean by "Lord Cavratt's flowers"? What flowers? The man had lost his mind!

Another knock. Crispin's jaw tightened and his eyes narrowed. Now what? No doubt Hancock would open to door to find every flower in London awaiting Catherine's approval.

He stood determinedly on the spot waiting for another nauseating bouquet to pass by. Instead, Hancock escorted a bespectacled man of middle years into the entryway.

"Mr. Brown," Hancock announced unnecessarily—Crispin would have recognized his family solicitor without the introduction.

Crispin firmly shook Brown's hand. Mr. Brown seldom came to Permount House. "This must be urgent."

"Quite."

Crispin had learned shortly after inheriting his father's title and all it entailed that Mr. Jebediah Brown was a man of vast knowledge and ability but very few words.

"Lady Cavratt will be needed as well."

"Of course." Crispin nodded to Hancock to send for Catherine. The butler immediately set out to fulfill the order. "Have you learned more of Lady Cavratt's inheritance?" Crispin asked as he led Brown to the library.

"I would prefer to wait for her ladyship."

That did sound serious. The silence between them hung heavy and thick as they waited. Was Brown's discovery good or bad? From the look of the man, he had not brought glad tidings.

The library door slowly opened some five minutes later. Crispin's heart beat a bit harder as a beautiful face framed by rebelliously loose honey locks peeked around the door and a pair of sapphire blue eyes locked with his. How did this woman who was receiving flowers from all and sundry wreak such havoc on his equilibrium?

"Come in, Catherine." Crispin tried to smile encouragingly.

She moved slowly, cautiously to where he stood. "You wished to see me?" Catherine hadn't seemed so uneasy in his presence since the first days of their marriage. The twinkle of amusement that had lit her eyes so often over the preceding weeks was entirely absent.

His frustrations seemed extremely unimportant in the face of her unhappiness.

"These came for you." He had intended to burn the notes that Philip and Finley had sent to Catherine. Doing so still seemed like the logical and sensible thing to do. Still, he handed them to her, simultaneously hoping and fearing that receiving such flattering correspondence from two eligible gentlemen would bring a smile back to her face. At what point had he become such a glutton for punishment?

Catherine took the cards with obvious wariness. Crispin watched closely as she read the note from Finley. Would she be pleased by his attentions? Embarrassed at Crispin's knowledge of them? To his surprise, and satisfaction, she looked almost ill.

"He sent flowers?"

Crispin nodded.

"Would it be bad ton to burn them?" Catherine asked with the slightest lift to one eyebrow.

Crispin felt a tug at the edge of his mouth. Catherine could see right through the man. An encouraging sign of intelligence.

Catherine laid Finley's note uncaringly on a side table and turned her eyes to Philip's.

Lizzie had masterminded that possible match. Crispin abhorred the idea. But how did Catherine feel?

"'Lord Cavratt's flowers'?" she reread aloud with confusion. Then she turned her eyes to him. "Did you get me flowers?" A hopeful smile unexpectedly lit her face. "Oh, Crispin. I love flowers."

"I . . . um . . ." Crispin struggled for a reply that wouldn't wipe the brilliant smile from her face. His reluctance seemed to answer her question, however.

"Oh." Catherine looked away again, her smile only a distant memory.

Blast Philip.

Mr. Brown hovered silently over the leather chair at Crispin's desk, waiting for his employer's convenience. Crispin indicated a chair nearby for Catherine, which she took without a word or glance in his direction. Who would have guessed that *not* giving his wife flowers could land a husband in such deep waters?

"What is it you wished to discuss, Mr. Brown?" Crispin opted to pursue a topic he stood some chance of comprehending, the female mind not being fathomable at the moment.

"I received this earlier this morning." Brown held out a crisp piece of parchment. "A letter from a solicitor representing the interests of Mr. Thomas Thorndale."

Crispin's back straightened abruptly at the name, every muscle in his body tensing. He glanced anxiously at Catherine, who had turned a touch paler.

"He plans to challenge the legality of your marriage," Brown said.

That made absolutely no sense. What interest did Thorndale have in their marriage? And why would he, of all people, question its validity when he had been the one to push it through?

"What does that mean?" Catherine quietly asked.

"The license under which you were married was not legally obtained," Brown said. "Based on that, he intends to claim in court that your marriage was never legally binding."

"Our marriage isn't legal?" Catherine's voice sounded so small.

"It is legal," Brown interjected, "until declared otherwise by an ecclesiastical court. But an annulment, as I advised his lordship, is fairly unlikely without also undertaking a criminal trial."

Catherine looked understandably confused. He hadn't told her about Mr. Brown's doubts. Marriages were extremely difficult to annul—the church having the exclusive right to grant them and being decidedly in favor of leaving marriages intact. Publicly charging Thorndale with criminal activities connected to Doctor's Commons, and, thus, the church, would help sway the ecclesiastical courts in favor of the annulment.

"Does Thorndale have legal standing to contest the marriage?" Crispin avoided the questions in Catherine's eyes.

"As her guardian, he has standing."

"But once she married, he was no longer her guardian." Crispin stopped at the desk. He watched Brown with growing alarm, a sense of foreboding quickly setting in.

"Unless the marriage never *legally* took place—something he has every intention of arguing."

"But Thorndale is the one who obtained the license." Crispin stood behind Catherine's chair, watching the solicitor for some sensible explanation. "By pointing out to the ecclesiastical courts that he did so illegally, he would implicate himself."

"Thorndale is not seeking an annulment directly," Brown said. "He is pursuing criminal charges."

Criminal charges? "Against whom?"

"Against you, my lord."

Crispin froze. Thorndale planned to bring charges against *him*? What in the blazes was going on? An uncomfortable hush settled over the room. All the color had drained from Catherine's face. Crispin sat in the chair beside hers and took hold of her hand—only because she was in obvious need of comforting, of course.

"Explain."

"His solicitor informed me that Mr. Thorndale will argue, in a civil court, that *you* illegally obtained a marriage license and then duped him and his niece into going forward with the unbinding marriage ceremony."

"Why would he do this?" Catherine sounded almost pleading. "He insisted on the marriage. He washed his hands of me and sent me off. He has been perfectly clear that he wants nothing to do with me."

"Has he renewed his interest in you, Lady Cavratt?" Brown asked. "Contacted you?"

"Several times."

"He came here three times." Crispin tensed at the memory. "He was cast from the premises on the third occasion. That was the last time."

"Actually, he has contacted me twice since then."

Thorndale had been in Permount House? Why wasn't he told? Why hadn't Catherine informed him?

"He sent a letter yesterday," Catherine said.

"What did he say?" Brown asked.

"He insisted I remove to Hill Street—his London home—and then return to Yandell Hall in Herefordshire."

"Asserting his rights of guardianship." Brown adjusted his spectacles. "And the other contact?"

"At the Littletons' ball last night," Catherine whispered.

"He was at the ball?" Crispin turned to fully face her.

She nodded. "In the gardens. He literally dragged me out of the ballroom."

She had been in the gardens with *her uncle*? Not Philip. Not Finley. Crispin had indulged in a bout of self-pity, leaving Catherine to the machinations of Mr. Thorndale. What a pathetic excuse for a husband he was.

"Did he reiterate his earlier instructions?" Brown asked.

"Quite forcefully."

"Why didn't you tell me?" Crispin's heart sunk at the thought of Catherine facing Thorndale alone.

"How could I? He wouldn't let me leave." Catherine took an unsteady breath. "If Lizzie and Edward, and Lord Lampton, for that matter, hadn't noticed my absence and cared enough to search me out, Uncle might very well have dragged me directly to his house with no one the wiser."

Her words hit their mark. He *had* noticed she'd gone missing, but she didn't believe he had—what was her word?—*cared enough* to look for her. In reality, he had cared enormously. But convinced he'd find her cozying up with someone else, he hadn't gone looking.

Crispin rubbed his face with his hands. "What does all this mean?" he asked Brown. "Why the criminal charges and not an annulment?"

"I believe it is an issue of time, my lord. Annulment proceedings are notoriously slow and often ineffectual."

"The most direct explanation would be best, Mr. Brown." Crispin rubbed his temple with his free hand, unwilling to release Catherine's.

"Our efforts at uncovering the amount and nature of Lady Cavratt's inheritance came to the attention of Mr. Thorndale. He had not been aware of the legacy and came to Town in order to ascertain whether or not he was entitled to a portion of it."

"The meeting with his solicitor," Crispin muttered. Thorndale had given that as the reason for his visit.

"The inheritance was, in fact, left to Lady Cavratt, through her mother but with certain unusual stipulations. She cannot inherit until her twenty-first birthday, which I understand is in two weeks' time."

Catherine nodded.

"And her ladyship only inherits if she is married or a widow."

"I have never heard of anything like that," Crispin said.

"It is unusual but legally sound."

"Since Thorndale is challenging our marriage, I assume he stands to benefit in some way from doing so?"

Brown nodded. "If Lady Cavratt is unwed on her twenty-first birthday, the entirety of her inheritance reverts to the Thorndale estate."

"My uncle gets it all." Catherine pulled her hand from his and rose, walking stiffly to the windows.

He felt helpless, frustrated. Thorndale continued to hurt her, and Crispin couldn't manage to prevent it. "Why is he not pursuing an annulment? That would make more sense."

"As I said, my lord, annulments take time. The inheritance is to be dispersed in whole the day of Lady Cavratt's birthday, based on her marital status at that time. The will does not allow for retroactive challenges. Thus, Thorndale's challenge must be upheld *before* Lady Cavratt's birthday for his argument to prevent her from inheriting. He hopes, I think, to have the legality of your marriage questioned enough for the inheritance to be given to him."

"And the criminal charges?" Crispin leaned his head against his fist. "At the risk of sounding arrogant, it is highly unlikely his accusation would stick when brought against a Peer."

"He wants the money," Catherine said from the window. "Wealth has always been paramount to him. Wealth and control."

Brown nodded his agreement.

"The inheritance must be substantial for Thorndale to go to so much trouble," Crispin said.

"Over fifty thousand pounds," Brown replied with a heavy look.

Crispin bit back a curse that would have left Catherine blushing.

"This is why he wished me to return home with him?" Catherine asked.

Brown nodded once more. "He would insist your husband sent you away and that Lord Cavratt views you as expendable."

"That is ridiculous." Catherine expendable? What utter rot! "He can't expect this to work."

"He only needs it to work *enough.* I understand he is on very good terms with a magistrate here in London—his suit would likely be heard by the end of the week."

"That is awfully convenient," Crispin muttered.

"Your options are, I am afraid, limited. You could counter his arguments with your own. Accusing him of obtaining the illegal license would certainly silence him, your word carrying far more weight than his."

"But still placing our marriage in an unflattering light," Crispin said. "Undermining its legality would do neither of our reputations any good." Especially Catherine's.

"You could file your annulment papers immediately," Brown continued. "He might very well abandon the criminal charges and use the pending annulment as argument against the marriage."

Crispin shifted uncomfortably. He'd been avoiding those annulment papers for weeks. The idea simply hadn't set well for a while.

"Or you can move forward with the marriage and hope your standing is enough to weather the inevitable storm."

How infuriatingly frustrating. A criminal trial and a marriage undermined by questions of legality. Catherine would never recover from such a public scandal. His standing would suffer despite the ridiculous nature of it all. They would both be the subject of censure and ridicule, though Catherine would inevitably suffer most.

"Please let me know as soon as possible what you decide." Brown rose to his feet and straightened his coat. "Criminal trials require the services of a barrister. I can contact one if you'd like."

Crispin shook his head. "I am on very close terms with Mr. Jason Jonquil."

Brown nodded in obvious approval. "A very respected and talented barrister. I will be awaiting your instructions."

Crispin let out a whoosh of air after Brown's departure. What a mess. He could feel Catherine's eyes on him.

He rose and turned toward her. She stood at the window, shoulders slumped, emotion heavy in her eyes. He had failed her again.

"What do you plan to do?" she asked.

"I'm not sure."

Something about his response upset her. Her expression crumbled, tears suddenly falling.

Feeling the need to do something, he held his arms out to her, and Catherine rushed into them, her open hands pressed against his chest, her head resting against his cravat. Crispin wrapped his arms around her and an emptiness he didn't realize he'd been feeling dissipated.

"I have had a very rotten few days," Catherine said quietly, her voice fluid and emotional.

"I'm sorry." Crispin rested his head on top of hers, taking a lungful of rose scent. He felt her lean more heavily against him. He could so easily imagine her always in his arms.

Why was he still debating with himself? He hadn't favored an annulment for weeks, if he were honest about it. They got along well and he had certainly grown fond of her. He cared for her. They hadn't been graced with the ideal beginning, but that did not necessarily mean they couldn't make something of their marriage.

Of course, Catherine's position on the issue remained a mystery. Lizzie firmly believed Catherine could not be happy in a marriage that had been forced on her.

"It seems we will need a great deal of cream to thwart my uncle this time," Catherine said.

Her unexpected humor brought a chuckle to the surface. "Gallons of it, I fear."

Catherine lifted her head and looked up at him. "Perhaps this magistrate friend of his also 'dislikes' cream."

"Did you not tell me that bribing a magistrate is a crime?"

"We wouldn't be bribing him."

"*Threatening* a magistrate is probably a more serious offense."

Catherine smiled at him. "It seems your criminal tendencies have rubbed off on me."

He adored that smile. She couldn't be completely opposed to their marriage. She wouldn't have turned to him for comfort nor felt reassured enough to laugh with him if she wanted nothing more than to be rid of him.

"What a mess he has made." Catherine sighed, leaning into him once more. "If only Uncle had waited two more weeks. He only wants the money, I'm certain of it. He would never have done this if not for the inheritance."

"It is unfortunate he didn't learn of the legacy after it was too late."

Catherine tensed in his arms. What had he said? Was she upset? She pushed away from him, a look of deep contemplation on her face.

"Two weeks isn't so very long," she said. To Crispin's disappointment, Catherine pulled away entirely but kept her eyes fixed on him. "If he could be . . . delayed, somehow . . . for only a fortnight . . ."

"He would lose his footing." Crispin suddenly grasped Catherine's point. "Without the possibility of claiming your inheritance, he would likely drop the charges. I doubt we would ever be bothered by him again."

"Is it possible, do you think? Could we stall him somehow?"

She hadn't objected to the "we" nor his insinuation that they would be together in the long term. Encouraging signs, indeed. Feeling lighter and more hopeful than he had in weeks, despite the legal entanglements hanging over his head, Crispin nodded confidently. "Philip's brother Jason, the barrister I mentioned, is remarkably good at his profession. If anyone can think of a solution, he can."

"Do you think he would help?" Catherine grasped his arm, her expression hesitantly hopeful.

He brushed one lingering tear off her cheek with his thumb, more shaken by her touch than he had expected. "The Jonquils are a reliable bunch." Even if they did attempt to win the heart of one's wife. Philip, however, would not find himself doing so much longer. Crispin fully intended to win her heart for himself.

Chapter Twenty-one

Catherine had hardly touched her dinner. Her appetite seemed to have fled with Uncle's latest attempt to destroy any hint of happiness that entered her life. Worse, he meant to destroy Crispin in the process.

Her gaze wandered to Crispin, leaning against the mantel. He was absurdly handsome, really. Catherine smiled to herself at her wayward thoughts. She had never met a kinder person—a touch moody, perhaps, but kind to his very soul. He could easily have made her life miserable after the difficult beginning they'd had. Instead, he'd been gentle and understanding, providing her with clothing and pin money, seeing to her comforts and needs, laughing with and smiling at her.

She pulled her feet underneath her as she sat in her favorite window seat and leaned her head against the cool glass. How easily she had fallen in love with him.

"Mr. Jason Jonquil," Hancock announced from the library door.

A young gentleman stepped inside. He bore a remarkable resemblance to Lord Lampton: golden hair, a tall and lean frame. Personally, Catherine preferred Crispin's dark hair and athletic build. But he likely did not prefer a relatively plain, soft-spoken lady.

Knowing her duty, Catherine rose and crossed the room to where the two gentlemen stood.

"Thank you for coming, Jason." Crispin shook Mr. Jonquil's hand. "May I introduce my wife?"

Catherine tried to look confident as she offered the appropriate curtsy and greeting.

"I read the information you sent me." Mr. Jonquil's serious expression stood in stark contrast to his brother's usually jovial demeanor. "Mr. Brown has accurately surmised your options, and I would, of course, be willing to serve as counsel in any case that might arise."

"We are, actually, hoping to avoid the predicament altogether," Crispin said. "We have reason to believe if the inheritance were out of his reach, Thorndale would drop the suit entirely."

Mr. Jonquil clasped his hands behind his back and pursed his lips, apparently thinking through the situation. "And you say this Thorndale has a magistrate in his pocket?"

Crispin nodded. Catherine's eyes darted between them. There simply had to be a way to stop her uncle.

"If this 'friend' of his agrees to hear it, there's very little to stop the proceedings from being pushed through," Mr. Jonquil admitted solemnly. "If Thorndale is determined enough, the proceedings could receive a great deal of attention—very little occurs in the courts that cannot be leaked to the press and the public with minimal effort."

"Would his charges hold up?" Crispin asked.

Mr. Jonquil shook his head. "Your word far outweighs his. The damage would still be done, however. Speculation would be rife, every accusation reiterated in papers and news sheets. He can easily cast enough doubt on the legality of your marriage to tie the hands of the ecclesiastical courts—they would have no choice but to settle the matter."

"Dragging both our names through the mud." Crispin had begun pacing again.

Catherine stood firmly in place, willing her brain to search out a solution. She had managed to deal with nearly every disaster Uncle had heaped upon her. She seldom emerged unscathed, but the outcome would have been far worse otherwise.

"It hardly seems right for him to choose the judge," Catherine objected quietly. "There has to be another who would be more just."

"Any number of magistrates could hear it," Mr. Jonquil said.

"Could we insist the question be heard by someone else?" Crispin asked, stopping his pacing to look directly at Mr. Jonquil.

"You could certainly make the request," Mr. Jonquil answered, hands still clasped firmly behind his back.

"You seem rather doubtful the request would be granted," Crispin said.

"There is no guarantee," Mr. Jonquil admitted. "Only time would tell."

"How much time?" Catherine asked, a glimmer of hope twinkling on the horizon.

Suddenly, Mr. Jonquil's very even expression turned thoughtful.

"If he could be delayed only two weeks, it would make a world of difference," Catherine pressed. "I could almost guarantee he would give up the suit if the question weren't heard before the inheritance was dispersed."

Mr. Jonquil regarded her intensely for a moment. Catherine held her breath. She glanced across at Crispin, whose eyes were firmly locked on Mr. Jonquil. No one spoke or moved for several moments.

Please, she silently prayed. *Please help us.*

"It may just work," Mr. Jonquil finally said. "With some ingenuity, we could tie this entire thing up until after Lady Cavratt's birthday."

"Are you sure you can create such a long delay?" Crispin asked, looking at Mr. Jonquil even more intensely.

"The legal profession is notorious for complicating the simplest of things. I believe this would be an enjoyable use of an otherwise wasted talent."

"What if Thorndale chooses to pursue the charges even after losing the inheritance?" Crispin asked.

Mr. Jonquil appeared deep in thought for a moment. How very different he was from his brother—so serious and businesslike.

"There would only really be two feasible options. You could file a counterclaim against him, accusing *him* of illegally obtaining the license, and begin the annulment proceedings in order to solidify your claim."

Catherine's heart sank. She hated the idea of an annulment, of living out her life without Crispin.

"Or you can petition the Archbishop of Canterbury to officially confirm the validity of your marriage."

Good heavens. "The Archbishop of Canterbury?" Catherine nearly choked on the prestigious name. "How can a person possibly accomplish such a thing?"

Crispin gave her a crooked smile that set her heart pounding once more. "He has a seat in Lords, my dear." The endearment brought heat to Catherine's cheeks. "Though we are only slightly acquainted, I would certainly be granted an audience with him."

"With the Archbishop of Canterbury?" Catherine shook her head at the absurdity of it all. Until she'd met Crispin, she hadn't been acquainted with anyone of more significance than their local vicar.

Crispin chuckled. "I can see you are suddenly very impressed with this ramshackle husband you have acquired."

"A *little* impressed." His teasing never failed to lighten her heart.

"Then I should tell you I am also acquainted with the infamous Duke of Kielder—that should render you speechless with awe at my elevated connections."

Catherine smiled and felt herself relax for the first time since Mr. Brown's visit. Crispin would not be laughing with her if the situation were dire. "I am afraid I do not know who the Duke of Kielder is."

"Then I shall be sure to introduce you," Crispin said. "His Grace is . . . one of a kind."

She followed Crispin's gaze as it shifted back to Mr. Jonquil, who stood silently watching them with a look of keen interest. Catherine abruptly dropped her gaze, something in Mr. Jonquil's expression telling her he'd seen far more than she was comfortable revealing.

Crispin cleared his throat. "My apologies, Jason. Where were we?"

Not even a hint of a smile touched Mr. Jonquil's face, though he did not look *un*happy. "I will discover which magistrate Thorndale is manipulating. You, in the meantime, need to decide which course of action to take."

Crispin nodded, his own expression growing more somber.

"Good night, Crispin. Lady Cavratt." The door clicked closed behind Mr. Jonquil.

After several drawn-out moments, Crispin broke the silence between them. "We must come to some decision about the an—"

"I don't want to talk about this." Catherine turned away, panic choking her words.

"We cannot avoid the topic any longer."

She moved to the window seat, trying to keep her breaths even and calm.

"Even if your uncle's charges against me can be prevented, bringing charges against *him* would call unwanted, negative attention to our situation." His voice was distant enough to tell her he had not followed her across the room. "Your reputation would be in tatters."

She pressed her hand to her heart. "And yours."

"Pressing charges against someone else would not hurt my reputation. Even the annulment itself would have less impact as a result of the criminal charges. Society would know the reasons, and while I might endure a few sideways glances and unflattering remarks, I would not be detrimentally affected. You, on the other hand, would be ruined. Utterly."

Catherine sat on the window seat, digesting what he said. *He* would emerge from the uproar of the annulment relatively unscathed. She, on the other hand, would not emerge with anything resembling a good reputation. She hadn't realized how enormous the consequences would be.

"I will not place such a burden on your shoulders, Catherine. You do not deserve to bear the weight of this."

"Neither do you," she countered quietly.

"There really is only one choice." A note of decisive determination entered his tone. "I will speak with the Archbishop."

Crispin had chosen against the annulment. He had chosen to continue their marriage. Catherine knew her heart ought to have been singing, but she felt numb, hollow.

"You would do that for me?" she asked, her heart thudding unpleasantly, painfully in her chest. She did not look back at him but kept her eyes fixed on the darkness outside, praying he would offer the smallest declaration of affection, confess to some degree of tender regard.

"It would not be fair otherwise."

The cold logic of justice. He would keep her out of a sense of fair play. Catherine closed her eyes against the tears that hovered too near the surface. She knew the loneliness of living in a home where she was not truly wanted—Uncle, too, had been forced to keep her, but by the stipulations of the law, not the dictates of his conscience. Crispin would come to resent her and she would be miserable. Chivalry was a poor substitute for love.

"I think you should file the charges, Crispin."

"I beg your pardon?"

"I want you to file the charges."

The sound of his footsteps warned her of his approach. One touch and she might lose her conviction. Catherine steeled herself. She had to be as fair to him as he'd thought he was being to her. A marriage without mutual affection would make neither of them happy.

"And the annulment?" He spoke directly behind her.

She took a breath to steady her nerves. "And the annulment."

Crispin didn't speak and didn't touch her. She could hear him breathing, could smell his shaving soap. The slightest movement would allow her to lean against him as she'd done so many times. But he did not deserve to be trapped by his own sense of honor.

"This is what you want, knowing the irreparable damage it will do to you?"

No. I want you to love me. Catherine could manage nothing beyond a nod. She opened her eyes and saw his reflection in the window. He stood perfectly still, his posture tense.

"We will have to wait and see what Jason can manage," he said tightly.

She nodded again, completely unable to speak. He had taken her suggestion without a single objection, with little beyond the briefest hesitation.

"Once we are more certain of your uncle's actions, we can proceed."

"That would be best."

He must not have noticed the catch in her voice. Crispin stepped away and walked, without a backward glance, to his desk. She watched him a moment as he flipped through papers.

Catherine wrapped her arms around herself and rested her forehead against the window. The cold glass soothed to some degree the throbbing in her head. She wished he would protest, insist he wanted her to stay because he cared about her.

She stared out at the rain-drenched garden and the sobbing skies and felt like weeping herself. She had fallen in love with a man who didn't love her in return. For a brief few weeks she'd had a glimpse of happiness and in a single moment it had disappeared.

Chapter Twenty-two

A CREATIVE MAN CAN THINK of countless ways to avoid his wife. Crispin discovered over the next week that he was a very creative man. Tattersall's. His club. Riding. The lending library. Staring out of windows. Pretending to read books in which he had absolutely no interest.

It wasn't that he didn't want to spend time with Catherine. In fact, the longer he stayed away, the more he realized the opposite was true. He missed her more each day. He missed the sound of her skirts swishing as she walked and the way she always smelled precisely like a rose in full bloom. He missed coaxing a smile to her face. He missed laughing with her at things only they would find funny.

Therein lay the problem.

He had grown far too attached to a lady who preferred ostracism and social ruin to a life with him. Thorndale's suit continued to be delayed by arguments of jurisdiction and other legal entanglements, compliments of the venerable Jason Jonquil, barrister. Jason seemed quite certain the point would not be heard before Catherine's birthday.

Her birthday. She would be free to leave after that, having sufficient funds to live on and no compelling reason to stay. Would she be relieved? Would she miss him? He'd given up trying to convince himself he wouldn't think of her after she left.

She had become too much a part of his everyday life for her to fade easily from his thoughts. He was simply accustomed to her presence. He had come to expect her to be around, much the same way he anticipated Hancock's presence.

No, he corrected himself again. Not at all like Hancock. He had no idea what Hancock smelled like. He didn't care what Hancock smelled like.

Crispin felt certain of only one thing. Her presence had grown excruciating. He found he couldn't bear to be around her twenty-four hours a day, knowing she wanted nothing to do with him, while he constantly battled the growing urge to beg her to give him a chance. But she knew her options and had made her decision. He had forced her hand once, however inadvertently, and would not do so again.

"You look like the back end of an overworked farm mule."

"Thank you, Philip. That is so relieving to hear." Crispin watched his oldest friend slide lazily into a leather wing chair directly beside his own in a secluded corner of White's. "Would you care to know which member of the animal kingdom you remind me of at the moment?"

"Peacock, I dare say." Philip straightened his aqua blue waistcoat. "No dandy would settle for any other comparison."

"You are no true dandy, and I know it," Crispin muttered, dropping the pretense of reading the *Times*. "Though I never understood why you bother with the act."

Philip shrugged. "We all wear masks of one kind or another."

"So what brings the swaggering bird to the mule's backside this time?"

"Your lovely wife."

"She sent you to find me?" Crispin knew he ought to feel affronted, but he felt strangely excited. Did she miss him too?

"Somehow I cannot see Catherine commissioning a team of spies to track down her negligent husband."

"You're using her Christian name now?" Crispin knew he was grumbling. He didn't particularly care.

"She gave me leave to," Philip said as though it were of minimal importance. "My name she has changed to Ph-Ph-Philip. I had no idea it was such a difficult name to pronounce."

The droll character Philip insisted on presenting to the world never ruffled Crispin the way it did just then. Was this really the man Lizzie thought so perfect for Catherine? He himself might be little better than a rusted, useless knight, but that was vastly more fitting for Catherine than a court jester.

"But I digress." Philip straightened his waistcoat and gave himself a drawn-out visual inspection. Apparently satisfied, he retook his tale. "I went by Permount House looking for you. Catherine insisted she hadn't seen you in days."

"I have been busy."

"You have been avoiding her."

"That is ridiculous."

"She is no empty-headed female, my friend." Philip picked up the paper Crispin had set aside. "In the past few days Hancock has seen you. Your housekeeper and cook have spoken with you. Several of the footmen have seen you in passing. Catherine realizes she is the only person at Permount House who has *not* seen you lately."

"Coincidence." Crispin wasn't even convincing himself.

"Rubbish."

The *Times* crinkled in protest as Philip folded back one page and then another.

"Why are you avoiding your wife, Crispin?" Now that sounded like the Philip whom Crispin had known for half his life. Intelligence and authority resonated in his voice. The look of mindless amusement had dissolved into one of discernment. "Have you two quarreled?"

"No." Philip was far easier to talk to when he abandoned his façade. "It is just better this way."

"Better for whom? For you, perhaps. But have you thought about Catherine?"

Thinking about Catherine seemed to be his sole occupation lately.

"Perhaps during your long sojourn inside these hallowed halls"—Philip motioned at the room around them—"you've chanced to riffle through the betting books."

"I have no interest in the betting books."

"You should. They are positively filled these last few days with wagers regarding the future of your rather famed marriage."

Wagers! Crispin began a heated jump to his feet.

"Don't be a dolt. You've drawn enough attention as it is." Philip really was dropping the act—he sounded almost angry. Once Crispin resumed his seat, Philip continued. "The odds are stacked heavily against the continuation of your marriage, Crispin. The two of you have not appeared in public together since the Littletons' ball, and that didn't go so well. Catherine's hasty departure—alone, I might add—did not go unnoticed. And now you are noted to be spending precious little time in her company, avoiding your own home, even."

Why couldn't society mind its own business for once?

"Catherine showed me this while I was at Permount House this afternoon." Philip handed the folded-back *Times* to Crispin, pointing out the opening paragraph of the society column.

Crispin read silently. *Lord and Lady C., subject of much conjecture since their hasty marriage, are rumored to be on the outs at last, with Lord C. going to remarkable lengths to avoid his bride. One close to the bridegroom reports an annulment is imminent, but Lady C. has, apparently, proven too undesirable a companion to make her company bearable during the interim.*

Philip leaned closer and lowered his voice. His eyes were penetrating in a way they hadn't been in years. "Are you planning to seek an annulment?"

"Why do you ask?" A suspicion lodged in his mind.

Philip shook his head in obvious annoyance. "Lizzie's scheme was outlandish from the start, and I am surprised you believed a word of it. Gentlemen do not pass around wives the way they do calling cards. She merely wanted to make you jealous so you would realize what a gem you married."

"That scheming brat." Still, a smile very nearly escaped him.

"I only went along after I realized that Lizzie was correct. You, my friend, married far above yourself. Regardless of the outcome of your time together, she deserves the protection of your public approval." Then in a mutter so low Crispin could hardly make out his words, Philip added something that sounded suspiciously like, "You have offered precious little else."

"My approval means little to her."

Philip gave him a look of utter disbelief. "Rubbish."

"*She* asked for the annulment, Philip. I explained that she would be ruined, that she would have no place in polite society. Her uncle would face a very public criminal trial, in which she would not be painted in a very flattering light. I told her I was willing to go forward with the marriage, that she need not endure all that. And she chose the annulment." He looked back at the now-crumpled news sheet in his hand. "Ostracism, it seems, would be more bearable than life as my wife."

"Yet she seemed anxious enough for your company when I spoke with her."

"That does not make any sense." Crispin slumped further in his chair.

"At what point did you decide a lady's actions were supposed to make sense?"

Crispin allowed a begrudging smile. The fairer sex ever had been a source of confusion to the both of them.

"Perhaps her more rational side was temporarily silenced by the splendor of my dashing new waistcoat." The lazy, not-a-care Philip was back in the blink of an eye.

Philip rose from his chair and painstakingly straightened his clothing, including the waistcoat that would be the envy of many a gentleman in Town. With a bow he strode away, leaving Crispin to gather his thoughts.

The protection of your public approval. It sounded so cold, so impersonal. But the tabbies had been drawing rather frigid conclusions about his feelings for Catherine. They would certainly go to great lengths to make her miserable.

"Blast it," Crispin muttered, getting to his feet.

He had simply been trying to make this easier. Easier on Catherine, he told himself. She didn't need the burden of his unreciprocated regard, but hiding that attachment had grown nearly impossible. Philip made it sound as though he'd been starving her in the dungeons.

Drat that man! Crispin was the knight in not-so-shiny armor, not the feudal executioner. Didn't Philip know anything about not mixing metaphors?

That, however, was not the problem at hand. Gossip, society's most viciously wielded weapon, needed addressing first. Seated inside the chaise, Crispin looked over the rather pointed report of his very irregular marriage.

"*Lord C. going to remarkable lengths to avoid his bride.*" "*Lady C. is too undesirable a companion to make her company bearable.*"

He let out a tense breath. In the few weeks since he'd met Catherine, his life had been entirely unpredictable. Nothing he did seemed to work out the way he'd planned. Fool that he was, he'd spent the better part of the past week wondering why a lifetime with him hadn't proven a promising prospect for her.

"*You owe her the protection of your public approval.*" Philip's words repeated in his mind. But how should Crispin do that? Bandy about his approval? Take out an advertisement in the *Times*? *Lord C. wishes to declare his unrequited affection for his wife and cordially invites society to stick their noses in someone else's business.*

He needed an actual plan. There were certainly any number of balls or musicales being hosted that very evening; they'd undoubtedly been invited to most. But suppose he dragged Catherine to one only to have her cut by every guest present? That would never do.

No. There had to be something more private yet public enough for them to be seen together, spending a harmonious evening in one another's company. He wondered if Catherine had ever been to Drury Lane. He hadn't taken her and doubted Thorndale ever had. It certainly met the requirements for a redemptive excursion. The theater was, after all, the place to see and be seen. She would probably even enjoy it.

So busy was he evaluating the soundness of his plan that he hardly realized he'd reached the music room. He hadn't had time to prepare himself for seeing Catherine again.

Lud, she was beautiful. She was seated at the pianoforte, hands on the keys, eyes on . . . him. He had to shake himself to focus his thoughts.

"Hello, Catherine." That sounded idiotic! Think, man.

She didn't even try to reply but simply watched him. Crispin would have felt less uncomfortable if she'd ranted and raved or looked daggers at him for all the difficulties he'd inadvertently caused her. He saw not a hint of anger or annoyance in those breathtakingly blue eyes. He saw disappointment.

"I . . . um." He cleared his throat. "I thought perhaps you would enjoy a trip to the theater tonight. I don't believe we've been since we came to London."

Catherine silently shook her head.

"Would you like to go?" He suddenly felt like a six-year-old begging Cook for a biscuit, completely unsure of himself.

"Are you sure you can *bear my company*?" she asked rather dryly.

Crispin recognized her almost verbatim reference. "The gossips can be vicious." And, on occasion, they could be frighteningly accurate. Catherine's company had grown remarkably difficult to bear, but not for the reasons they insinuated. "I am hoping tonight to—"

"Stand them down?" Catherine finished for him.

Crispin nodded. Her utterly lifeless tone was disheartening.

She sighed, her gaze drifting to the piano keys. "I have discovered that doing so is both exhausting and fruitless."

"It is infinitely easier when you aren't alone."

She plunked out a stilted few notes. "I will have to take your word on that. This past week I have done everything alone."

Frustration pushed out a cynical reply. "Annulments are like that. In the end, one is left doing a great many things *alone.*"

Her hand froze above the keys before dropping into her lap.

What was wrong with him? He hadn't resorted to cutting remarks in weeks—least of all with her.

She rose from the pianoforte and walked toward the door, not sparing him so much as a glance. The swish of her skirts. The smell of roses. He would be without her soon enough and couldn't leave things as they were. "Wait. Please, Catherine."

She stopped only steps past him but didn't turn back around to face him.

"I'm sorry about all of this," he said. "The gossip and the mess. I wasn't trying to make the situation worse by staying away."

"Then why did you?" She didn't look back at him.

It was a direct enough question with an answer he knew well. *Because I've never felt this way about anyone and I don't understand it. Because being in the same room as you is torturous.* He couldn't seem to verbalize an answer.

They stood in heavy silence until Catherine left without a word or a backward glance.

Chapter Twenty-three

"There must be a thousand people here," Catherine whispered, staring in awe at the mass of humanity that stretched out beyond Crispin's private box at the Theatre Royal.

"The Theatre holds just over three thousand," Crispin said. "And I'd guess nearly every seat is taken tonight."

"Good heavens."

Three thousand people in one place. Until coming to London, a crowd of three hundred would have been all but impossible for her to imagine. The sight was so overwhelming she might not have trusted her legs to remain steady beneath her had she been standing.

She had yet to account for Crispin's offer to bring her. He had quite obviously been avoiding her. Now that there was no question of their not seeking an annulment, she never saw him. Perhaps his affectionate behavior had been a futile attempt to force himself to care for her should they be required to remain wed.

"Now." Crispin leaned closer. Catherine commanded her heart to remain calm. He had made his relief at their pending separation quite clear, and she must not misinterpret a moment of kindness as anything more than that. "Time for a tutorial on theater-going. Of the three thousand or so people here tonight, five or six might actually watch the production. The rest will watch the audience."

"The audience?"

"The point of the theater is to see and be seen. Everyone will be on the lookout for fresh gossip."

Catherine shuddered at the word. "I am heartily sick of gossip," she muttered under her breath.

Crispin's fingers wrapped around hers. Catherine kept very still. He pulled their entwined hands to his lips and softly kissed her gloved fingers. Why would he do such a thing?

"Yet another thing for which I must apologize." Crispin spoke in a low whisper. Despite the dull roar of the enormous crowd, his every word reached her ears with amazing clarity. "I have been inexcusably inattentive."

Catherine couldn't pull her gaze from Crispin's eyes. Their color never seemed the same from one moment to the next. Brown with varying flecks of gold and green. Sometimes dark as night. Other times the color of creamed coffee. Regardless of their hue, his eyes could be positively hypnotizing—ofttimes the only window into Crispin's often shuttered feelings.

He smiled at her, lightly rubbing with his thumb the hand he held. She could almost believe, in that moment, that he cared for her beyond a desire to be civil. It was the gesture of an affectionate husband, not a man anxious to end his marriage. Yet he had jumped at her offer to walk away.

Crispin continued tracing a slow, lazy circle along the back of her hand. Catherine nearly snatched her hand away, too confused and overwhelmed to endure his touch. Why must he torture her like this?

The curtain rose, though the crowd did not quiet down at all. Catherine forced her gaze to the stage, attempting to ignore the tingle his touch sent up her arm. She'd longed for his reassuring presence the past two weeks. The temptation to lay her head on his shoulder was nearly too great to withstand. How perfectly natural it would feel at that moment to lean against him for the remainder of the night, to pretend he would always be with her.

"I understand from Mr. Brown that Mr. Jonquil has successfully stalled your uncle's suit," Crispin whispered in her ear, sending a shiver down her spine.

"It seems we chose the right course of action." Only a Herculean effort kept her voice calm and steady.

"And it was your suggestion, if I recall. When Brown retires, I'll have to hire you as his replacement." Crispin's breath tickled her ear. "You apparently have a remarkable legal mind."

Catherine forced herself to take a breath despite the tension in her lungs. "Are you certain you can afford the outrageous fee I would require?" Catherine whispered. Somehow she managed a teasing tone.

"It is to be highway robbery, then?" Crispin leaned a little closer. Heaven help her, she would burst if he didn't put a little distance between them.

"You, sir, are a hardened criminal." The joking banter relieved a little of the tension building in her. "You know what they say about honor among thieves."

"Could I, perhaps, pay you in fairy cakes?" Crispin slipped his arm around the back of her chair.

She pulled herself excruciatingly upright, desperate to keep his arm from brushing against her. She could not endure much more.

"That would require an awful lot of fairy cakes." Did he hear the catch in her voice?

"Perhaps I could pay over time."

"I rarely extend credit. You would have to be extremely trustworthy. Or my most important client."

"And how does one become your most important client?" Crispin leaned closer, his breath rustling the strands of hair framing her face. She closed her eyes. "I could take you for a ride in Hyde Park. Ices at Gunter's." He kissed her cheek. "Dinner at Vauxhall Gardens." Kissed her temple.

"You do all this with Mr. Brown?" Catherine tried to steady her breathing. Crispin's nose still brushed the side of her face. "No wonder he's so loyal."

Crispin's quiet, warm laughter reached her ears. She'd come to adore that laugh, rare as it was. His arm slipped across her back and she felt him gently squeeze her shoulders. He pulled her closer, so she had little choice but to lay her head against his obliging shoulder.

Catherine barely held back a sigh. She would allow herself this moment, though she knew it would make leaving that much harder. Years down the road, when she was little more than a vaguely familiar name amongst Crispin's many acquaintances, Catherine would pull this moment to the forefront of her own thoughts and perhaps find some comfort in the recollection.

"You aren't asleep already, are you?"

Catherine managed to shake her head slightly but didn't open her eyes.

"The Prince Regent has arrived in his box," Crispin whispered.

Catherine glanced across the theater, along with three thousand others. "Who is that with him?" She did not recognize a single soul who had arrived in the Prince's company.

"Lord Alvanley is seated beside the prince," Crispin said. "Beside him is Beau Brummell."

The list continued and expanded beyond the Prince's box. Crispin seemingly knew the entire Upper Ten-thousand. Such information would, undoubtedly, have transfixed the attention of any lady of the ton, but Catherine found she could hardly concentrate. Crispin kept his arm snuggly wrapped around her shoulders and caressed her hand as he spoke. Her heart would ache when he let her go, but she hadn't the strength to pull away.

Heaven help her, she was in love with him. What she wouldn't give to hear him say he loved her in return.

The first intermission arrived, and Catherine hadn't watched a single minute of the play. She'd spent the first act memorizing everything about being held in his arms. When he broke that contact, her heart plummeted.

"Champagne, I believe." Crispin rose to his feet.

"Champagne?"

"Tradition, my dear. One must have champagne at the theater."

"I have never known you to drink champagne."

"Special occasion," Crispin explained with another trademark lopsided grin. "I shall return shortly," he said with a brief bow and a wink.

Catherine pressed her hand to her thudding heart after he left. That organ would certainly never be the same again.

Footsteps sounded from the back of the box and Catherine spun around, expecting to see Crispin. Had he decided her company was preferable to obtaining refreshment? Instead, she came face-to-face with Miss Cynthia Bower.

"Lady Cavratt." Why did Miss Bower always sound on the verge of laughter when she greeted Catherine?

"Miss Bower," Catherine returned as civilly as possible. "To what do I owe this honor?"

Miss Bower gave her a very condescending look. "I am looking for Crispin." She gave Catherine a look of utter contempt, as though her mere presence was an inconvenience.

"Lord Cavratt will return shortly. If you would rather not wait, I can tell him you were here."

"I'll wait." Catherine did not at all trust the gleam in the lady's eye.

Then came a voice she not only didn't trust but couldn't bear: Mr. Finley's.

"Dear, dear Catherine," he intoned, stepping to where she stood and reaching for her hand. Catherine slipped around and out of reach.

"Mr. Finley," she replied, hoping her voice was as icy as she felt.

"I have brought you a restorative," Finley said, a seductive glint in his eye.

"I am not in need of one." She had been in need of a respite and was rather in need of a rescue at the moment.

"You most certainly are, having endured Cavratt's company when you could have been enjoying mine." Finley inched ever closer to her.

Miss Bower watched the entire scene, her expression indicative of equal parts disgust and triumph.

"A change of companions would do you good," Finley said.

"Your leaving would do me far more good, Mr. Finley."

"Afraid your husband will return?"

"Please leave."

Finley opened his mouth to reply, but a third voice cut him off. "Ah, Finley. I thought I detected the faint smell of horse excrement."

Philip! Thank heaven. He entered the box, inspecting Finley through his quizzing glass.

"Lampton." Finley spoke with no hint of warmth or congeniality. "Come to take advantage of an old friend?" Catherine didn't like the way Finley emphasized "advantage." Why did she get the feeling she'd just been insulted?

"On the contrary." Philip smoothed the sleeve of his jacket. "This box seems to be the center of attention at the moment. I've come to be seen."

Philip traipsed to the front of the box, leaned calculatingly casually against the high column, and fixed his eyes on Finley with a look of ennui.

"Useless fop," Finley grumbled, eyeing Philip with utter contempt.

"This is quite a scene." Crispin's voice joined the jumble. He didn't sound amused.

Catherine looked from Philip's look of nonchalance to Finley's glaring eyes to Crispin's noticeably tensing jaw. Her eyes settled on Miss Bower's look of triumph. She was enjoying this scene, wasn't she? Catherine had stomached quite enough.

"You seem to have torn a flounce, Miss Bower." Amazingly, she managed to infuse the lie with an aura of truthfulness. "Perhaps you should see to it lest someone suspect you've been misbehaving."

Miss Bower flushed a blotchy red and offered a quickly muttered excuse before scurrying from the box. She would, of course, be quite put out when she realized her flounces were entirely intact. Catherine couldn't care less.

"And you, Mr. Finley." Catherine spun around to face the second intruder. "You may take your leave as well. I, as I have assured you, have no need for your offer nor any desire for your company."

"Good show, Catherine." Finley smiled at her.

"You will not use my Christian name, Mr. Finley."

Much to her consternation, Mr. Finley stepped even closer, as though her words had actually been encouraging.

"Cavratt does not want you, love," Finley whispered as he closed the distance between them. Catherine had no room to back away. "I do."

Crispin appeared behind Finley. "You have quite overstayed your welcome, sir." His hand clamped Finley's shoulder. "You will be leaving now."

"And the dandy?" Finley snapped his head in Philip's direction. "You really think his intentions are honorable?"

Crispin shot Finley a look that should have leveled him.

"Keep your copy of tomorrow's gossip sheet, Cavratt." Finley made his way out of the box. "After this spectacle, it should prove an interesting read."

Crispin's gaze never left Finley as the man disappeared from view.

"Finley got his handful of fame," Philip said, walking to where Crispin stood glaring at the back of the box.

"His intention, no doubt." Crispin let out a tense breath. "Thank you for coming in after him. I couldn't get through the crowd."

"I would much rather make Finley uncomfortable than face the horde of rabid gossipers following you around hoping for a juicy tidbit."

Crispin shook his head in obvious displeasure. "What a mess this all is."

Catherine cringed at his words. She had tried to keep the situation under control. She'd sent Miss Bower packing, hadn't she?

"I shall leave you to see to your lovely wife," Philip said. He stopped a few steps short of leaving, turned back to the two of them, and offered one more bit of advice before leaving. "Give the tabbies something to claw each other over."

Crispin picked up the two flutes of champagne he'd brought with him and held one out to Catherine.

"I don't think I could," Catherine protested. "My stomach is a bit unsettled as it is."

"Finley has that effect on people."

"I really did try to persuade him to leave," Catherine said. "But he wouldn't go."

Crispin took a generous sip of bubbling wine. "He is rather like the plague, isn't he?"

"Deadly. Painful. Putrid." Catherine nodded. "An appropriate comparison."

He smiled after another swallow. "*Putrid*? He would be mortified."

"He ought to be mortified more often," Catherine mumbled.

"Finley was right about one thing, though." Crispin finished his glass—Catherine didn't remember ever seeing him drink, let alone finish an entire glass so quickly. He must have truly been upset. "This will, I am afraid, further fuel the gossips."

"Do you think anyone noticed?"

Crispin motioned with his head to the audience behind Catherine. She glanced covertly over her shoulder. An inordinate number of eyes were, indeed, focused on their box. She turned back to Crispin, closing her eyes to steady herself.

"What should we do?" she asked when she finally trusted herself to speak.

He didn't answer for a moment. Catherine opened her eyes to find him watching her closely. "We have to convince them you weren't inviting Finley's attentions. Or Philip's, for that matter."

"I wasn't."

"I know," Crispin stepped closer to her, setting his empty glass on an obliging table beside her still full one. "But *they*"—He eyed the theater beyond—"don't know that."

"How do we convince them?" Catherine's heart beat harder as Crispin stepped closer.

"To begin with, you could smile." Crispin matched his expression to his suggestion. "Much better. No point convincing them we're quarreling."

"We couldn't be quarreling—there's no fountain," Catherine replied.

Crispin cupped her chin with his hand and kissed the tip of her nose. She would never survive another onslaught. "If there *were* a fountain . . . ?" He let the phrase dangle.

"You wouldn't be afraid to let the ton see you in a tizzy?"

"I don't have tizzies, Catherine."

"Really?" She arched an eyebrow at him, grateful for the return of his teasing tone.

"Now that is a look I cannot possibly be expected to resist."

What did he mean by that?

In the next moment, Crispin kissed her. He kissed her in his box at the Theatre Royal in front of three thousand people. It was not merely an obligatory peck, but a thorough, more-than-a-few-mere-seconds'-long kiss. Warmth spread through her entire body as his arms wrapped around her.

Catherine touched his face with her hands, memorizing the feel of him. He could not possibly kiss her so deeply and not mean anything by it. She poured her heart into returning the kiss, praying he would feel just how much she needed him, that he would want her to stay with him.

"If we leave now," he whispered against her mouth, "the gossips will be entirely convinced."

The gossips. He had kissed her for appearance's sake?

Her heart dropped. His performance as the doting and affectionate husband would certainly convince the gossip-hungry members of society. For a moment, *she* had actually believed he cared for her.

Chapter Twenty-four

THE COLD NIGHT AIR OUTSIDE the Theatre Royal went a long way to cool Crispin's thoughts. He'd told himself, even as he leaned forward to kiss Catherine, that he was doing so merely to convince any interested onlooker that he and Catherine were not at odds with each other. Somehow that motivation had all but disappeared the moment his lips had touched hers.

Blast! He wasn't a schoolboy who couldn't keep himself in check. Yet he found it absolutely necessary to sit opposite Catherine during the carriage ride home instead of beside her. What kind of spell had Catherine cast over him that he couldn't trust himself to keep a proper distance now that they weren't putting a spoke in the wheels of the gossip wagon?

The situation had grown nearly unbearable. Only one more week. One week. She'd be gone and he could breathe again. Lud, that wasn't at all comforting.

Why, by George, did he feel like his mind couldn't quite keep up? Perhaps the champagne hadn't been a good idea, after all.

He was not foxed—descending from the carriage and taking the steps into Permount House was easy enough. His surroundings were holding still and his eyes were focusing just fine. He wasn't completely inebriated, and yet . . .

Crispin rubbed his face as he stood in the doorway of the sitting room. He generally avoided alcohol. He was not one of those gentlemen who could spend a night in his cups and still remain unaffected. It had been a source of endless taunting in his Cambridge days.

"Are you all right, Crispin?"

Catherine's voice pulled him back to the present. She was watching him from just past the sitting room doors. He did his best to look unaffected.

"Fine."

"You look a little unwell."

"I'm not ill."

Her unwavering gaze proved decidedly uncomfortable.

"The champagne?" she asked, her voice a little lower, her forehead wrinkled with knowing concern.

He was not jug-bitten. His pride suffered a severe blow at the idea that she thought he would get roaring drunk while escorting her. Gads, he was responsible for her safety, her well-being. He wouldn't allow himself to become cup-shot.

"You never drink more than a few sips of wine with dinner. I simply assumed you do not care for spirits." Catherine crossed to where he was standing, eyeing him quite penetratingly. "Do you need to sit down? Shall I ring for coffee?"

"I am far from foxed, Catherine, just a little—"

"Light-headed?" she finished for him. "Come, sit down." Catherine motioned toward a chair not far off in the sitting room.

"I am fine. Really. I think I'm more tired than anything else."

"Then perhaps you should lie down," Catherine said.

He shook his head. Catherine took gentle hold of his arm. As it had earlier at the theater, her touch shook him to the core. He stepped back, needing a little space and time to clear his foggy mind. Foggy enough, in fact, that he backed directly into a hall table and managed to topple a flower-filled vase. He barely managed to right it in time.

"I really think you should at least sit down, Crispin." Catherine led him by the hand toward the stairs. "You will feel better if you do."

He followed mutely, unsure where they were headed but enjoying the touch of her ungloved hand in his too much to ask or object. A moment later—a very short moment later—she released him. He sat in an armchair beside the fireplace in the library, pondering just how he could convince her to hold his hand again. Low embers cast a soft glow around the room but not a lot of warmth.

As if reading his thoughts, Catherine snatched a throw from the nearby sofa and draped it over Crispin's lap.

"I am not in my dotage, Catherine," Crispin objected, feeling like an octogenarian. "Nor am I in my cups."

"Uncle never could stop drinking before becoming thoroughly foxed." She ignored his objection. "He never was one to exercise restraint." She stepped away to stoke the fire, bringing a little more life to the barely glowing coals.

Restraint! Did Catherine have any idea the Herculean effort required to exercise restraint in her company, especially with her hair quite enchantingly escaping its knot and her perfume filling the room? He doubted it. In fact, he knew she didn't. Catherine wanted nothing to do with him. Catherine was walking out in a week.

"Was your father that way?" Catherine took a seat opposite him, wrapping a second blanket around her shoulders.

What way? What had she been talking about? Ah, yes. Drunkards. "He was not particularly susceptible to alcohol."

She shook her head. "I meant, was he willing to accept his limits? An exerciser of self-control?"

Did Catherine view *him* that way? Was a man of restraint her ideal, or did she equate it with weakness? And why, he demanded of himself, did he care so blasted much? Somewhere along the way he'd become sentimental and maudlin. Caring about people never did any good.

"I suppose," was all Crispin managed to offer.

Catherine gave him the oddest look, as if searching his very soul for some bit of crucial character-evaluating information. Perfect! Sketch his character while he was three sheets to the wind. Or at least a sheet and a half. Calculating the exact sheet percentage of one's drunkenness was particularly hard when one was just a touch cut.

Where were they? Ah, yes. Catherine was evaluating him and, apparently, his father.

"My father was a good man," Crispin said. "He was a fair landlord and an attentive father and a devoted husband." His father had not been a fool, wearing his heart on his sleeve or pining after a lady who wanted nothing to do with him.

"Did your parents love each other, then?"

"They rubbed along well. And I think they were fond of each other."

"But they weren't in love?"

"Of course not."

"Why 'of course'? Love between married couples isn't such an outrageous occurrence."

It was proving more "outrageous" all the time. He'd gone his entire life with a reasonable and logical view of relationships and attachments. A few weeks of Catherine's company and he'd gone soft. He didn't need a clear head to see the result of that egregious miscalculation. "Love is the invention of poets, Catherine." Malevolent, vicious poets.

If her gaze had been searching before, by the end of his declaration it look turned positively dissecting. "I knew you sometimes gravitated toward cynicism, but I hadn't realized you espoused skepticism, as well. To dismiss an emotion so entirely . . ." Was that disapproval in her eyes? Or simply confusion?

He was feeling a little muddled himself.

"That is a rather bleak assessment," Catherine said, her brows knit in concentration. "You cannot truly say you do not love your sister."

Lud, his head was far too foggy for such a philosophical discussion. "It is not the same thing."

"Love is love, Crispin."

"All families love each other, in that familial sort of way." He leaned his head back against the chair. "You were referring to love between spouses." *Ironically enough.* "Men and women. Romantic love. That . . . nonsense."

"First of all, not *all* families love each other. And secondly, I don't believe the love between a man and a woman is nonsense."

Was Catherine glowering? She seldom looked anywhere near upset—disappointed at times, borderline annoyed. But glaring at him?

Why in heaven's name was he discussing this with her in the first place? He never spoke to anyone about his frustrations with the hypocrisy in the world. He'd seen too many unhappy marriages, been pursued by too many avaricious young ladies to have much faith in the promise of love. Catherine hadn't particularly helped in that regard. She had dropped him like a hot rock.

"I daresay you don't understand." There. Let Catherine glower over that. Even with a clear head he found the topic confusing at best. He refused to have this discussion with his wits dulled and unreliable.

"I understand quite well that you discount an emotion I have believed in all my life." Lud, she really did sound upset. "What I do not understand is why. You were loved by your parents. You are loved by your sister. You are loved by . . . by *others.* Yet you are willing to dismiss the emotion so entirely."

"And you are willing to argue about it incessantly."

"Perhaps you dismiss it because you have always been loved. If you had ever felt its absence, maybe you would more willingly acknowledge its existence and value its role in your life."

"Love plays absolutely no role in my life, Catherine." He wouldn't allow it to. Caring for . . . *people* hadn't turned out well. He would be indifferent. Unaffected. "Outside of my parents and sister I have never known a single person who inspired in me anything more than detached notice or annoyance. At the moment, you are tending toward the latter."

Even in his mild stupor Crispin recognized his mistake immediately. Catherine's face instantly drained of all color and her gaze dropped.

"Catherine—"

"I hope you sleep well," Catherine cut across him. She rose from her chair. "Black coffee in the morning may be helpful as well."

"Catherine, please." He rose to follow her, knowing he owed her quite an apology. She was gone before he'd uttered another word. Down the corridor and around the corner he heard a door close—her door, no doubt.

Crispin rubbed his eyes and ran his fingers through his hair. What had possessed him to say those things to Catherine? Annoyance? At what? Her concern? Her solicitous attentions while he was less than himself? The fact that she could speak so passionately of love and feel nothing for him?

He'd lashed out, protected himself by implying that he felt little more than a detached awareness of her presence. Heaven help him, his awareness of her lately had been far from *detached*! That, in fact, had been the heart of the problem. Catherine had become ingrained in his life, in his very being, and he had no idea what to do about it. He'd never cared about anyone the way he cared about her. Those unrequited feelings ate away at him, left him empty and bitter. So he'd reverted to his usual self and offered a cynical and entirely undeserved put-down.

He couldn't really blame her for wanting to leave him and this chapter in her life far behind her. For the briefest moment, while he'd kissed her in his box at the theater, he'd actually contemplated trying to convince her to reconsider. But hearing his own harsh words repeat in his mind and remembering the look of pain he'd brought to her face, he wondered if, for her, a life without him might be best after all.

Chapter Twenty-five

A PARTICULARLY PLAINTIVE TUNE FILLED Permount House late the next morning. Crispin stood outside the closed doors of the music room, debating what he ought to do. He remembered enough of his conduct the night before to feel like a complete cad. Catherine's pale, disappointed face came unbidden into his thoughts. He ought to apologize but wasn't sure she wanted to hear it.

A clean break was best, he told himself. She would leave in a few days and his cynicism and sharp words wouldn't hurt her again. But he ought to do something to make amends.

He left the house without a word to his wife. Crispin rode the short distance to Philip's house on Park Lane. He owed Catherine some kind of apologetic gesture. Philip would know which one, surely.

"Come to extol the perfection of my Mathematical, no doubt," Philip said when Crispin joined him in his book room. "My valet swears he never tied a better looking knot. What a shame the Beau is not here to fawn on me."

"I believe Brummell favors the Waterfall," Crispin answered dryly, dropping into a chair beside Philip.

"Only because he has never seen such a fine Mathematical."

"Can you not be serious for a moment or two, Philip?"

"Did your man nick you with the razor this morning?" Philip eyed him quizzically.

"I need your advice on a . . . personal matter." Lud, it was difficult admitting that.

"I always have been a source of wisdom." Philip smiled a touch arrogantly but with enough of a laugh in his eyes to make the expression humorous.

Crispin, however, was not particularly in the mood to be entertained. "I said something thoughtless to Catherine last night."

"Finally told her how you feel?"

"I guess I was—What did you say?"

"Never mind." Philip shrugged as if it didn't matter much.

"What do you mean 'how I feel'?"

"We've known each other since we were thirteen years old, Crispin. I've seen the way you look at her."

"You know full well the nature of mine and Catherine's connection."

Philip lounged lazily in his chair, watching Crispin with obvious amusement. "Fustian! I *know* how it started. I *know* about the annulment proceedings. And I *know* you were ready to toss Finley—and, I half suspected, myself—from your box to his very disreputable death last night."

"We weren't discussing Finley!"

"No, we were discussing Catherine."

"And what possessed you to ask for leave to use her Christian name? Do you have designs on my—" Crispin bit back the rest of his lecture.

"Your wife?" Philip pressed. "Or '*your Catherine,*' perhaps?"

Blast Philip!

"Face facts, old friend. You've committed the most inexcusable offense known to Polite Society."

Crispin truly hated when Philip added dramatics to his already affected demeanor. "What would that be?" As if he needed to ask to get an answer.

"You've fallen in love with your wife."

"You know perfectly I don't put a great deal of confidence in love and all that."

"I knew a Crispin Handle once who did." Philip's right leg, draped elegantly over his left, swung lazily. "Then he inherited a fortune and an ancient title and found himself thrown into the company of the hypocritical ton—mercenaries and liars the lot. Deuced messy way to lose faith in humanity."

"Thank you for that glimpse into my past." Why had he even come? Philip was no help at all.

"You didn't actually drink the champagne you brought into your box last night, did you?"

"What does that have to do with—?"

"You, my friend, grow exceptionally morose when in your cups."

"I was *not* drunk." Catherine had jumped to the same conclusion.

"It does not take much. Tell me, did you wax eloquent on the doomed future of the kingdom or, my personal favorite, the impossibility of love and happiness and anything remotely pleasant?"

"I did not come to discuss me."

"But *you* are the problem." A sudden flash of the knowing, intelligent Philip whom Crispin knew from years before emerged. "Admit defeat, Crispin. Your Catherine has completely destroyed your peace and undermined your determination to distrust and dislike anyone and everything you encounter."

Crispin rubbed his weary eyes. "She's all I think about," he admitted, a man beaten. "I miss her after ridiculously short separations. She looks in another man's direction and I'm jealous as a greenhorn. I'm willing to make a cake of myself just to see her smile or hear her laugh. It's pathetic."

"Sounds like love to me."

"It's torture."

"Sweet torture." Was that a smirk on Philip's face? The brainless dandy Philip insisted on being returned in full force and Crispin knew he'd get no more advice from him.

The book room doors flew open and Jason rushed inside, looking anxious.

"Crispin. Glad you're here."

Philip swung his quizzing glass in a lazy circle. "What panic-inducing crisis has brought you here this time?"

Jason ignored his brother and spoke directly to Crispin. "Thorndale's solicitor came by my office this morning. He'd had an unpleasant meeting with his client."

"An unpleasant man took part in an unpleasant meeting?" Philip raised an eyebrow, his quizzing glass still going 'round. "This *is* an emergency."

Crispin had no patience for theatrics when in the best of humors. In his current mood, the dramatics tempted him to land the both of them a facer and storm off.

"Thorndale has accepted that his legal challenge will not be heard before Lady Cavratt's birthday," Jason said.

"So you've come for a celebratory glass of champagne." Philip's comment earned him a less than amused glare from his brother.

"Thorndale has found a loophole—one that needs no ruling from any court. Knowing Thorndale for the dastard that he is, Clayton is afraid the man will take advantage of the technicality."

"What's the loophole?" Crispin's head pounded anew. The introduction of another legal technicality brought the headache he'd been fighting all morning back with a vengeance.

"No stipulation was made regarding the disbursement of the Lady Cavratt's inheritance should there be no one available to inherit it."

What was Jason yammering about? Crispin's head hurt, deuce take it. And he still hadn't figured out a way back into Catherine's good graces. Couldn't they have a legal debate later?

"Pay attention, Crispin!" Jason's patience had clearly gone. "She has to be twenty-one to inherit—"

"Which she will be in six days." Must the man be so obtuse?

"Thorndale gets it all if Lady Cavratt can't claim it." Jason spoke slowly, as though Crispin were the biggest dunderhead.

Philip seemed to have caught on to whatever his brother found so crucial. He'd risen from his relaxed pose and was staring mouth agape at Jason.

Crispin rubbed his face. The ramshackle knight was tired, blast it.

Philip stepped directly in front of him and shook him by the shoulders. "Think, man!" he demanded, his look fierce. "The only way he gets the blunt is for her to forfeit. The only way for her to lose the inheritance is by default." Philip shook him harder in rhythm with his words. "Not being alive to claim it."

Crispin felt as though someone hit him just under his ribcage. "He wouldn't . . . he wouldn't really . . . kill her."

"Thorndale's man of business is afraid he might."

"I'll take her to Kinnley." Crispin rushed to the door.

"Thorndale will know to look there, Crispin," Philip said. "All your properties are easy targets."

"I have to keep her away from him!" Crispin continued his mad rush to the stables.

Philip kept up with him. "Take her to any of the Lampton holdings. I'll come around to Permount House shortly to help with any arrangements."

Crispin nodded, mounting as quickly as possible.

His mind turned dozens of directions as he frantically maneuvered through the London traffic. Where should he take Catherine? Which destination would Thorndale be least likely to think of searching? What if he was watching Permount House? Perhaps Philip's Scottish hunting box would serve. It sat further from London than the other Lampton properties, and few people knew of it.

Crispin burst unceremoniously through the back entrance of Permount House. A few steps inside, he encountered Hancock.

"Where is Lady Cavratt?" Crispin frantically looked inside each room he passed.

"I believe she is still in the music room. She has not yet rung for tea, though she seems to be finished with her practicing."

"Have Jane pack a trunk for Lady Cavratt." Crispin kept his voice low. "The necessities only. Have her pack for a cold climate. And have my man do the same for myself. They are to tell no one—not even any of the servants."

Hancock bowed and disappeared up the staircase.

Crispin reached the closed music room doors in record time. He flung them open, not waiting for the footman to do so. The sooner he got Catherine beyond Thorndale's reach, the better.

He couldn't help a sigh of relief when he spotted her, unharmed, leaning against the frame of the open French doors. She turned her gaze toward him as he closed the music room doors and crossed the room. Not surprisingly, she didn't look particularly overjoyed to see him. He'd fix that problem later. Right then, he needed to get her someplace safe.

"Hello, Crispin." Her eyes didn't quite meet his.

"We have a problem, Catherine." A direct approach seemed best—faster, at least. "With Thorndale."

"Uncle?"

"It seems he's figured out that he'll receive your inheritance if you don't claim it." Crispin rushed through the explanation, afraid even the slightest delay would ruin everything. "As you stand between him and the inheritance, he sees you as an impediment. I believe your life may be in danger."

Catherine's eyes grew large, her face drained of color. Perhaps a direct approach had been a bad idea after all. "Pistols," she said in a strangled whisper.

Crispin took hold of her hand. "You must be out of London as soon as possible."

She nodded, her eyes still enormous with obvious trepidation, tears gathering on her lashes.

"There is no time for tears, darling. We must leave immediately."

"*We*?" Catherine's eyes jumped to his face. She looked alarmed. "Are you coming with me?"

"Of course." Did she think he would simply abandon her? He was an imbecile at times, certainly, but he wasn't heartless.

"But you would be in danger," she protested. "I cannot allow you to—"

He placed the tips of his fingers against her lips and quite effectively cut off her words. "I will brook no arguments, Catherine."

She stepped backward enough to free her mouth from his fingertips. "This is madness. If I go alone, you will be safe. We need not both be in danger."

"Just how do you propose arriving at a destination I have not yet revealed to you?" Why was the infuriating woman arguing with him on this? They were running out of time!

"You can give the direction to the driver. Or did you intend on driving the coach as well?"

"You cannot travel unprotected, Catherine. Even without Thorndale's threats, you would be in peril on a highway alone."

"But you wouldn't be in danger if you remained here."

So Catherine had a stubborn streak, did she? Crispin, too, could be unflinching in his resolve. "I am accompanying you, Catherine, and I will hear no more arguments about it."

"I will not place you in danger." Catherine attempted to tug her hand free of his. A futile effort, to be sure. He had no intention of releasing her hand until she was at least six counties removed from London. Perhaps not even then.

"Confound it, Catherine! We do not have time to quibble about this."

"But there is no reason for you to come with me."

"There is every reason," Crispin countered. "Please, Catherine." He wasn't above begging. "The sooner we are out of London, the better."

Crispin tugged her by the hand toward the music room doors. If he had to drag her kicking and screaming all the way to Philip's hunting box, he would do just that.

"But I don't understand."

"That you're in danger?" Crispin's anxiety and frustration began to boil over.

"Why you are making this your concern."

Pushing down an exasperated growl, Crispin took gentle hold of her chin so she would be forced to see the determination he knew must be obvious in his face. "I am not going to sit back and let some madman threaten you, Catherine. And I will not send you off alone. Not now. Not ever." Why in heaven's name was she not moving more willingly? A violent man was after her—she ought to be running!

"But why?"

"Because I love you, blast it!"

"You said you didn't believe in love."

"I know!" Crispin pulled away and threw his free hand up in the air, allowing his bewilderment and frustration to show in his action and tone. "Apparently I am losing my mind along with my temper."

"Crispin?" Catherine's voice was suddenly so small and uncertain.

Somehow he had to convince her to come with him. She *had* to listen to him. They *had* to get away from there. "I know I'm not making any sense. I don't understand it myself. But I need you to do this. I need you to just come. Where you will be safe. And I *need* to be there, too. I need to know that you're safe. I . . ." Crispin felt himself shake with the frustration and confusion of it all. "I can't explain it. I just—"

Catherine's fingers pressed to his lips the same way his had moments earlier to hers. "I love you, too," she whispered.

Crispin's shock muted any reply he might have produced. She loved him? Truly? He shook his head. He'd sort all that out later. First matter of business: safety.

"So you'll come?" he asked.

Catherine nodded and smiled. Crispin allowed a sigh of relief. He pressed a quick, affectionate kiss to her lips and another to her forehead. "We have to hurry," he whispered. With every ounce of determination—for the temptation to stay there and kiss her far more thoroughly was quite strong—he turned toward the door, her hand still firmly held in his own, and reached for the handle.

"Don't touch it, Cavratt."

Thorndale.

Crispin heard the distinct click of a gun cocking.

Chapter Twenty-six

UNCLE. CATHERINE'S HEART SEEMED TO stop for a moment. They were too late.

"Come here, wench!"

Catherine shook as she turned to face him. Uncle held one of his Mantons aimed in her direction.

"Thorndale, be reasonable." Crispin, too, had turned to face the foe.

"This is a family matter. None of your concern."

"You have threatened my wife. That makes this my concern." Crispin spoke with excruciating clarity and obvious anger.

"Get out!" Uncle yelled, purple-faced.

"No." Crispin released Catherine's hand and stepped between her and Uncle.

"Not a step closer," Uncle shouted. "I am aiming for your heart Cavratt."

Catherine felt her own heart nearly stop at Uncle's words. Crispin was in danger, precisely as she'd feared from the moment Crispin informed her of his suspicions.

"Put the pistol down, Thorndale, and let us work this out."

"There is nothing to work out. That wench owes me!"

"I will give you the fifty thousand pounds. The entire sum of her inheritance." Crispin waved his hand behind him where only Catherine would see it. What did that mean?

"This isn't about the blunt!" Uncle kept the pistol pointed at Crispin's chest, though it shook violently.

Catherine stared in panic at Uncle's wide, nonsensical eyes. Something in his demeanor bordered on insanity. "It would have all been mine without her. It should have been mine."

"Name your price." Crispin's voice remained steady despite the trembling pistol aimed right at him. "I'll give you anything you want to simply walk away and forget about all of this."

Uncle shook his head, his eyes fiery. "Can't do that."

"You certainly can. Take my offer. You'd be a very rich man."

"It's not about the money."

Catherine would have expected Uncle to shout, to rattle the windows with his anger. He spoke no louder than he would have for a calm conversation. No one would hear him outside the room. If only he would bellow, someone might come to their aid.

"I came here for the chit and I won't leave without her."

"Stealing another man's wife? Holding a gun to an unarmed man? You are apparently no gentleman."

What in heaven's name was Crispin doing? He had questioned the honor of an obviously deranged man—a man who held him at gunpoint. Sheer madness! And he hadn't stopped waving behind his back.

"How dare you, sir!" Uncle's eyes narrowed angrily. "You dare to insult me?"

"Crispin," Catherine pleaded desperately with him. Making Uncle more angry couldn't be a good idea.

"Stay out of this, Catherine." Crispin's eyes remained glued to Uncle. "This bounder was simply making a spectacle of himself."

"*Bounder*?" Uncle's voice raised a fraction more. "You'll answer!"

"Fine."

Fine? Catherine grabbed Crispin's arm, Uncle's many lectures on the efficiency of pistols to eliminate enemies and sources of discontent plaguing her thoughts.

"But I choose weapons," Crispin continued, undeterred.

"Crispin," she frantically whispered. He could not do this. Uncle would shoot him dead.

"And we settle it now," Crispin said. "Here."

"Perfect," Uncle growled.

"Fisticuffs."

"Impudent pup." A foreboding chuckle escaped Uncle's chest. "And by the time you regain consciousness you'll be a widower. My condolences."

Crispin shrugged off his jacket and began fumbling with the buttons of his waistcoat.

"Crispin." Catherine pulled on his arm, turning him enough to look into his face.

He smiled tensely at her as he undid the last button of his waistcoat. "This will distract him," Crispin whispered. "You can get out and alert the staff. Do not come back in."

"I will not abandon you, Crispin," Catherine insisted sotto voce. "Uncle is dangerous when he is angry." She took Crispin's discarded waistcoat, hoping Uncle would believe she was merely helping her husband prepare for the impromptu duel.

"Believe me, Catherine, I have been wanting to do this since the day I met you." Crispin's eyes flashed with obvious anger when he glanced past her to where Uncle waited.

"But he has a gun." She couldn't help the tremor those words sent through her. Uncle would have no qualms about shooting a man dead in his own house.

"He set it on the mantel." Crispin's gaze fixed firmly on her. "Bring someone back here."

Catherine nodded. He placed his long, crumpled cravat in her hand and gently squeezed her fingers before stepping around her to face Uncle. Catherine laid his discarded clothes on a nearby chair and watched the two men approach each other. Uncle had, indeed, set his pistol aside.

If only she could get around them and to an exit without Uncle noticing. Catherine kept her eyes firmly fixed on the two men looking daggers at each other. Each was down to his shirtsleeves, fists held in ready position, circling one another. Catherine inched closer to the terrace doors—the brawl about to explode prevented her from reaching the door leading to the corridor.

Catherine inched along the wall. If Uncle noticed her trying to escape . . . She wouldn't think about it—the plan simply had to work.

Uncle's massive fist flung through the air. Crispin slipped out of reach, untouched and unharmed. Another swipe from Uncle. Another near miss. In the next second, Crispin's fist connected with Uncle's jaw, sending him stumbling backward.

"Not as easy facing a grown man as an innocent woman or child, is it Thorndale?"

Catherine had never heard Crispin sound more livid. She didn't think even Uncle looked as viciously angry as Crispin did at that moment.

"Greedy, grabbing wench! I ought to have strangled her the minute I laid eyes on her!"

"And I should have called you out the first time I saw you lay a hand on her."

Neither man seemed to notice her moving further away. Encouraged, Catherine increased her pace. She reached the terrace doors just as Crispin landed a resounding blow to Uncle's jaw.

Catherine hesitated. Suppose Uncle noticed she had left? What if he did something horrible? Went for his gun again?

The sound of quiet footfall up the terrace steps made Catherine's heart race in panic. Did Uncle have others there? Accomplices?

In an instant, however, she recognized Philip. She ran toward him and the red-vested man at his side.

"Philip! You have to help! My uncle!" She pointed back to the open door. "He has a gun."

"Hancock heard commotion." Philip's demeanor was uncharacteristically serious, almost authoritative. "We didn't want to risk startling your uncle into anything rash by bursting through the other door. But if you are safe—"

"Crispin is still in there!"

Philip and the other man bounded from the edge of the terrace toward the doors, Catherine hot on their heels.

"Not used to your sparring partner fighting back, then, old man?" she heard Crispin bark as she stepped back through the doors.

Uncle's face was bloodied and purple with rage. Crispin stood with his back to her. Catherine's heart hammered. Philip's friend inched carefully inside—Philip did the same, only moving toward the opposite side of the room.

Help him! Why weren't they jumping in?

Crispin landed another punch, and Uncle bent over in pain. Perhaps Crispin didn't need help after all. She had never in her life believed anyone could overpower Uncle.

Her breath caught in her lungs when Uncle straightened again. He held in his hand the tiniest pistol Catherine had ever seen.

She saw her husband stiffen at the sight of the gun aimed for his heart. Philip and the other man stood stock still, eyes focused on the weapon no one had expected.

"You are a fool, Cavratt."

"Murder is a hanging offense." Worry touched Crispin's expression.

Please, no.

"You can't inherit if *you* are dead."

"This is not about the money!" Uncle's voice rattled the windows and doors of the room. He looked demented. Deranged. There was no telling what he would do.

"Put down your weapon." Crispin's voice was calm.

Catherine held her breath, watching Uncle in horror. His jaw was set. His hand flinched. He was going to shoot.

Blinded by panic, Catherine shouted, "No!" and ran toward Crispin.

She felt his arms wrap around her. He turned her, placing himself between her and her uncle just as the air exploded.

* * *

For a moment Crispin couldn't move. Couldn't think. Had he been fast enough? Was Catherine safe? Had Thorndale shot before he'd sufficiently shielded her?

He looked down at her pale face, panic threatening. Her eyes were open—a good sign.

"Are you hurt?" He clasped her face with his hands, nearly unable to breathe. If she was hurt . . . !

She shook her head. "Are you?"

"No." Crispin's heart raced. He had to keep Catherine safe. How long before Thorndale shot again or came after her in another way? Could he get her out? Crispin turned back toward Thorndale, prepared to do whatever he must.

Thorndale wasn't there. An unknown man in a red vest stood over what Crispin was certain was Thorndale's unmoving form. A Bow Street Runner? What was a hired investigator doing in his music room?

"I have impeccable timing," a familiar voice observed from the direction of the French doors.

"Philip?" A Bow Street Runner *and* Philip? What was going on? And what had happened to Thorndale?

"Thought playing the hero would be the dashing thing to do." Philip shrugged. "So I brought a Runner. Good thing, too. Grimes here is a crack shot."

"He shot Thorndale?" Crispin looked from Philip to the Runner and back again. "You saved our lives."

"I'll send you my bill later." Philip tugged at his canary yellow waistcoat.

"Is he dead?" Catherine's voice shook.

Crispin pulled her tightly into his embrace. His heart had not yet stopped furiously pounding.

"No, m'lady," the Runner replied. "There's a doctor at Newgate. He'll see to 'im."

"Jason's on his way." Philip dropped into a chair near the pianoforte. "He's bringing Thorndale's solicitor and a couple of Grimes's colleagues. His idea of a regular society gathering, no doubt."

"The group o' us can handle ol' windbag, here," Grimes assured them, motioning at Thorndale's prostrate form on the floor. "And don't you worry none, m'lady. He won't bother ya no more. We'll be sure of it."

"Th-th-thank you."

"Thank you, m'lady, for yelling out like you did. Distracted the blackguard just long enough . . ."

"He would have shot my husband."

Crispin stroked her hair, closing his eyes a moment in an attempt to convince himself she was truly well and whole.

"I hate to contradict a lady," Philip rejoined the conversation, "but Thorndale was aiming for you, Catherine. Not Crispin."

Crispin's heart dropped to his feet. He'd nearly lost her. The thought kept repeating in his mind. He'd almost lost her.

"I should have left when you first asked me to," Catherine said from within the circle of his arms. "If I hadn't argued with you—"

"Shh." He didn't blame her, not in the least. But at the moment all words escaped him. The sight of Thorndale pointing a gun at her remained far too fresh yet. "You're safe now. You're safe." He spoke to himself as much as to Catherine. She was safe. She was safe.

He spent the next half hour giving directions and overseeing the removal of Thorndale, who had regained consciousness, though he remained incoherent, out of Permount House and into a coach bound for Newgate Prison, where Thorndale would, if he recovered, await trial.

Jane retrieved Catherine within minutes of Thorndale's being felled by Grimes's bullet. Catherine's pale countenance and clearly distressed eyes worried Crispin. She needed to lie down. She obviously needed to be away from the chaos and blood. So he'd reluctantly let her go.

Crispin pulled Philip into the sitting room before letting his lifelong friend leave. "I cannot thank you enough." He dropped one hand firmly on his friend's shoulder. "For myself and, especially, for Catherine."

Philip began his trademark shrug.

"No! Stop! I am being serious. Drop all this and listen to me. You saved my life. You saved my Catherine. You have no idea . . . how . . . indebted I am . . ." No words seemed sufficient.

Philip's face transformed one more time to the person he had been years before, to a man Crispin sorely missed. "I'd have shot the man myself, but Grimes has better aim. I didn't want to accidentally kill my best friend." Philip actually looked a little shaken.

"It was rather a close-run thing, wasn't it?"

Philip nodded without a hint of the dandy he pretended to be.

"I am in your debt," Crispin said.

"Well, then, if I ever find my life threatened by a lunatic, I will fully expect you to rescue me." Philip smiled—not the empty-headed smile he usually affected, but a true smile.

"It's a deal. And thank you again."

Philip waved off Crispin's gratitude as if it weren't important. "You rather beat old Thorndale to a pulp before I arrived to save him from your violent temper."

Crispin knew he was grinning like a schoolboy. "Cannot tell you how good that felt."

"Do you still plan to flee London, then?"

"I hadn't given it much thought," Crispin admitted.

"Suffolk is quite a sight in the late fall," Philip suggested with a raise of his too-knowing brow. "Catherine would love it."

"You mean Kinnley?"

"Unless, of course, you're still planning to ship the poor woman off, leave her dangling on the edge of society. With her uncle no longer a worry, you wouldn't have to wait on the annulment. This attack would probably strengthen your arguments, in fact."

"I . . . It's not like that . . . Things have changed . . ." How did he put it in words? "I can't let her go like that."

Philip nodded with understanding. "I'm happy for you," Philip said genuinely. "You will be good for each other."

"And if she doesn't agree?"

"Tell her. Convince her," Philip replied, making his way out of the sitting room. "Better yet,"—He turned back, a look of pure mischief on his face—"*show* her."

Hancock bowed as he opened the doors of Permount House to allow Philip to leave.

Philip tugged foppishly at his waistcoat and offered an affected smile. "Perhaps I should go home by way of Hyde Park," he said. "I appear to be quite in looks today."

Crispin shook his head in bewilderment. He would never understand why Philip acted the way he did at times, nor what had affected the drastic change in his friend. Perhaps someday Philip would confide in him.

Before Hancock had closed the door behind the baffling Earl of Lampton, Crispin was halfway up the stairs with one destination in mind.

He slipped almost silently through the door to Catherine's rooms. She was pacing in front of the fireplace and looked up as he entered.

"Oh, Crispin!" Catherine threw herself into his arms, precisely where he needed her to be. "Is everyone all right? Is he gone?"

"Thorndale is on his way to Newgate." Crispin hugged her close to him. "He will not be coming back."

"I have never been more afraid in all my life." She trembled as she spoke.

Neither had he. Thorndale had nearly succeeded. Crispin had almost lost her forever. He laid his chin on the top of Catherine's head.

She leaned more heavily against him. "I've been a great deal of trouble, haven't I?"

"As a matter of fact." He couldn't help a smile. *Trouble* did not begin to describe Catherine's impact on his previously predictable life. "To begin with, you've turned this home into a hothouse."

"I can hardly be blamed for being irresistible."

She was decidedly irresistible. Crispin stroked her hair, not particularly caring that her hairpins weren't equal to the task of holding her locks up against his interference. "For another thing, you turned me to a life of crime."

He felt her laugh. "I thought we agreed your mother bore the blame for your tendency to steal pastries."

"Either way, I have become a hopeless criminal—most ladies would object to that."

"As well they should." Her fingers rustled the open collar of his somewhat bloodied shirt "Worse yet, you are bruised like a prizefighter."

"Just how do you know what a bruised prizefighter looks like?"

"Furthermore, you threaten me with your fountain."

"I'm shameless." He looked into her sparkling eyes and smiled despite himself.

"And . . ." Her expression clouded a little. "You claim you do not believe in love."

"A belief I am beginning to doubt." Crispin lightly kissing her forehead.

"Doubt?"

"Dismiss." He kissed the tip of her nose.

"Dismiss?" She still seemed unsatisfied.

"Renounce, then."

"Much better," Catherine managed to say before Crispin covered her mouth with his.

Show her, Philip had said. Show her how much he cared for her, needed her, loved her. He did, desperately. He could never have imagined that when he kissed her in that garden—it seemed like ages ago—that kiss would lead him to this.

He held her as tightly and closely as possible. She returned the embrace with equal determination and didn't pull away from his kiss.

"Catherine." The word rasped out of him as he broke the seal of their lips. He closed his eyes and pressed his forehead to hers, breathing in the familiar scent of her. He could not bear the thought of her leaving him. "I cannot do this."

He felt her pull back. Crispin dropped his hands to her shoulders, holding her in place. He opened his eyes and locked his gaze with hers.

"Please reconsider," he said, desperation making his heart thud anew. "I know I haven't been the ideal husband, and I often say and do stupid things. But I cannot simply let you walk away. Give me a chance, Catherine. Please. Come with me to Kinnley—even for just a fortnight or so. Give me a chance to court you properly before you insist on an—an annul—" Lud, he couldn't even push the word out. "Just allow me a chance. Please."

"You want me to come with you?" Catherine asked.

"I want you to *stay* with me," he answered. "I won't force you, but, heaven help me, I will fight for you. I'll do whatever I must. If that means raiding every hothouse in the county or throwing myself in the fountain or begging you shamelessly, I'll do so without a moment's hesitation. I swear to you I will."

"You don't want an annulment?"

Crispin shook his head. "I haven't for some time now."

Her gaze dropped, a look of uncertainty on her face. Crispin brushed a strand of hair back from her face, waiting anxiously for her next words.

"Because you feel sorry for me?" she asked.

He placed a lingering kiss on her forehead, knowing if he kissed her lips he'd never manage to say what he needed her to hear. "Because I can't live without you."

He felt her sigh, and her entire expression lightened. "Then you don't regret walking in that garden all those weeks ago?"

"Providence, my dear. The heavens knew I needed you."

She very nearly smiled. "You needed an *accidental* wife?"

"It seems to me"—He pulled her closer once more—"those are the very best kind."

Her smile bloomed fully, and Crispin was lost. Who initiated the kiss that followed he did not know. He simply savored her, knowing he didn't deserve the treasure he'd been given. When he attempted to break the kiss, Catherine didn't allow him to, a turn of events he hadn't foreseen but to which he didn't object.

"I love you," Catherine whispered against his mouth several moments later.

The old, rusted, battle-weary knight straightened his creaky armor as he bent his neck to kiss her once more. "And I will forever love you."

About the Author

Photo by Claire Waire.

Sarah M. Eden read her first Jane Austen novel in elementary school and has been an Austen Addict ever since. Fascinated by the Regency era in English history, Eden became a regular in the Regency section of the reference department at her local library, painstakingly researching this extraordinary chapter in history. Eden is an award-winning author of short stories and was a Whitney Award Finalist for her novel *Seeking Persephone* (2008). You can visit her at www.sarahmeden.com.